Discovering Darcy

A Modern Pride and Prejudice

By Barbara Seidle

Edited by Tamara Eaton

This is a work of fiction. Similarities to real people, places, or events are entirely coincidental.

DISCOVERING DARCY

First edition. November 10, 2021.

Copyright © 2021 Barbara Seidle.

ISBN: 979-8227777478

Written by Barbara Seidle.

Dedication

For my husband, Jay, who is my very own Darcy right down to the part where I told him I wouldn't marry him if he was the last person on earth. I'm a lot of work, and he's a patient man. I am so grateful he pursued me.

1: Beth

"It's not good for a man to be alone. It's in the Bible. The new renter is single and a Christian. He's plenty old enough that he must be thinking about marriage." Mom puffed out her chest and continued to spread butter on a slice of crusty Italian bread during our weekly family dinner.

"The Bible also says that singleness can be preferable to marriage. Paul called it a gift," I said.

"Beth, stop talking nonsense. You sound like a feminist." Mom spit the words out like a curse.

"Being self-sufficient and independent is not a terrible thing. I hardly think valuing the equality of the sexes is something to look down on." I was wasting my breath. We had circled through this same tired conversation over a million Beckett family dinners. Each time it was as if my mother had never heard my proclamation of beliefs.

"Henry, do something before she infects the rest of the girls with her bitterness."

Dad barely even glanced at Mom when he replied. "Gwen dear, I hardly think you need to worry about her sisters being influenced by any form of reason."

Lydia, my youngest sister, tucked a tendril of her highlighted ash-blonde hair behind her ear and piped in without any apparent recognition that our father's words might be insulting to her or our sisters. "Beth is just jealous. She knows she isn't as hot as the rest of us, save perhaps Mary, and she knows she'll never turn a man's head. Maybe if she did something about her hair and clothes, she might trick someone into marrying her, but that's doubtful."

I knew I was plain. Short. Flat. Pale. My most remarkable feature was my black hair, and considering it never did anything but hang limply around my face, that wasn't saying much. Still, Lydia's words stung, mostly because they parroted the words I'd been hearing from my mother since I was thirteen. Sure, I could spend my time in tanning beds and salons, but there was too much to see and do in this world to be bothered with all that. I had a wanderlust that my budget couldn't satisfy. I had learned early on that I was more likely to find satisfaction in books than in boys.

I could see Jane's conflicted expression. Unlike Lydia, who spent an exorbitant amount of time and money to perfect her look, Jane was a natural beauty. Her dark brown hair was always twisted into a classic updo. Her deep brown eyes with the simplest of make-up reflected her kindness. The oldest, at twenty-five, Jane's maternal instincts made her a peacemaker. She couldn't bear to have anyone insulted in such a manner, but she also abhorred confrontations. She shot our sister a look with a muffled, "Lydia," but said no more.

In an attempt to change the subject, I turned to twenty-one-year-old Mary, the most serious of us all. "Mary, what are you reading now? It must be fascinating to be keeping your attention even in the midst of such an intense theological debate."

Mary rolled her eyes as she pushed her glasses higher on her rounded nose, but she didn't look up. "If Lydia and Cat can text at the table, there is no reason I shouldn't read. As if you actually care, I'm reading Augustine's *Confessions*. And for the record, I don't think you can classify a conversation about using make-up to attract boys as a theological debate."

"I have a confession. I'm starving. Could you please pass the spaghetti?" Cat smiled as if she found herself amusing. Lydia's snicker indicated that the two of them shared the same dull sense of humor. Cat beamed. Older than Lydia by eighteen months, Cat in many ways emulated our youngest sister, but she lacked the equivalent skill with a make-up brush and had yet to master our sister's flirtatious ways.

From there, the conversation turned to Lydia and Cat's upcoming summer plans. Lydia was finishing her junior year in high school, and Cat was finishing up her first year at community college. However, with the number of credits Cat had earned, she would still be considered a freshman when she registered for the fall semester. Dad interjected into the conversation briefly with a feeble demand that they both find jobs and forget their plans to sunbathe and flirt the summer away. Mom waved him off the same way she dismissed all of his attempts to encourage industry in their daughters. I could only assume the result of this conversation would be the same as every previous dinnertime discussion. My father would give in to mother's incessant drip, drip, dripping.

At the conclusion of dinner, Jane and I cleared the table, packed up the leftovers, and washed the dishes. I stared out the kitchen window while I wiped down the sink. My father had grown up in this house. The wooded acres that surrounded this home had been in the Beckett family since the late 1700s. Of the original eighty plus acres, only this small groundskeeper's house on a one-acre plot were still in our family's control. I loved the history of this once grand estate. How many generations of Beckett women had done this same post dinner dance in this precise spot? Jane and I had performed this routine practically every night until this past September when we moved to the old dormitory, now an apartment building, on the southern end of the Beckett Grounds. I would have loved to see my younger sisters take up their share of the load, but that didn't appear to be happening. The little help we offered in Friday chores meant one less complaint our father would need to endure. That was a price I was willing to pay.

"Do you want to take the scenic path back to our place?" I asked Jane.

With the May air cool and smelling of sweetness, I was confident she would agree. Actually, she would agree to anything I wanted. It was part of what I loved best about Jane. She was all goodness.

The direct route to our apartment was only a two or three-minute trek, but we took the nature trail that led down to the canal path and snaked through the woods before it passed the old cemetery. The scent of honeysuckle made us slow our steps. We had always made a habit of finding its source and then tasting the sweet nectar that came from the flowers. Spotting the vines near the canal's edge, I scampered down the steep edge, plucked off a few blossoms then climbed back up. I knew my mother would disapprove, but at twenty-three years old, I hardly felt it was dishonoring to my parents to be "reckless" as Mother would call it.

Handing two flowers to Jane, I let out a satisfied sigh. "The first plunder of the season."

We gently pinched the end of the flowers, not so hard as to cut straight through the fleshy base, but just enough to break the outer layer. We slid the stigma down through the petals releasing a miniscule drop of sweetness. We each repeated it again with our second flower. Just as I was about to proclaim this the most glorious of evenings, up ahead I noticed the shimmering green flash of a lighting bug. I had never seen one this early in the year. "Look." I pointed.

Jane smiled in recognition. "What could be more perfect than honeysuckle and fireflies? The school year is just about a wrap. All is right in the world."

With a flutter of laughter, I clasped Jane's arm and led her away from the canal up towards our apartment. "I don't believe I have ever seen you in any state other than bliss. You practically sing your lessons each day. Those rug rats are the luckiest kindergarteners in the world, and with you as a sister, so am I."

Jane, unable to simply accept a compliment, had to return the favor. "Your students are just as lucky. Certainly, we have different dispositions, but your energy and creativity are perfect for 4th grade. Better yet, I get to work with you every day."

As we came over the rise that led to our building, I couldn't help but pause to take in the beauty of the setting sun casting an orange glow on the mid 19th century structure that was home. Frustrated by a lack of educational opportunities for his daughters, the late John Beckett built the first girls seminary in New Jersey. It was a simple structure to house classrooms and living quarters for a small number of young women. He swam against the current of his day, but time had not done any favors in preserving his legacy. Hard times and mismanagement of the family estate resulted in the seminary's closure and the family land being sold off piece-by-piece.

The newly converted staff apartments still catered mostly to women, primarily young teachers like us. The ivy that grew along the walls of the brick structure had weakened it over the last century or so and the chinking was eroding away. I pushed hard to force open the old heavy wooden door that led in to the dimly lit lobby. The stucco on the walls was cracked and water stains marred the ceiling near the doorway that led into our apartment. Yet underneath layers of paint you could still see the workmanship that had gone into the building's original banister. It had been built to last.

The units lacked central air, but not even the sweltering days of summer would be too high a price for cutting the apron strings that had been choking me since my teen years.

I followed Jane into our one-bedroom apartment. I placed my bag on the kitchen counter and flopped down onto the couch. "I think we should move to Wyoming. I'm sure there are teaching jobs there."

"Why on earth would you want to move to Wyoming?"

"Lowest people per square acre in the continental United States. Sounds pretty good, doesn't it?"

"We don't have friends or family in Wyoming," Jane replied.

"Exactly!" I snatched my laptop off the table and began booting it up. "I'll see what kind of jobs are available."

Jane, in all of her goodness, didn't say anything to the contrary. She probably knew me better than I knew myself. She'd watched me search for degree programs at universities around the globe; plan out vacations to Hawaii, Peru, and Norway; and research life in a Kibbutz, all after Friday family dinners. She simply put on the kettle and began making us tea while I verbalized all the benefits of open space and fresh air awaiting us in the Rocky Mountains.

2: Beth

Worship service had been just what I needed to give my attitude the adjustment it needed. The stress of the last few weeks of school seemed to wash away as we sang the closing hymn.

My best friend, Joy Douglas, rushed over to my spot in the sanctuary. "Are you going to make it to Bible study this week?"

"Don't I always? It's practically lifeblood for me."

"Well, yes, but I wanted to be sure. I am trying out a new muffin recipe for the café, and I wanted you to be my guinea pig." Her family owned the Douglas Café, and I enjoyed reaping the benefits of the test kitchen. Joy masterfully hosted the women's Bible study that Jane and I had attended faithfully every Tuesday evening for the past two years.

I feigned exhaustion. "Oh, if I must. But only for you will I force myself to eat carbs."

Joy laughed. "Oh, and can you help out next week at the Grounds Association Meeting? The college kids are all busy with finals. Jane already said yes."

"For you, anything." I wrapped my arms around her shoulders and pulled her into a hug.

We spent a few minutes catching up with other friends before heading to our parents for lunch. My parents' church ended earlier than the church Jane and I had been attending since Jane finished college a few years back. We had barely stepped through the front door before Mom began what could only be described as a dramatic monologue. And just like that it seemed my peace was ebbing away. Sigh.

"Really, Henry, it's unconscionable. I spent years homeschooling our girls to make sure they had a proper education to prepare them for the most holy work in the Kingdom, marriage and motherhood. Yet, you are unable to even spend a few moments of your time to assist our girls in their future. It's not every day that a new business rents space on these decrepit grounds. A millionaire nonetheless. Smart. He runs a company that helps students pass the SAT for college. But our girls won't even need to go to college in order to find a rich man if you could introduce them to some wealthy men now. Oh, no. You don't want to impose. He was right there in the back row of the church building. You could have welcomed him as a deacon. Besides, you're the head of grounds. You know all the other business owners. A lot of good they have done us so far. Not one of our girls is fulfilling their call to marriage and child bearing."

"There is more to life than a husband." I knew my words were a waste of breath, but to devalue my education and my career was more than I could handle.

"You're right, Beth dear, money matters too. Do you think your teaching salary is going to be enough to support you forever? Life isn't a lot of fun when you don't have a pot to piss in. Do you want to live in those dorms when you're my age? An old maid? You won't be living here, your father made sure of that with that lousy business deal. Now, when he dies, the house defaults to his old partner, and we'll all be homeless. Where will I live? I can't exactly move in with you and Jane into that tiny nothing room you live in. What will happen to me? Your sisters? There'll be nothing left of the Beckett Estate. What comfort will your career be to you on those long nights knowing your mother is out on the streets?"

If Oscars could be given for mealtime performances, Mom would have no trouble finding a career after her husband's passing. Her greatest accomplishment had likely been the training she had provided to her youngest two daughters in the art of drama. I had been subjected to the same upbringing as all of my sisters. I wondered how we could have all turned out so vastly different. My mother's approach to homeschooling was really more un-schooling. We had access to our father's extensive library, the public library, and the Internet. We could all pick and choose from a myriad of online courses, but our mother neither pushed nor checked on our progress.

Father laid out the general educational plan for each of his daughters on an annual basis. Jane, always wanting to please, followed it out of obligation and love. I on the other hand had fallen in love with stories. "Beth dear, the entire world is within your grasp. Drink it all in." Father's passion touched me. I devoured books. Not wanting to miss out on some of the references made in stories or desiring to more fully grasp the clues in a murder mystery, the context of a historical fiction, or the science behind a sci-fi thriller, I branched further and further into non-fiction books on every subject. Math had been my least favorite, but spurred by the desire to be well rounded, and with aspirations of college, I worked my way through each math class systematically and with determination, though without affection.

I wasn't sure of Mary's motivation. She certainly was smart, and she read more with violence than passion. She read non-fiction nearly exclusively and had no interest in being well rounded. She read to support her opinion and win arguments, theology mostly. The rest of her studies were merely a means to an end to complete her undergraduate degree in Biblical Studies. For what purpose, I was clueless. Future careers were never brought up, and her unaccredited, online bachelor's degree program didn't offer career counseling. Mary spent her days shut up in her room, so our sisterly bond was nearly non-existent.

The younger two had embraced our mother's carefree approach to education and read little and studied even less. Unlike Jane, Mary, and myself who had homeschooled through high school, my two youngest sisters had gone to Asbury Christian Academy during their high school years, which was the only reason they weren't completely ignorant. Their grades were poor, but Cat had managed to graduate and head to community college, while Lydia was expected to graduate next year. They were capable, but lazy.

I was drawn from my reverie by Dad's voice. "Gwen, he was speaking with the pastor. I'm sure his family felt plenty welcome. And while I understand your desire to see your daughters well married, it's not in my job description to become the grounds matchmaker. While I would never meet with the new owner of Academic Success for the sake of your marital aspirations for our daughters, I did need to meet with him for actual work. You will be relieved to hear that I invited him to the Ground's Association meeting next week. Now, perhaps we can eat in peace."

Peace was not to come. Mom would guarantee that. "How could you let me think you didn't care? It's like you want me stressed. You know I have anxiety. So? What did he say? You can't just end the conversation now."

"Dear, you can judge for yourself at the meeting. I, however, am finished with this conversation."

3: Beth

I wasn't particularly looking forward to the Ground's Association meeting today. I loved teaching at Asbury Christian Academy, but I had to fulfill my obligation to Joy to fill in as a server. I could do without being on my feet another two or three hours after teaching all day, but the extra cash would go towards my nest egg. The cheap rent was a nice perk to my current apartment, but I was dreaming of buying my own home. One a little further away from my family.

I dressed in white button-down shirt and black slacks along with my most comfortable flats. To ensure I didn't look like a waiter while at school, I grabbed a bright green and blue scarf, a chunky bracelet, and long dangling earrings that hinted of peacock feathers. Once the day was over, I'd take off everything of flair and head to the business meeting on the far west side of the grounds in the building that once held the stables and carriage house, but now was restored into a rustic yet elegant banquet hall.

The small Methodist school where Jane and I worked was the sole tenant in the main building that once served as the home for my ancestors. Providence had brought the school here a few years back. I loved to look out the old windows, wavy with time, and imagine the way the land would have looked in their day. I would slide my hand across the dark wood railings that led down the grand staircase. I wondered who slept in the room where I taught, now adorned with posters and cubbies, while the scent of sharpened pencils permeated the room. There is nothing like teaching Colonial history from inside the walls of a building that witnessed those days. Sure, things had changed over the years. Upgrades to the building made the interior look more modern, but nothing could steal the charm of the old stone walls. I loved this place and all the history it held not just for my family, but my community as well.

At the end of the day, I instructed my students to pack up their things. "Remember, tomorrow is Pajama Day. Don't forget to wear your pjs and bring your favorite storybook and a stuffed animal or blanket to snuggle up with while we read together. You've done such a great job this year, and you've earned this treat." While I spoke, I removed my scarf and carefully wrapped my bracelet and earrings inside the folded scarf for safekeeping. I tucked my laptop and a folder of papers to grade along with the scarf inside my workbag.

"Katie, come here a second." I crouched down to be closer to eye level when Katie reached my desk. "I want you to read that story we were working on today to your little brother. He'll love the attention, and it will give you practice before you read in front of the class tomorrow. Remember that Patricia Polacco story I read in class?"

Katie's head bobbed up and down. "She didn't learn to read until she was older than me."

"Exactly, but she didn't give up. And now?"

Katie smiled. "She's a famous author, just like I want to be someday."

"Precisely. The class is going to love your story tomorrow."

When the final bell rang, I led my class down to the cafeteria for dismissal. Once I had them settled, I grabbed a walkie-talkie and headed outside with the other teachers who would be escorting children to their cars.

Just as the cones were being set up, a black Tesla pulled up to the third spot, directly in front of the main entrance to the school. The driver hurried from his vehicle, seemingly unaware that he couldn't park here.

"You can't park there. Excuse me. Sir. Sir!" I called out.

The stranger rushed past me locking his car with his key fob and not even slowing for a moment to acknowledge my existence. I spun on my heels. "Unbelievable." Trailing him, I stepped through the doors into the school lobby. The man was speaking to the receptionist at the front desk. Wendy appeared to be providing him with directions.

I stepped up next to him. "Excuse me, but you can't leave your car there. Carpool is about to begin. You're blocking all the traffic."

The man didn't even turn his head as he spoke but continued filling in his name on the visitor's log. "And you are?"

I let out a slow breath and spoke using my teacher voice. "I am Miss Beckett, the 4th grade teacher. And I'm going to need you to move your car."

He held out his key chain. "I'm late for a meeting. Here, take these and move it for me. Just leave the keys here at the front desk." Peeling the visitor name badge off of the backing, the man finally looked up.

I clenched my fists. *The nerve of this man.* "We don't offer valet service."

He looked me over up and down twice and his mouth broke into a smile. "Looks like you do." And without so much as a response, he tossed the keys I had refused to take and strode off down the hall.

It took me several seconds to recover from my astonishment. In the moments I had been standing there while that despicable man ogled me, I had read the man's nametag. Darcy Williams. Was that the Williams of Williams Holdings that owned the Beckett Grounds? I had snatched the keys from the air out of instinct rather than compliance, but there I stood with his keys in my hand and Wendy's eyes on me. Her mouth hung open, obviously feeling the same shock as I had experienced, but likely without the humiliation. I was in fact dressed in service attire, and now I either had to move this man's car or deal with the frustration of an excessively long and complicated carpool.

I drove the fifty feet to the adjacent lot and parked the car, making sure to leave the seat pulled fully forward to accommodate my small frame. With his height, getting in would prove to be a challenge. I wasn't a vengeful person, and that was all the uncharitableness my conscience would allow. I stormed back to the lobby. Without even looking at Wendy, I dropped the keys on her desk and headed back out to carpool, which was now half over. My heart was pounding so hard I could feel it in my ears. I sensed the heat in my checks, a mixture of rage and indignation. It wasn't that I considered the job of a valet beneath me, it was more that I prided myself in having a comeback for every situation, and this man had bested me with his boorish words. I'd stood there dressed like a valet holding his keys like an idiot, and then I'd moved his car. When carpool was over, there would be questions from the other teachers. I needed to escape. I grabbed my bag from where I'd left it just inside the main doors and set off to the banquet hall. *Please, Lord, don't let me see that man again. If I do, it just might cost me my job,*

As I crossed the grounds, I ruminated over all the things I could have said or done to that infuriating man. It was my own internal walk of shame, reminding me of my silent defeat. I should have dinged up the door on his fancy car. No. That would surely cost money I didn't have. I could have thrown the keys at his back. No, that really could get me fired, and honestly my aim is so horrendous I would have missed and only added to my humiliation. Why couldn't I have said or done something? Anything would have been better than standing there dumbfounded. I clenched and unclenched my fists a dozen times before I reached the banquet hall where the meeting would take place.

The meeting wouldn't start until four, but Joy would already be there. Joy's parents had bought a small café in the strip mall right down the street when Joy and I were nine and Jane eleven. The three of us became fast friends and had become practically inseparable during our homeschooling days. Most of the people who worked on the grounds ate lunch at the Douglas Café, not necessarily because the food was fantastic, but because it was just about the only place in the vicinity. The café provided the coffee and treats for the monthly meetings and in turn, Mr. and Mrs. Douglas were unofficial members of the association.

I worried about Joy. Ever since high school, she worked hard to help her parents' failing business, recently taking over the catering portion. She seemed neither content in her position nor motivated to change her situation. I couldn't do much about that, but I could make her afternoon a little more tolerable by helping her serve today. Jane slipped through the door and paused to give me a quick hug before settling her things next to mine.

****

Dad's small crew of grounds workers was busy getting ready for the meeting. Tall tables for standing were spread around the room with scattered chairs in clusters for conversation areas. While Joy draped the tables in long tablecloths, I placed the coffee carafes, mugs, creamers, and sugars on a cart to bring out to the self-service coffee bar.

"Jane, could you grab the baked goods and follow me out?" I called over my shoulder as I pushed through the swinging doors.

"Sure thing." I heard the door swing again a moment later.

Joy, Jane, and I got right to work, wrapping the folding chairs in white covers to give the illusion that they were more dignified than they actually were.

Jane spoke as she worked. "Chapel was great this morning. I'm so glad they started bringing in some new faces. The new children's pastor from Trinity really kept my class's attention."

"I agree. His illustration about hurtful words damaging hearts led to a great conversation in my class regarding forgiving one another after a rather rambunctious game of kickball during recess." I smiled, recalling my students practicing giving and receiving apologies. Guilt struck me for my completely ungracious response to the stranger a few moments ago. *Lord, I am sorry. I can be so pig-headed. Help me become more like You.*

Dad leaned over to kiss my cheek and then Jane's as he stepped past us. Though Dad served as the head of Buildings and Grounds on the tract of land that rightfully he should have inherited, he never seemed bitter about spending his days surrounded by all that could have been. He served God with all his heart and that carried over into the pride he took in his work. He woke early each day to pray and read his Bible before work. He had taken more than one young man on his crew under his wing and led them to the Lord. I looked over to where my dad had moved and saw him working side-by-side with his crew setting up rows of chairs on the opposite end of the room for the more formal business meeting that would precede the social hour. Never one to stand by and supervise, Dad was a quiet leader who led by example. With the head of Williams Holdings, the company that now owned the Beckett Grounds, largely absent, Dad had become the face of the grounds. His friendly demeanor helped him build rapport with each of the various businesses both on the grounds and in the surrounding community.

A motion at the door pulled my attention from Dad and onto my mother entering the room. Mom had found Dad's job beneath him. While many spouses attended these meetings, Mom rarely showed her face. There was no doubt what had prompted Mom's attendance at tonight's meeting. She headed straight for the untouched refreshment area and fixed herself a plate. Mom set her coffee and plate at the table closest to the door and kept watch as the first few people began entering. This was my cue to leave.

I headed back into the kitchen where I had left my folder of papers to grade. I played the farce with myself every time I came. I wasn't going to do any schoolwork. I rarely got any further than pulling my papers out and setting them on the kitchen counter along with my red pen before being called away or engaging in a conversation with Joy. I never really minded. That's just what best friends did. We were comfortable working side-by-side and never minded the interruption.

Joy called Jane and I over to where she stood gazing through the glass windows on the swinging doors. "Look, there's Chad Woods. He owns Academic Success. They haven't even opened their doors yet. He's here with his two sisters and his brother-in-law, who all work for him. Rumor has it that he's not only single, handsome, and wealthy, but a Christian. He donates tons of money to charity, and he provides tutoring to Christian schools. And that fine specimen next to him is Darcy Williams. He owns the grounds, which is probably how Chad Woods was able to lease the space so quickly after the lawyer's office moved out. Darcy Williams is probably a gazillionaire, and isn't he super hot?"

I felt my face harden as Joy spoke. Of course, I would have to see him at this meeting. I'd never seen him at one of these meetings before, why would he start today? Now, I'd have to spend the evening cleaning up his trash. And I'd have to be on my best behavior, because my boss was also at this meeting. Could today get any worse? "Mr. Williams may be rich, but he is most certainly not a Christian."

I guess I spoke too loudly, because Joy shook her head. "No, he is. He inherited The Agape Foundation from his father. It's this huge charitable organization that helps people around the world."

"That doesn't make him a Christian. You don't inherit your faith. He's probably just the figurehead. I think if you are ever so unfortunate as to meet him you'll agree with me." I heard the hostility in my voice, but whatever.

Joy continued, "Darcy's main job is running this cyber security corporation mostly helping banks so they don't get hacked. I Googled him."

"You're proving my point. He can't be running two big companies and manage tons of real estate. Money is his business, and it shows."

Jane put her arm around me. "Beth, this isn't like you. What's going on?"

I took a deep breath and relaxed my shoulders so that Jane could feel me calm under her embrace. "Sorry. Long day. I'm fine."

I watched as Mr. Williams was called forward at the beginning of the meeting to welcome everyone. He said how busy his schedule is, and how he always read the meeting minutes and took them into consideration as he managed the property. Yada Yada Yada. He then introduced Mr. Woods the owner of Academic Success and his sister and brother-in-law, Heather and Nick Hurst, who would be heading up their newest location here on the grounds, asking the members to welcome the newcomers to their group.

With the meeting adjourned, the crowd moved toward the refreshment area. For the association members, the networking was more valuable than the business portion. I had hoped that Mr. Williams's busy schedule would have forced him to leave at the end of the business meeting, but no such luck. I found him speaking not only with Chad Woods, but also with my boss, Dr. Cooper. It made sense. This was a chance to connect Academic Success with a local Christian school.

For the first half hour, I encouraged Jane to circulate on the far side of the room. Jane was gathering the trash abandoned on an empty table near Mr. Williams when Dr. Cooper called her over. From my place refilling the coffee carafes, I could see Dr. Cooper gesturing introductions to the group that included Mr. Williams and Mr. Woods. Jane, always lovely, smiled and chatted with the gentlemen for several minutes before continuing to clean up and check on everyone. Just as I was relaxing, I heard something that made the hairs on my neck stand up. The piano. Mary. No, this couldn't be happening. Mary was allowed to practice on the baby grand that sat in the ballroom, but not while an event was going on. What was Mary thinking? Mary was a loner in every sense but one. She enjoyed an audience as long as she didn't need to speak. Piano was her outlet. Mary was reasonably accomplished, but lacked in social graces. The crowd grew silent and then the murmurs and haughty looks began.

I moved my way toward my father and quietly implored him to interrupt my sister. Slowly, Dad maneuvered his way through the attendees.

The moment that Mary's song ended, Mom began clapping emphatically. "Bravo! Such talent. Never mind her weight. She'll make some man very lucky."

The rest of the crowd began a hesitant applause as Dad closed the lid to the keys and whispered into Mary's ear. At that moment, I looked at Mr. Williams who was staring directly at me. I couldn't pull my eyes off of him as he turned his head toward Mary, then back toward me. His face was grim as he returned to his conversation. The gentleman he was conversing with began speaking, looked over at my dad and drew Mr. Williams's attention to the piano. Then both men looked at Jane. There could be no mistaking what they were saying. I was sure my face had reddened enough to be noticeable even from across the room. I spun on my heel and stomped into the kitchen.

4: Beth

"Jane, have you called on Chad yet?" My mother's voice echoed from the kitchen the minute we stepped through the door for our Friday night dinner.

"Of course not, why would I do that? I barely met the man." Jane's face reddened.

"He clearly had eyes for you, but men won't wait. You best come up with a plan to snatch his attention or he'll be looking at the next cute thing. And trust me, as beautiful as you are, your looks won't last forever. And then what?"

Mother's words were likely to have the opposite effect than she hoped for. Jane was shy, and she withdrew when uncomfortable. I tried to change the subject. "What did you think of his friend?"

"How a nice man like that could be friends with the likes of Mr. Williams is beyond me. That man practically stole our home out from under us. Your father actually talked with the scoundrel. Might as well be consorting with the enemy."

Mom's diatribe lasted the remainder of dinner. By the time Jane and I had cleaned up I was almost sorry I had tried to rescue Jane from Mom's matchmaking. Twenty minutes into dinner, I found myself wanting to defend Mr. Williams. Clearly, I needed to clear my head. At least, I had girl's night to look forward to.

Once a month, depending on Joy's work schedule, we planned movies, chocolate, and wine. Joy arrived only minutes after we returned, and she let herself in without even knocking, the way it should be with your ride-or-die chicks. While not prone to much in the way of gossip, we were still inclined to some girl talk.

"Chad Woods is hot." Joy laughed as she spoke the words. "But his friend is even hotter. Did you see his body? He has to be at least six-two, and those arms. To be wrapped up in those arms."

Jane blushed. "Joy! Stop it."

Joy and I giggled at Jane's reaction. Ever proper and sweet, Jane was certainly not going to allow the conversation to continue down this path. Sensing the need to ensure Jane's innocence, I at least attempted to stifle my giggle. "So, Jane, I saw Dr. Cooper introduce you to the men of the hour. What are your thoughts on them?"

Jane spoke with her typical grace. "Mr. Williams is every bit a gentleman, intelligent and polite. Mr. Woods, he's," she thought for a moment before continuing on, "He's sweet, thoughtful, and gorgeous." She looked surprised by her own admission and covered her mouth with her hand. Joy's eyes showed the shock of what we'd just heard. I don't believe Jane had ever said so much about a man.

Joy wagged a finger in Jane's direction. "Well, well, well, who's turning those nice gentlemen into pieces of meat now?" Then she burst into laughter.

Jane's neck turned bright red, and she hung her head.

I didn't like seeing my sister so uncomfortable, but Joy wasn't going to let this drop. I just needed to change the direction of the conversation slightly. "What do you mean about him being thoughtful?"

She looked up as if unsure whether she should speak or not. She looked at Joy's grinning expression and then back to me. I sat near her without even a hint of a smile tugging on my lips. After letting out a long breath, Jane spoke. "Chad asked me all about my job at the school. He introduced me to his two sisters, Missy and Heather. He told me that they'd be moving to the area. Heather and her husband Nick purchased a place in town. Missy and Chad will be staying with them while they get the business established. He asked me to offer recommendations for his sisters as to places to get their hair done, go shopping, grab a bite to eat, that sort of thing. Dr. Cooper invited Chad to join the men's Bible study at our church. Sounds like he might go, but his sisters didn't seem as interested when I invited them to join our women's study." Jane hesitated and then seemed to back pedal. "His sisters were incredibly sweet. I didn't mean anything by that remark. They're both brilliant and tutor students and teach test prep classes. We chatted for far too long before I needed to excuse myself to finish clearing. Chad obviously cares a great deal about his sisters, and he never once appeared to look down on me, even though I was there to clean up the trash."

The microwave beeped and Joy grabbed the bag of popcorn. As she poured it into a bowl, burning her fingers slightly in the process, she spoke to Jane. "If you like this man, and it seems like you do, you need to be a little more aggressive. You're shy and reserved, which is sweet, but it's not going to get a man interested. Guys might like a little challenge, but no man wants to be flat out rejected. If you don't give him a few signals that you're interested, he's not going to take the risk. You're going to have to flirt." Without waiting for a response, Joy crossed the room and sat on the couch, pulling up the menu on the TV and logging into our online movie library.

I glanced over at Jane's pensive face. Joy was probably right, but I couldn't see Jane making the first move. Heck, I wasn't sure if she'd even respond to a move made by Chad even though she was clearly interested. I wondered if there would be a way to help them along. Jane wouldn't be bulldozed into it like mom wanted, and she certainly wasn't going to flirt like Joy insisted. Jane needed things to move slowly, and Chad had to be able to read her subtle cues. This would be tricky.

5: Beth

The next morning, I woke up to Jane's sweet singing. Pulling myself off the floor by the edge of the couch, I tossed the throw pillow and blanket onto the cushions and rubbed my hands over my face a few times to force myself awake. Jane had already cleaned the kitchen, cleared away all the trash, and washed the dishes from the night before. Joy was in the bathroom, so I headed to the kitchen area in need of caffeine.

"I checked the weather app. Seems perfect for biking up the canal." I snatched a mug from the cabinet to pour myself a cup of coffee.

"Where do you want to eat?" Joy's voice filtered through the bathroom door.

"I'm thinking Jammin' Crepes. I think the Brownie in a Blanket is calling my name."

Jane shook her head. "I don't think you can call a brownie and ice cream stuffed crepe, 'breakfast.'"

I feigned shock. "You mean a thin pancake made of grains filled with a dairy product isn't acceptable?" I laughed. "If I can't eat ice cream for breakfast at my age, I don't really know what the perks of being an adult are."

Just as we were walking out the door, Jane piped up. "Lydia and Cat will be joining us." They had undoubtedly been reluctant when they agreed to bike along, but the car being unavailable left them no choice. I went from the anticipation of a morning with friends, to the dread of spending the entire day trying to keep the two of them from finding trouble.

Mary rarely came into town, unless the seminary was offering a lecture that she deemed conservative enough to warrant the exertion.

We arrived in Princeton mid-morning. The bike ride only took about 25 minutes, and the few miles each way made for a peaceful and serene start to our day. Jane and I tried to ride our bikes into town at least a couple of times a month when the weather was pleasant. Between the public library and the university, there was always something going on.

"I'd loved to stop by the bookstore if you guys don't mind." I tried to remain balanced while turning my head backwards to call over my shoulder as we came up to Nassau Street. "On a gorgeous day like this, the discount table should be set up along the sidewalk."

They both mumbled their agreement as we parked our bikes in a bike rack near one of the gated entrances into the University campus. While Joy preferred the clothing stores, she humored my love of literature. Jane never led the way through town. She always claimed to be content to window shop and spend time with Joy and I, and there was no reason to doubt her assertions. None of us could afford to buy anything not marked for clearance.

Before we had taken two steps, Lydia had already set her pleading face towards Jane. "Jane, can I borrow ten dollars to grab breakfast? You know Mother didn't make anything this morning. I'm starving and that bike ride is so long and exhausting, Look how sweaty I am." She swiped her sleeve dramatically across her forehead. "Ugh! I don't know if I'll have the energy to ride back."

Inwardly, I began predicting the conversation that unfolded in real life almost word for word.

Cat's face lit up and she joined in. "Yes, Jane. Please. I'm starving, too. I'll pay you back after I get my summer job. You know I don't have time to work during school. It's so hard to be a college student, I work just as hard as my teachers, but don't get paid for my work."

I knew these were hollow promises. Neither girl had yet to ever apply for a summer job.

"I'll buy you something if you come with us, but I'm not giving you cash. And I expect to be paid back as soon as you get your first paycheck." Jane tried to be firm, but she taught kindergarten and her lectures always sounded cute. They also didn't come across with a force that cried out to be obeyed.

We crossed the street and entered the quaint eatery. Cat and Lydia ordered more than was reasonable, but I supposed they didn't care as it was on Jane. Once they had their meals in hand, they waved their goodbyes and raced out the door. They headed straight for campus. I guessed that their first stop would be the sand volleyball pit, and then if they found the area void of shirtless undergrads, they would meander across campus to the fountain in search of the same thing.

Joy shook her head. "Those girls are going to get in over their head one day. All they do is hunt out invitations to parties. Neither one of them has a clue as to what a college party is really like."

Joy wasn't wrong. The girls had been doing this for years, but up until recently, they were too young to be taken seriously. Cat, a grade older than Lydia, might have been noticed earlier had it not been for Lydia. Lydia's more outgoing personality meant that she would often lead off their conversations and once the boys discovered her age, they withdrew. Though still in high school, Lydia, beautiful and flirtatious, had still managed to secure the attention of a number of undergrads.

"I don't know what to do about it. Every time I bring it up, Dad brushes off my concern and Mom only says things like 'Such pretty faces. How can you blame them?' I've intervened on a few occasions, but I can't always be around. And once their curfews get later, they might just make it to some of these parties." I felt a gnawing sense of dread deep in my gut. I really hoped Lydia and Cat would come to their senses sooner rather than later.

Joy, Jane, and I took a more leisurely exit from the shop, bringing our crepes across to the university campus and seating ourselves on the curved stone bench in Stockton Court just outside the Richardson Auditorium. The location was close enough that my ice cream hadn't melted, and shaded enough to cool us off from the exercise. As we chatted, we were surprised to see Chad and Darcy striding across campus.

6: Darcy

"Lexi is going to be fine taking over Williams Holdings. You've done a great job training her up, and you've set up a full year to transition." Chad's words eased my mind.

"I know you're right, but she's still my little sister. I worry about her. I'm not at all worried about her competency, just her stress with school and work." I'd been raising her since she was a teen, and it was hard to go back to being just her brother.

"The real question is how you're going to use the extra time once you release your grasp on the company?" Chad slapped my back.

"I think I'll be plenty busy with Williams Security and the Foundation." It would be nice to have a little more free time. Maybe I could get back to traveling again. But was Lexi ready? Was I?

"Darcy, God called you to a hard thing. Raising Lexi while still in college, taking over the family business, starting your own. And He faithfully saw you through all of that. But there is more to life than just work. It's time to find what makes you truly happy. Fulfilled. Lexi wants that for you too. I know she does. We talk."

"You better not be talking to her." I shot Chad a sideways glance. Chad raised his hand in the surrender pose.

"Not like that. I promise. She feels like you've sacrificed so much for her. It's why she's been prepping to take back Williams Holdings even while she's finishing her MBA. She's ready. It's time, man."

I nodded. He was right. Letting go was hard, but it was time.

We had just passed by the auditorium when Chad caught my arm and pulled me to an abrupt stop. Apparently, he had noticed the woman he had been speaking with at the association meeting. He had regaled me with his opinions on her beauty and charm. She was the most lovely, most sweet, most interesting woman he'd ever met. Chad told me similar things frequently enough that I barely listened anymore. His appraisal of Jane's looks wasn't overstated; she was gorgeous. Jane mentioned that she taught kindergarten. She truly was enchanting, but she wasn't my cup of tea. No offense to her. She was delightful in every way. Soft spoken and saccharine sweet. Chad adored sweet girls, but I was looking for someone with a little more spice.

Chad led us over. "What a lovely surprise to see you here, Jane."

Jane's eyes dipped down. "It's nice to see you too."

"You remember my friend, Darcy." Chad gestured my way.

"Of course. Mr. Williams, it's nice to see you again as well.

"Please, it's Darcy."

"Let me introduce you to my friend Joy, and my sister Beth. Joy's family owns the Douglas Café, who catered the business association meeting, and Beth teaches 4th grade at Asbury Christian Academy with me." Jane pointed to each one in turn. "And perhaps you two haven't met Chad Woods. He's the owner of Academic Success, which is going to open up in the old law office. Mr. Williams, I mean, Darcy, actually owns the grounds." Jane's gaze was directed slightly downward, but she occasionally glanced up at Chad.

There were the usual acknowledgments and waves as everyone became acquainted. Beth seemed uncomfortable, and I couldn't keep my lip from turning up a bit. "Joy, nice to meet you. Beth, I believe we're met already. Thanks for taking such good care of my car." Both girls' heads shot toward Beth. Joy's grin was enormous. I wondered if they had heard that story already.

Beth squared her shoulders and landed her feet flat on the stone path. She made herself as fierce as possible for a woman eating ice cream for breakfast. "I'm sorry about the key marks on your door. Not being a valet, I wasn't prepared for the task." For a woman barely over five feet with freckles on her face, she had spunk.

"I didn't notice. If this teaching gig doesn't work out, I think you can find your calling in parking cars." A chuckle escaped my lips, not that I had tried too hard to hold it back. The fire in Beth's hazel eyes screamed that she didn't appreciate my humor.

Jane, clearly uncomfortable, interjected, "What brings you men into town today?" Her gaze settled on Chad.

"Actually, Darcy and I both went to Princeton. We usually come down each year for Reunions, which was last weekend, but this year with me in town for a bit, Darcy figured he'd stay for a while as well. He can do most of his work remotely, and he likes to check up on his properties from time to time. We were just heading over to meet up with the man who served as the faculty advisor to our Christian fellowship back when we were students. He's retired now, but still prays for the likes of us fools."

Chad shoved my shoulder jovially and then turned back to Jane. "Do you ever come to Reunions?"

Jane smiled softly, and her voice came out mildly. "No. We've been to Communiveristy Weekend before, but we prefer when things are quieter. Less traffic, Fewer people."

"And what summer plans do you have, besides enjoying this deserted campus?" Chad quickly looked at all the girls to include them in his question, but his focus appeared to be on Jane alone.

"Summers are usually rather quiet for us. This summer, Beth and I are attending a conference, which should be nice. Our headmaster, you know, Dr. Cooper, asked Beth and me just yesterday about attending a teacher's conference in Jersey City. We'll be in workshops during the day, but there will be time to see the city."

I shot a look at Chad who caught my eye, and I knew he was thinking the same thing I was. This could be entertaining.

7: Beth

Ugh! Not that it matters what these men think, but Jane's description of our big summer plans being a work conference probably sounded highly pathetic. Who equates a work conference with a vacation because you get to see a new city? And not even a well-known city like LA or Chicago. This was Jersey City. And from the fact that both men smiled and shot a glance at each other, that's exactly what they thought. Whatever. It's not that we didn't have any money; it's just that a down payment on a house isn't cheap. My blood began to boil. Just because they happen to have more money and could afford to go on expensive vacations didn't make them better than everyone else. I heard the crackling as I clenched the Styrofoam take-out container in my hand, but decided against confronting the arrogant looks I had seen.

Chad and Darcy made small talk for a few minutes before Darcy ended the conversation. "We'd hate to keep you from your meal. It seems like Beth's ice cream is melting. We don't want to spoil your breakfast." And with that, the two men strode off. Just then, I felt the cold sticky liquid running down my leg. I looked down to see melted chocolate ice cream leaking out of a crack in the bottom of my container and the remnants of a soggy brownie. Irritated at both the loss of my treat and my peace, I stormed off and tossed everything in the trashcan.

Jane pulled a few baby wipes from her purse and handed them to me. Of course, Jane had wipes on her. I swiped angrily at the brown rivulet that ended at my once white socks.

"Well, Joy, what do you think now? Did you hear the condescension that dripped off Darcy's tongue? He was all arrogant smirks and cutting barbs. I don't know if anyone has ever gotten under my skin like that man."

Joy smiled. "I don't know Beth. He was a fine specimen of a man. I bet I could put up with a little sass if a guy was willing to spoil me with the kind of money he has."

I huffed. "Joy Douglas, you can't be serious. I would much rather marry a poor man who respects me than sell my soul to the devil for some financial security. And I don't care what you say, that man is not a Christian."

Joy's eyes looked a little hurt, but she recovered quickly and laughed it off. "Darcy Williams is not the devil, and a little practicality goes a long way. You need to stop reading all those romance novels. Real life isn't all sweet kisses in the moonlight and princes sweeping peasants off their feet. Marriage is more like a business contract than a Hallmark movie."

8: Beth

With the school year over, and the AC units in the dorm apartments unable to keep up with the late July heat, my anticipation of the upcoming Educational Advancement Foundation conference grew. I loved to explore new places, and despite being a mere hour away, I had barely spent any time in Jersey City. When I was younger, it had a bad rap, but the revitalization in recent years had made it more of a haven for millennials who worked in Manhattan. When Dr. Cooper had asked Jane and me about attending, we readily agreed. We felt less honored when he explained that many of the other faculty members already had summer plans. No doubt the faculty who had spouses with lucrative jobs could traipse around the world. Not Jane and I. He also mentioned that some of the workshops appeared to touch on the younger grades, including a cross curricular emphasis on art and science.

Jane and I thought through our plans. Jane wondered aloud, "Maybe we can extend our trip a few days and spend some time with Aunt Erica and Uncle Bert. I bet the kids are getting so big."

"Yes, that sounds perfect. I love Aunt Erica." Aunt Erica married my mother's younger brother Bert. Bert, eight years my mother's junior, was a lawyer in NYC. He was my mother's polar opposite. Reserved, quiet, and scholarly. We always got along just fine. Aunt Erica on the other hand, a few years younger than Uncle Bert, was much more like an older cousin than an aunt. We were close, but she was even closer to Jane. Perhaps Jane's more maternal side connected with Erica who was mother to our two young cousins.

I shot off a text. *Jane and I are coming up to Jersey City early in July, We hoped to see you.*

I waited while the text bubbles appeared on my screen.

Erica: *Shoot. We leave to visit my parents in Michigan right after the kids get out of school. Won't be home until late July.*

Disappointment filled me.

Me: *Ugh. Bad timing. When you get back, we'll have to plan something. Enjoy your trip. Kiss the kids.*

Jane sighed, but continued her travel research.

While excited about learning new things, we were more interested in a free stay in a fancy hotel with a daily food allowance that would allow us to enjoy some of the local dining. We weren't exactly foodies. How could we be on our income? But we knew how to use Yelp and Tripadvisor to find the best bang for our food budget buck. We had little in the way of an entertainment budget; however, that wouldn't stop us from having fun. I had already researched Jersey City on a shoestring and had found dozens of options that would require little or no money. We had found places to eat from bagel shops to food trucks, with a few nicer sit-down restaurants. This was going to be almost as nice as a vacation, something neither of us had taken in years.

***

The first sign that things wouldn't go smoothly came as we stood facing the registration desk of the Hyatt Regency in Jersey City. I noticed a gentleman who looked an awful lot like Darcy Williams in the back-office area, but his back was toward me as he spoke to several people.

My attention was drawn back to the woman at the front desk when I heard a confused "hmmm" come from her mouth. The woman stepped away from the desk and into the office, interrupting the conversation. She spoke too quietly for me to understand what she was saying, then nodded a few times and returned with her lips tight. She appeared worried. "I'm very sorry. There was a mix up with your reservation. We accidentally double booked your room. We've made arrangements for you to be placed in a nearby apartment. Though it's not in this building, it's a fully furnished apartment with a lovely view just a short jaunt along the riverfront. It's a private rental, but I am sure you'll find it to your liking." She lowered her voice. "It's a huge upgrade. You're incredibly lucky."

Jane looked at me and smirked. Jane, who could never let anyone feel bad for even a moment, smiled at the woman. "Thank you so much. We're sorry to cause you trouble. I'm sure it'll be great. Just point the way." Just like Jane to apologize for the hotel's error.

I continued to split my attention between the woman at the front desk and the familiar looking man in the back, but I couldn't get a decent look at him. Finally, I gave up and turned my full attention to the conversation at hand.

"We'll have our bellhop bring your bags over for you. Here's the information for the keyless entry, and we've included a fifty-dollar credit for you to enjoy at any of our restaurants or the gift shop. Before you settle in, you might want to check in at the conference registration table to get your registration packet and welcome bag so you can take it all over at once. Just let me know when you're ready, and I'll send someone to transport your bags."

Jane thanked her, and we headed over to registration. I tapped Jane and leaned closer to her. "Was that Darcy Williams in the back room?"

"I don't know. I hadn't noticed. He lives in Jersey City, but it'd be odd for him to be in a hotel if he lives here. Unless it's for his job."

I pondered that thought as we navigated our way through the lobby. As we reached the front of the registration line and checked in, I noticed the large banners that stood around the table advertising the sponsors of the event. One sign was for something called Jersey Strong, an afterschool program funded by a major financial institution. It had something to do with getting children excited about STEM subjects. Next to that was The Agape Foundation with pictures of some of educational programs around the world that their charity supported. There were pictures of kids in school uniforms in Haiti, Uganda, Thailand, and Jersey City. The hair on the back of my neck stuck up. Darcy's foundation was one of the sponsors of the event. That could explain his presence in the back office.

My stomach dropped. It wasn't likely I'd get through the next four days without seeing him.

Across the main room stood a collection of vendor booths and the familiar face of Chad Woods caught my eye. I pointed him out to Jane and pulled her through the crowd. Chad was chatting with a conference attendee, so Jane chatted with his sister, Missy.

I missed what Jane said, but Missy's response was crystal clear. "Dear, stay close to the waterfront while you're here. It's lovely and there's plenty to do. You start straying beyond this area and you never know what kinds of people you'll run into. Some areas are dangerous. Poor people everywhere." She lowered her voice as she said the word poor, like it was a dirty word. I'm sure in her mind poor people were dirty.

I looked at the brochures and display. I'm sure the school would have some interest in these things, but I wasn't exactly prepping my 4th graders for college entrance exams.

It was evident by the conversation I had overheard that Chad was trying to wrap things up with the other man. Once his attention turned to us, he was all smiles.

"Jane, Beth, so nice to see you. Did you sign up for our drawing?" he asked.

"No. Not yet," Jane replied. "I don't think it would help my kindergarteners, and I'd hate to take the chance away from someone who could use it."

"Nonsense. I can just scan your badge right here, and you can pass it on to your school if you win." With that, Chad scanned both our nametags. "See. Easy. Did you guys need any tips for things to do in the area? Here, take my card." He began writing his personal cell number on the back of the card. "Call or text me anytime. Maybe we can meet up for dinner." Chad was talking fast. He seemed nervous around Jane, which I found rather endearing. From the look on her face, Missy was noticing the same adoration in Chad's eyes and didn't appreciate it at all.

Jane clumsily accepted the card then readjusted the bag of free goodies and the large conference packet we'd received at registration. We thanked Chad and Missy and then began pulling our suitcases out the door and down the waterfront path that led to the building where we would be staying. Jane would never want to be a bother anyone, and I hated getting help for anything I could do on my own.

**

Honestly, I couldn't believe the accommodations we just stepped into. The space included two bedrooms, a full kitchen, a living room with huge windows, and a top floor balcony with a view of the NYC skyline. If this had been a hotel, it would have been the presidential suite. For a few minutes, I contemplated skipping all the sessions. I was right in the middle of *The Count of Monte Cristo,* and I was sure I could easily fill my days lounging on that balcony reading. The tasteful décor spoke of money but not opulence. A large screen TV took up the entire space above a gas fireplace. The art on the walls wasn't the kind you find in a hotel, with its pastel colors or the splatters and smudges of modern art. Rather, the walls held photographs of incredible scenery, presumably from around the world. The furnishing was sparse, but homey. I had a feeling that the bathroom was going to have a tub with jets, and if that was the case, I was going to spend an evening soaking in a warm bath. Peeking in, I was not disappointed. Perhaps this mix-up was going to be rather fabulous.

We had settled into our suite but the kickoff wouldn't happen for three more hours. Together, we spent some time reading through the workshop choices and deciding which events we would attend together and which ones we would rather split up and then share notes.

"I would love to attend one of Chad's workshops, but attending a session on AP classes when I teach kindergarten feels like I'm taking advantage of Dr. Cooper sending me here."

"He is one of the keynote speakers. It says he's speaking on educational changes in the post-COVID era. That should be valuable. So, we'll definitely hear him speak." I was less excited to see that Darcy was also a plenary speaker. He was the final speaker of the event. For a moment I wondered if Dr. Cooper would be upset if we were to head home a little early. "What are your thoughts on the most important decision of the day?"

Jane looked at me quizzically. "What's that?"

"Dinner, of course." I smiled.

We headed down to Newark Avenue. to eat at one of the smaller restaurants along the strip. I was leaning towards the Gypsy Grill. As we came upon the Grove Street Station, we stumbled upon a farmers market. Booths were set up selling fresh fruits and vegetables but also nuts, pickles, popcorn, and even prepared dinners. I considered just grabbing dinner right there, but we decided we could come back another night. Meandering through town we stopped to enjoy the murals scattered along Christopher Columbus Boulevard. Jane and I marveled at the beauty despite the paint peeling in places. The urban art was so different from the streets of Princeton. I decided that I might need to reconsider some of my prejudices that the city was ugly. I clearly hadn't accounted for the view of the river, the skyline, and the murals.

Dinner was another treat. Newark Avenue was a pedestrian street. The shops and restaurants opened up to a wide avenue. Tables littered the edge of the road, while in the center there were kids doing skateboard tricks, a person played guitar at a bench near the center of the lane, and a magician was even giving a small show. I paid for my shawarma and followed Jane and her salad out to a picnic table. How could such a sense of community exist in an area so populated? It had the feel of a Palmer Square in Princeton only with taller buildings. Dinner finished, we headed back to the Hyatt for the beginning of the conference. We saw neither Chad nor Darcy. The mere fact that Darcy had once again entered my thoughts irritated me. My plans for a fun working vacation would be anything but that if I was subjected to the likes of Darcy Williams at every turn.

9: Beth

The follow morning, way too early to be up on summer break, we decided to check out Wonder Bagels. They had great reviews online and the weather seemed pleasant enough to make the walk several blocks there and back. We left enough time so we'd be back for this morning's plenary speaker. There was a line out the door when we arrived that snaked past a small outdoor seating area that was comprised of several small café tables and chairs. The line seemed to be moving fairly quickly. Even so, we did our best to peek through the door and read the menu posted on the wall behind the counter. As we finally reached the front and placed our order my eyes caught the small sign by the register. This was a cash only establishment, or at least under $10 was. Jane and I both started searching our purses for enough cash to cover the order. Then from behind me, I heard the same deep voice I had been hoping to avoid this week.

"Allow me." Darcy placed his order and handed the cashier a twenty.

I felt the heat rising in my face. I steadied myself before I turned around. "That won't be necessary."

Jane placed her hand on my arm and turned her eyes to Darcy. "Thank you so much. I hardly ever carry cash. We hadn't realized we couldn't use our cards."

I mumbled, "Who carries cash anymore?"

Darcy leaned down so that he was mere inches from my ear and whispered, "Just about everyone in the city." I felt the fire behind my eyes, but refused to allow the source of that anger to have the satisfaction of seeing me react.

"If you're heading back now, I'd be happy to offer you a ride." Darcy directed his question to Jane.

Personally, I would have preferred crawling back on my hands and knees over broken glass, but Jane quickly accepted. Traitor!

Since it was her idea, I forced her into the seat closest to Darcy, providing me with a buffer.

Darcy's black town car was not the car I had driven. This "ride" came with a driver. Figured. Obviously, his entitled attitude came from his easy, pampered life. Yet, the car was comfortable and even I had to admit that the trip back was far nicer than sweating outside in the warm, humid weather.

"What add-on activities did you pick from the conference listings? Ellis Island? The Broadway show?"

I was willfully silent.

"We don't have much in the way of fun money," Jane said. "We're planning to swing by the farmers market and check out the mall. Oh, and I heard sometimes there are street performers."

I would have liked to have crawled under the seat, not because I was ashamed of our financial situation, but rather because I hated freely giving Darcy any more reason to look down upon us.

Darcy nodded. "Text Chad, he knows the best places to eat."

When we arrived at the Hyatt, we parted ways, and I breathed a sigh of relief.

**

The first two days of the conference were a blur of workshops and speakers. Between events, we took in the waterfront. We played chess with oversized pieces in the lobby of a nearby mall, treated ourselves to the local cuisine, and basically enjoyed ourselves immensely for two girls who would not have declared ourselves to be city people. Obviously, if done right, one didn't need to have money to enjoy oneself. Jane's text to Chad had supplied us with more eateries than we could possibly try in our few days, but each one had been affordable and delicious.

Chad appeared at almost every turn. Okay, so maybe I dragged Jane into the vendor booth area several times a day, but it was our obligation to thoroughly check out the curriculum and resources available to best help our school. And sure, I might have considered room assignments when planning my workshops so we were mingling in the hallway adjacent to a conference room Chad was presenting in. Jane needed the help. But even my attempts at casually bumping into Chad didn't account for the number of times we saw Chad. Often the places Chad suggested we visit were the places he was going as well. I hoped this meant he returned Jane's feelings.

I wished it hadn't come with the baggage of his best friend and his sister, Missy, who was bound and determined to hang on Darcy's every word and when possible his actual body. Ick. Whenever we roamed the waterfront or were on our way to grab a bite to eat, Jane and Chad would lag behind. I was often stuck with Missy and Darcy. Missy seemed to squeeze her way between Darcy and myself regardless of how inconvenient it was. Several times, I was nearly forced to walk into the street to avoid colliding with someone or something. Not that I had any desire to be near Darcy, but seriously, how about some common courtesy? If she considered me a threat to her conquest, she was gravely mistaken.

"Darcy, your session today was absolutely wonderful. Who knew grant writing could be so interesting." I tried not to roll my eyes as Missy gushed over Darcy.

I didn't listen to Darcy's reply. My ability to school my face into something resembling friendliness was getting old real fast. I wouldn't have done it for anyone other than Jane.

At the end of second day, when the two men, this time without Missy, had discovered Jane and I at the mall in an animated, oversized chess game, I relinquished my position to Chad, citing this having been my third game and touting Jane's superiority. Darcy suggested we take a go at shuffleboard.

"I'm sorry. I can't play. I'm not eighty years old yet," I quipped.

Darcy laughed, and I wasn't sure if it was irritation or appreciation for the joke. I hadn't thought my rejection through. Now I was left alone with him and an awkward silence. He seemed subdued maybe even nervous tonight. Maybe Missy acted as a buffer for him, Now, with no one to keep the conversation going, he'd be forced to try with me.

After a painful few minutes Darcy broke the silence. "How has your time in Jersey City been?"

I stammered my reply. "It's been nice. Informative. Pleasant."

"What are your impressions of the city? I know you enjoy Princeton. This is a far cry from what you're used to."

Was he honestly assuming I had no experience with cities? "I have traveled, you know. My Aunt Erica and Uncle Bert live in Manhattan. It's not like I'm some sheltered child. If you must know, I enjoy cities very much."

Darcy let out an exasperated sigh. "Beth, I didn't mean to irritate you yet again. It seems like everything I say rubs you the wrong way. What I was asking was how you feel about this City. My city. I've lived in Princeton myself. It's a different lifestyle. I was curious as to whether you enjoyed this lifestyle as well. This city in particular?"

Was he judging my personality or making small talk? I wasn't sure. I relaxed my shoulders. "I'm sorry. You do seem to get my goat." I smiled sheepishly at him. "I'll admit to being pleasantly surprised by my time here. When I was younger, I remember hearing how run down and dangerous Jersey City was. My dad nearly forbade me from coming up here for a college retreat. The city looked different back when I was younger, The only thing I saw on the retreat was the inside of the college where we stayed. Dad's orders. I had no idea there were million-dollar condos and hip restaurants around. The revitalization here has been remarkable. I can definitely see the appeal of living here."

Darcy smiled at me. "You think you would ever want to teach in one of the schools around here?"

I eyed him warily. Darcy held up his hands to me. "I'm curious. I'm doing informal research. I ask teachers questions like this all the time. It helps me understand how to find what teachers are looking for in positions so we can staff our programs well."

I nodded my head. "Honestly, I wanted to teach in the inner-city. I did my student teaching in Trenton. I thought God had called me there. Like a mission field." I paused as I thought back. Darcy nodded for me to continue. "It didn't go well. I felt like such a failure. I was naïve. I didn't understand what it was like to grow up in the city. I had read all these books on urban education, but the kids had more street smarts than I did. I was idealistic. It took a while for me to figure out that kids can't learn when they're hungry and tired, and parents who don't speak English can't read in English to their kids at night or help them with homework when they can't read the instructions. Math homework was less of an issue. Universal language and all." I collected myself.

"I think in some ways I did more damage than helping those kids. It was pretty eye opening. But that wasn't the worst. There were security guards in elementary schools. I was shocked at how lacking in nutrition the free breakfast and lunches seemed to be. The hoops we had to jump through for State tests. I think educators are burnt out. My boss used to swear at us in staff meetings. I hated that.

"The day one of my kids' parents told me I had a white savior complex I was really offended. But looking back, maybe she was right. I wasn't the right fit for the job." I looked up at Darcy who was staring at me with compassion in his eyes. "Maybe I would be better at a job like that now, I've grown up a lot since then. And, while I never saw myself teaching in a private school, I love my job and the freedom I have to share Christ with my students. It's a different mission field than I thought I would have." I shook my head to clear it and looked back to Darcy. "Sorry. You probably didn't want to hear all that.

Darcy touched my hand for the briefest of seconds. "No. I did. Thank you for sharing that with me." I was surprised by how much comfort I drew from his sincere compassion.

I wanted to reciprocate some deeper questions but found myself unsure as to what to ask. His interest in me seemed almost genuine, yet I couldn't muster up that same level of thoughtful inquisition. Fortunately, Jane and Chad joined us.

Darcy looked at Jane and back to me. "Will you be joining the tour of the schools tomorrow?"

"No, sadly it was all booked up before we registered for the conference." Jane said.

Chad piped in, "We could get you ladies on that tour if you wanted. It's not a problem. Darcy always holds a seat or two open. Isn't that right?"

Jane beamed at Darcy as if it were his idea. He simply nodded.

"Perfect. Meet us at the bus stop tomorrow. We'll make sure to have the list updated." Chad nodded toward the door.

Darcy cleared his throat. "And on that note, I think it's time to call it a night. I look forward to seeing you tomorrow on the tour." Then the men silently strode off.

Did I just bare my soul to Darcy Williams?

10: Darcy

Beth stepped from the bus at our fourth and final stop of the day. She sure wasn't the kind of woman I had pegged her as when I first met her. I followed her through the doors of the enrichment center. Beth took in the brightly colored walls, reading the posters and gazing on the murals. Her face lit up with joy. A small child was coming down the hallway carrying a tray with several cups filled with paintbrushes. Beth approached her, crouched beside her, and spoke softly. I couldn't make out what she said, but moments later the girl placed her tiny sneakered foot on Beth's bent thigh while Beth reached up to place a steadying hand on her arm. Beth quickly tied her laces and then patted her foot twice before the girl removed her foot and rewarded her with a grateful smile. Beth stood and quickly caught up with the group.

We entered into a large cafeteria where groups of children were working with teachers in several areas. One group was building bridges, another was working on a drawing of a skyscraper, and another group was doing some sort of experiment with scales and weights.

Our guide was explaining the importance of stirring excitement in the kids for the STEM subjects. "Not only are those jobs more lucrative, but they are the fastest growing career fields. Traditionally girls and ethnic minorities are underrepresented."

Beth spoke up. "How do the students get into this program? Is it expensive for families?"

"The program is free to qualified families. If a student qualifies for free or reduced lunch, they probably qualify for our program. And another benefit is they get those lunches throughout the summer program as well. We fill our classes through a lottery system. We can't accommodate all the students who apply. We'd love to open more locations, but we need teachers. We don't have the staff to expand our program. All of our teachers are volunteers. Mostly college students on break, building up their resumes. We have a few paid positions for supervisors and site directors, but mostly we run on generosity."

Without skipping a beat, Beth piped up again, "Do you have housing for volunteers?" She bumped Jane with her shoulder and smiled at her sister.

"Actually, we've been looking into a grant for that. If we can offer room and board for volunteers, we could potentially recruit more college interns and expand our program."

Our guide seemed hopeful as Beth nodded her head. Could Beth be interested in spending more time here? That grant might just be worth funding. I shot off a text to my assistant at the Agape Foundation to check into this. Maybe my sister, Lexi, could head this up. College internship, study abroad options, continuing education credits for teachers. I'd have to think this through more. Beth had given me some food for thought last night when she detailed her personal experience. How could we better train teachers coming in from the suburbs? I glanced up at Beth, who was following our guide out into the courtyard. My gaze followed her as she put distance between us. I lingered for just a moment to take in the sight of the light coming through the door and reflecting off her black hair. I stepped toward her. Beth Beckett was worth pursuing.

11: Beth

The last day of the conference, Jane and I ventured out to the food trucks to grab a quick bite to eat. There were so many to choose from that it took far longer to get lunch than we had expected, but I'm a sucker for food trucks. You can't think too hard about calories or fat content or even sanitation. If you can push those pesky thoughts from your mind, a well-chosen food truck item might be the best meal you'll eat all week. We ate on a bench soaking in the view of Manhattan and the Hudson River. Our time away had been just the rest we had both needed. Forty-five minutes later, we were headed back to the conference when Jane started to wince in pain. She slowed her pace, and I turned to face her. Jane's face was pale, and beads of sweat were breaking out. Her chestnut hair was sticking to her forehead.

"Jane, what's the matter?" I'm sure my worry was evident in my expression.

"I need to go back to our room. I'm going to be sick."

Thankfully, our place was closer than the hotel. As rapidly as was possible considering Jane's condition, I ushered her back to the apartment. I lent her support. She seemed to be getting weaker and more ill with each passing moment. As we struggled down the hallway, we encountered Chad entering the apartment adjacent to our own.

"Jane, what's the matter? Are you okay?" He left his door ajar and rushed to help support Jane, who didn't speak. I knew this was a bad sign.

"We just finished lunch. It came on so fast. Thank you. I didn't know if I could make it back by myself."

"I should call the doctor." Worry lines ran across Chad's forehead.

I knew we couldn't afford the kind of doctor who made house calls. "Thank you for the offer, but I'm sure it won't be necessary. I'll check with our insurance company and see if there is an urgent care center nearby if it comes to that. I can call my Aunt Erica. She lives in New York City. She'll be able to help." Then I remembered why we hadn't seen her already. "Shoot. She's away."

Chad glanced between Jane and me. He helped to settle Jane into her room and pulled out his cell phone. While I was trying to make Jane comfortable, I heard him requesting a doctor. My worry for Jane quickly eclipsed my worry about the money, so I didn't even try to stop him. Chad exited our apartment, but left the door open. The next thing I heard was his apartment door close, then open a few minutes later, and close again.

Moments later, Chad was standing in Jane's bedroom with a thermometer and a bag. He handed me the thermometer and started pulling things from the grocery sack. First there was a selection of medication. There was ibuprofen, acetaminophen, and a couple of medications for upset stomachs and even allergies. Next, he pulled out a can of ginger ale and a package of crackers. "I've called the doctor. She'll be here in a little while. Please, don't argue. I want to do this. I've already told her to bill me. Do you need anything else? Let me give you my number."

I handed Chad my phone. "Thank you. You didn't need to do all this."

"I'm just next-door. Missy and some of our employees are covering the table today, so the only time I won't be around is when Darcy is speaking tonight, but even then, if you need me, just text. I can be back in a few minutes."

"I'm sure we'll be fine," I said.

"If the doctor prescribes anything, have the pharmacy deliver it and charge me. Don't argue." I saw the determination in his eyes.

Gone was his cheerful disposition. Chad's face showed his concern. I was impressed by how calm he was under pressure. He thought of everything. I was the complete opposite. I couldn't put two thoughts together. Before I could speak, I saw Jane sitting up and the look on her face alerted me that a race to the bathroom was coming. Chad, equally perceptive, rushed to her aid and together we got Jane there before the retching began. Once again, Chad left for a few moments, but this time he returned with several small blankets. Together we were able to get one blanket on the floor to make Jane more comfortable as she emptied her stomach. The rest he laid at the foot of Jane's bed. I was glad she had taken the master bedroom with the attached bath.

**

The doctor arrived before Chad left and determined that a trip to the hospital wouldn't be necessary unless Jane's condition worsened. Rest, fluids, and fever reducing medication would be enough. She assured me that in a few days, Jane would be back on her feet and confirmed my suspicion that it was probably food poisoning. "Give it a few days. But if her fever increases, or if she can't keep down liquids and is becoming dehydrated, I want you to bring her to the emergency room."

Chad and I left Jane resting in bed and accompanied the doctor to the door with our sincere thanks. Chad promised to have broth sent up for Jane along with other necessary supplies. Once again, he made me promise to call him if Jane needed anything.

"I am so incredibly grateful for you, Chad. I don't know what I would have done without you. I guess God was watching over us today. Is there any chance you know if we can extend our stay here? We were actually supposed to be in the hotel and somehow ended up over here. I don't know who to contact, but we were supposed to check out tomorrow morning."

Chad seemed surprised by the question. "I'll take care of it, but I don't think it will be a problem to stay as long as you need. Darcy owns this place. We were neighbors before he moved closer to the marina. He rarely rents the space out. Assume it's fine unless you hear back from me."

"Darcy Williams? This is his place?" He couldn't have said anything more shocking if his goal had been to unnerve me.

Chad laughed as if he had enjoyed the joke. "I'm going to take care of a few things, but expect a delivery in a little while."

I thanked him for the umpteenth time and gave him a hug before he strode away. When the door closed, I slumped down on the couch and tried to collect my scattered thoughts. What the heck? I was sleeping in Darcy William's house? Did he know that?

When a knock finally came, I found two deliverymen carrying flowers and several bags. They placed items on the kitchen island as instructed, but declined a tip, assuring me that it had been taken care of. I snuck into Jane's room and placed the enormous arrangement of flowers on the dresser so that she would see them when she awoke.

Unpacking the grocery bag, I discovered a case of small water bottles, lip balm, tissues, tea bags, and some more ginger ale. The other bag appeared to have come from a local restaurant. It contained a quart of chicken noodle soup, several small packages of saltine crackers, a small loaf of bread with some butter packets, and a Styrofoam container. I carefully opened the container to reveal a medley of pasta dishes: spaghetti and meatballs, chicken fettuccini alfredo, and a pasta with sausage with pesto sauce. Considering the choice of food, I assumed that Chad had sent up the Italian dishes for me. There was no way someone in Jane's condition could eat such heavy foods. He must have been unsure as to what I would want to eat, so he provided options. Jane was right. Chad was incredibly thoughtful. Not for the first time this afternoon, I sent up a prayer of thanks for him and asked God to bless him for his kindness. I texted my thanks. Chad was one of the good guys, and I couldn't be happier for Jane to have found a man like him.

12: Beth

Throughout the night, Jane's condition stayed much the same. She was sick off and on, but she seemed able to hold down enough fluid to compensate for what she lost. She slept fitfully, and I chose to remain nearby rather than retire to my own room. A knock at the door in the morning brought a delivery from Wonder Bagels. I took the cup holder with two hot teas and the bag from the young man's hand and placed them on the entryway table. I began fumbling in my wallet for a tip.

"No tip. Thank you, but it was already covered. Enjoy." He spun around and headed out.

I pulled out the rainbow bagel with butter like I had ordered the first morning and smiled. I hadn't been able to resist the bright colors. It had been the perfect carb-filled start to the morning. Other than the plain bagel coming with butter on the side, this was the exact order Darcy had already purchased for us. I was starting to feel like a free loader.

I texted Chad, *Thank you for the bagels. We both appreciate it. Jane's doing a bit better.*

The morning came and went with Jane feeling only slightly better. When a knock came around noon, I was expecting a lunch delivery. The direction my thoughts took was solely based upon Chad's generosity rather than any feelings of entitlement on my part. Instead, I opened the door to Darcy.

"How's your sister?"

I tried to settle my nerves from the shock of the sight. "Uh, she's doing a little better. She's still sick, but certainly in a better state than yesterday."

We stood in silence looking at one another for a few moments before he spoke. "I wanted to let you know that the place is yours for as long as you need it. No worries at all."

"Thank you. I don't know how we will ever repay you and Chad for all this."

"There is no need to repay anything. Anyone would have done the same."

"I hardly think so. Everything Jane or I could have possibly needed has been sent right to the door. I haven't had to leave her once. I am incredibly grateful."

Darcy smiled with a look of contentment. "I'm glad to hear that. Chad wanted to make sure you were both comfortable." His voice dropped as he caught my eye. "So did I."

The look Darcy had just given me had my stomach aflutter. It was neither one of compassion or pity. It was more interest or even desire. The thought that Darcy Williams, wealthy business man, could harbor feelings for me was ludicrous. The stress of the past day must be messing with my head.

"I...I... uh... we're definitely comfortable." Great, now I was stuttering. I pulled myself together. "I have to admit I was surprised to find that we were staying in your place. It's amazing. I can't imagine what your new home looks like, because to leave views like this must have been difficult."

"I'm glad you're enjoying the view. Though, if Jane is feeling better later, maybe you'd be interested in a change of scenery. This evening we could get outside for a bit? You've been cooped up in here for quite a while. Missy volunteered to stay here to give you a break? Say six? We can grab something to eat while we're out."

Did Darcy Williams just ask me if I want to go to dinner? What the? "I...I guess that would be alright. As long as Jane is feeling okay and Missy doesn't mind."

"Excellent. I'll be by at six. Are you set on food until then? Do you need anything?"

I assured him that we'd been more than provided for. I thanked him and closed the door. I was starting to get used to having no idea what was happening in my own life. It was as if I were watching a strange story unfold on a screen. I considered Darcy. He had to have been the one to send breakfast. At the very least he had to have been the one to tell Chad about our order. Were Jane and I just another charity for him to support? Or was there more? Honestly, I just didn't have it in me to overthink this right now. I was sure I'd analyze it to death in due time, but right now I was too tired to think.

After reading on the balcony for an hour or so, I checked in on Jane. She was resting comfortably, and I decided the best way to clear my head was a nap. I had barely slept last night and was sure I looked it. I was awoken at 5:55 by a rapping on the door. Completely out of sorts, I couldn't figure out exactly where I was or when it was. I stood from the couch and collected my bearings. Yes, I was sleeping on Darcy Williams' couch. The second tapping had me staggering to the door. I am sure I was completely unsuccessful at hiding my embarrassment at my appearance when I opened the door to Darcy. He was wearing jeans and a short sleeve button down shirt. I was just as surprised to see him in jeans as I was to see him at all. My words tumbled out. "Come in. I'm so sorry. I must have fallen asleep. I can be ready in a few minutes. Oh, I have to check on Jane."

Darcy touched my arm and waited until I looked him in the eyes. "It's fine. There's no rush. Take your time. Check on Jane. I'll just make myself at home." He grinned.

I nodded before rushing into Jane's room.

She was sitting up in bed sipping on some water and reading a book. I discussed the plan for the evening and confirmed with her that all was well. She assured me that there was no need for Missy to babysit her. "Go on. Get out of here."

"You're sure?"

"I can text if I need you. Promise. Just go." Jane texted Chad and let him know that there was no need for Missy to come over.

Chad responded right away, but let her know that both he and Missy would be right next door all evening if she needed anything.

I warmed up some soup for Jane, made sure she had the remote for the TV, and then brought her the pills she'd need before heading to my room to get ready.

I flipped through the things I had brought for the conference. I was running low on clean clothes, but a little digging through my luggage, and I found a cute green top to pair with the jeans I was already wearing. I grabbed my brush and then groaned when I looked in the mirror. If Darcy had harbored any feelings towards me earlier today, seeing the mess I was tonight certainly chased those thoughts away. I forced myself to remember that I didn't care about his feelings on my appearance. I swiped my brush through my hair, deciding it was best left down. I slipped on comfortable sandals and grabbed a sweater.

Darcy was sitting on the couch when I came out. His eyes glanced over my form, and immediately, I began to feel self-conscious. But he smiled as he stood, and I forced my shoulders to relax.

He gestured to my sweater. "You do realize it's July."

"I'm always cold, and if at any point in time we are inside or there is a breeze, I'm going to need it."

He let out a laugh as he shook his head. "Missy isn't here yet. Should we wait?"

I filled him in on the new plan.

"Good. Shall we?" He headed for the door.

13: Darcy

Beth was exhausted as evidenced by her eyes. Not only were they drooping, but they didn't have the same luster I was used to seeing in her. I suspected it was not so much physical fatigue as it was emotional. I slowed my pace to meet hers. While a good foot shorter than me, she usually moved significantly faster than she was doing tonight.

"What are you in the mood for?" I asked.

"Are the food trucks closed for the night?"

I cocked my head. "Isn't that what led to this current situation? Surely you want to avoid the same fate as Jane."

"Let me guess, you don't eat at food trucks? Too unsanitary." She playfully bumped into my arm, but then staggered. I reached out to steady her. Her sheepish glance at me was kind of cute.

I enjoyed this playful side of her. It seemed to occasionally appear, unbidden, before her conscious mind took over, and she closed up. Then, she would seem irritated by my very breathing. She never clammed up with Chad or Jane. Of course, Chad was a master at chatting with anyone and everyone and Jane was Beth's favorite person in the world.

"You might be surprised to know that I am not a food snob. But you're right, I'm leery about food trucks and those hole in the wall joints that show up on TV shows. I am a huge fan of not getting food poisoning. On that note, let's pick a place that allows us to sit down and relax."

"Well, considering this is your neck of the woods, what do you suggest?"

I didn't want Beth to think of me as pretentious. I was pretty sure she hadn't forgiven me for my little valet stunt from the day we met. I had been tempted to apologize to her several times since that day, but I didn't think she would appreciate my confession that I'd only done it because she had looked adorable being so tiny and fierce, and I just couldn't help poking the beast. "How do you feel about tacos? I know a great place. You won't find a better taco outside of Mexico."

"Considering I've never been to Mexico, I guess these will be the finest tacos someone like me has ever eaten. Is it far?"

Did I just step in it again with her? Good grief, woman.

"It's a few blocks away, but if you're too tired, we can find some place closer or grab a cab. I hadn't thought about the fact that you probably didn't get much sleep last night."

Beth shook her head. "No, it's not that. I don't mind the walk, but I must admit I don't think I can go much faster than this. And I don't want to be too far from Jane, but I'm sure she'll be fine."

I turned to her. "If Jane needs anything, we can grab an Uber back. Is that okay? Or we can pick something right here by the water instead." Her affection for her sister was admirable.

Beth was making me uncomfortable as she stared at me. She must have been weighing her decision. However, when she let out a slow breath, I wondered if I made her nervous. She nodded. "I'd love some tacos. Thanks."

As we strolled along the waterfront, Beth stopped to read the signs at a giant sundial. She studied the long shadows on the ground and read the charts to calculate the time then checked her watch to confirm she'd done it correctly. She seemed frustrated that she hadn't. "I teach astronomy at school. I make a remedial sundial out of a can and a spoon. We wait for the perfect sunny day and then mark the changing shadow. The class predicts where the shadow will move and how fast. I think it would be a lot of fun to have a nice sundial at school. Maybe not as large as this one, but one that the kids could actually use to figure the time."

"Are you always thinking about teaching?"

A snicker escaped her lips. "Actually, yes. I can't help myself. I love what I do, and when I see things that could make me better at my job, I check them out. I never took astronomy in college, so I've tried to read up on the topic so I don't look foolish. But the questions my class asks." She smiled as she shook her head. "So many hard questions. I am sure they must question how I became the teacher." She let out a real laugh that tossed her head back. "I think it's all part of doing everything for the Lord. It's my calling. I want them to love learning."

"My father always instilled that same value system in me growing up. He reminded me that it didn't matter if it was in the business world or on the mission field. I was called to serve God first and foremost. It's nice to talk to someone with the same mindset." It probably wouldn't be that hard to get a sundial. I'd have to check into that.

I offered her my arm hoping she would take it. She hesitated, but when she reached up her hand and held on to the crook of my elbow, my heartbeat sped up.

The trip to Tacoria was predominantly silent. I wasn't sure what had changed.

"Did you enjoy the conference?" I asked.

"Yes."

Another single word answer. I'd try again.

"What was the best part?" That's a better question. Open ended.

"The tour of the school, I suppose." She stared off. Quiet once again.

"Were you thinking about volunteering to teach in the summer program next year?" That was a question I was definitely interested in hearing her answer to. I turned to give her my full attention.

Beth furrowed her brow. I waited, not patiently, but I waited. Finally, she responded. "No, not seriously. I mean, it certainly piqued my interest, but it's not practical. I need to save money if I'm ever going to have enough for the down payment on a house. I also need enough free time over the summer to rejuvenate for the new year.

I'd be worried that even if they offered room and board, I'd spend more money living in a place like this with so many things to do, and paying for transportation. It was just a pipe dream. Maybe in a few years."

Finally, Beth was opening up. Could we finally move past this awkwardness? I knew the problem hadn't been just on her side. While Beth hadn't asked me a single question the entire evening, I never seemed to have problems engaging people in a business meeting. Yet with Beth I felt tongue-tied. I was trying too hard.

"Maybe not a pipe dream. Even if it doesn't work out for next summer, if it's something you want, I'm sure you'll make it happen. You're obviously motivated and hard-working."

That was an understatement. She was intelligent, well read, kind, sassy, and beautiful. I loved when she laughed and even more so when she dropped the walls that kept her reserved around me. Why did her manner always seem to alter the moment I entered into her space? If she hated me, why did she agree to come tonight? Could she be nervous around me for the same reason I was nervous around her?

While my thoughts took me away, the conversation stopped yet again. I tried once more. "What had you hoped to do while you were in town but didn't get around to?"

Beth was thoughtful for a moment. "I saw that they had kayak tours of the Hudson."

I grimaced. "Do you know what's in the Hudson?"

She giggled. "Yeah, The Statue of Liberty, Ellis Island."

"Disease, germs, pollution. You don't want to be that close to the actual water. If you want to go in the river we could take my boat."

"You have a boat?"

Did I just invite her out on my boat? What am I doing? I tried to act casual. Best to stop talking before I say something truly stupid.

14: Beth

Tacoria was not at all the kind of restaurant I'd expect Darcy to enjoy. The exposed brick and colorful tiled walls made the place quaint.

"Will I seem like a chauvinist if I order for both of us?" Darcy said.

"I think if you ask, you negate that possibility." I tried to flash a sweet smile, so he would know I was sincere.

We each grabbed drinks from the refrigerated case by the register. Darcy ordered us eight tacos, two street corns, and an order of chips and pico de gallo. He handed me the paging coaster and grabbed our drinks from the counter.

I looked at him incredulously. "I hope you're hungry, because I am certainly not going to able to eat that much." Another thought crossed my mind. "But I can certainly pay my half." I began fumbling through my purse. I was still working on little sleep and had forgotten my manners.

Darcy's hand came into my view and landed on my hands, stilling them. "Beth, I've got it. My treat." He gave me a charming smile. "I'm sure I'll be eating more than my fair share, because I couldn't bear to let this delicious food go to waste." Then he winked at me.

What the heck? Was he flirting with me?

We grabbed seats at the counter facing the street. The outdoor seating area was already filled up, but I figured the conversation would actually be easier side-by-side and closer together. More accurately, the silence wouldn't seem so awkward. Besides, it's hard to talk while eating something as messy as tacos. I definitely didn't want Darcy to judge me for sauce running down my face.

After placing our tray of food on the counter and sitting, Darcy held his hand out towards me. "May I pray?"

Cautiously, I placed my hand in his and nodded. Darcy closed his eyes. "Father, we ask that you take care of Jane tonight and heal her. Help her to recover her strength. Bless this food to our bodies. Be in our conversation this evening. Amen." He squeezed my hand, let go and immediately grabbed a taco. It took me a little longer to recover and do the same.

Darcy had been right. The food was fantastic. The tacos were small but filling. I ate two tacos, a corn, and a few of the chips. True to his word, Darcy finished the rest. I wasn't sure if I had ever gone through so many napkins on a date, not that I had been on many dates, and not that this qualified as a date. Had it been a date? Considering how Darcy had offered me his arm and how nice it felt maybe it was? He was a gentleman. No guy had ever offered me his arm like that. Perhaps Chad had asked Darcy to do him a solid so he could check in on Jane. I wondered if he had twisted his arm to force this evening. This was more like a pity outing. I'm sure that was the case.

Before we headed out, I texted Jane. She assured me that Chad had texted her several times throughout the evening. I was hopeful that his attentiveness went beyond neighborliness. Maybe we could take a little longer to return home, just in case that was Chad's plan. I could tolerate Darcy for the sake of Jane. I'd do anything for her.

Darcy might have had a similar thought. Perhaps he was enduring for the sake of Chad. "The best place to get ice cream is just across the street. They have some crazy flavors. I'll take you, but you have to promise to try something you've never had. None of this chocolate or vanilla."

I put my hands on my hips. "Do I strike you as the kind of girl that's afraid of a little adventure?"

"Not at all. Completely the opposite."

I chose pumpkin pie. I felt a little rebellious eating a fall treat at the height of summer. Darcy chose Oatmeal Cookie. He offered me a taste, but I declined. Definitely too date-like.

With Jane's assurance that all was well, Darcy directed us on a more roundabout course back to the apartment. We stopped to look in a few windows on Newark Avenue, gazed at some murals, and we even sat on a bench along the waterfront. I pulled my sweater on as we sat, and he laughed. "You realize it's almost eighty degrees out, right?"

I stuck my tongue out at him like a petulant child, but immediately regretted my flirting. I must be more tired than I realized. Sleep drunk makes you do foolish things. "I told you I'd need a sweater. I'm always cold. The absolute worst is air conditioning. It makes summer miserable."

"You realize we're in the 21st Century. Air conditioning is almost considered a necessity in life."

"Well, I have never been terribly concerned with what everyone else thinks. I suppose that is one of the few traits I inherited from my mother." At the mention of my mother, I sensed a shift in Darcy. He straightened, but his smile seemed forced. Just then my phone chimed. Of course, it was my mother. "Speak of the devil." I tilted my head down and shamed myself. "Sorry, that was uncalled for."

I read Mother's text.

Mom: *I hope Jane's illness hasn't affected her beauty. Make sure she wears make-up. It's bad enough you won't wear any.*

Me: *Seriously? That's what worries you? Not how she feels?*

Mom: *She won't die from food poisoning, and she won't snag Chad if he sees her like this.*

"Ugh!" I grumbled while I shot off a reply. *Too late Mother, he helped carry her to the room last night. I guess you will never get those grandkids.*

I wasn't sure if Darcy could see my texts, but I was done with this conversation with my mother. I let out a frustrated sigh and shoved the phone in my pocket. Darcy seemed even more distant than earlier after our brief moment of flirtation.

We didn't stay out too much longer. Darcy mentioned an early morning meeting and led me back to the building. I wondered if it had more to do with what I'd said than with the meeting. I recalled a similar look on his face at the business association meeting after Mary had played the piano. Perhaps his opinion of my mother was more unfavorable than even my own. Was Darcy truly so bothered by my mother that he couldn't even stand to have a conversation with me?

All of my defenses went back up. I matched his formal posture and attitude. *How dare he judge my family.* By the time we reached the door to the apartment I couldn't seem to suppress my indignation. Darcy wished me a good night and thanked me for the evening. I thanked him for dinner and stepped inside, closing the door before he even stepped away.

15: Beth

The following day, Jane and I watched a few movies and ordered some take-out that Jane felt she could handle. There were no more deliveries and no more visitors. Jane had been texting Chad and Missy throughout the day. She told me that we had both been invited next door for a game night. She wasn't quite ready to spend the night out, but begged me to go without her.

"Chad and Missy have been so thoughtful. I would hate to offend them. Please go. I know you despise game nights, but could you do this for me? I promise to come by for a few minutes and bring you back home at a reasonable hour or whenever you text me to come save you."

I could never let Jane down. "If any one of my friends invited me to a game night I would be looking for new friends, but for you I am willing to subject myself to this. I might, however, need to pay you back for it." I smiled so Jane would know I wasn't as put out as I was implying. We would be heading home the following morning. I had endured game nights with my sisters; I figured this couldn't be worse.

When I arrived next door, I found Chad's company included Missy, his sister Heather, her husband Nick, and Darcy. The men were all playing some sort of video game, while the women were standing around in the kitchen setting out snacks. Even though I hated such overt sexism, I offered my service in the kitchen.

"Is there anything I can do to help?"

Missy's smile seemed forced. "I think we've gotten everything in hand. I had someone stop by earlier and set everything up."

I refrained from rolling my eyes, but only physically. Who had half a dozen close family and friends over and hired help? And this was snack food, not a sit-down dinner party? I sensed that Missy wanted me to feel out of place in this world of wealth. If that was the case Missy had misjudged me. I had grown up the poor girl in a wealthy town. I could adapt better than a chameleon.

The conversation among the sisters was forced and awkward, and I suspected that was only the case since my arrival. When loud unhappy screams erupted from the other room, I figured the game had ended. Shortly after, the men entered the kitchen and grabbed some snacks. When the men started back, Darcy declined the request to play another round. Nick tugged on Heather's sleeve, leading his wife willingly to take Darcy's place before Chad could persuade him to reconsider.

Missy's eyes turned to Darcy and she flashed a flirtatious smile. "Well, I guess it's just us left. What game would you like to play?"

"Missy, you know I hate games. I can barely tolerate a round or two of Chad's video games."

Missy moved next to Darcy and placed her hand on his arm, practically hanging on him. "I know, darling. But it's game night. We have to play a game."

Darcy stepped away, but she moved with him as if unaware of the signals he was sending. He turned to me. "What about you. What games do you like?"

"I don't really like games either." I was still annoyed from the way the night before had ended. I couldn't think of anything less pleasant than playing games especially with Missy fawning all over him. Pushing down my disgust I declared, "I can tolerate a few, but usually only with close friends." When Darcy's lips tightened, I added, "But I guess after all the time we've spent together this week, I guess you qualify." I looked at Darcy as I spoke though I had directed my last remark at Missy. I didn't want it to appear to her that I was throwing down the gauntlet, but I wanted her to know that I wasn't going to be made to play third wheel in her delusional play for Darcy's affections. Darcy's eye widened and he stifled a laugh.

"Perhaps a puzzle, Darcy? That's not a game, and we can catch up. It's been far too long since I've seen your sister. It's a shame she wasn't free tonight." And there it was. Missy letting me know her relationship with Darcy ran deep. I wonder what she would think if she knew I had no interest in Darcy myself. I simply didn't want to see him saddled with someone like her. Well, unless he really wanted that. *Did he want that?*

We both reluctantly agreed. As we sat, Missy moved her chair as close to Darcy as possible, and with him already positioned near the window there was nowhere for him to retreat. I almost felt sympathetic towards his plight. Almost.

Darcy's neck and jaw tensed. "Lexi has a lot on her plate preparing for her upcoming position at Williams Holdings and finishing up school. I probably should be helping her now instead of hanging out."

"Nonsense. You dote on her too much as it is. She's plenty grown. I'd have sold off the company and given her a trust fund instead of keeping it going. She could have forgotten about work and lived perfectly comfortably."

Darcy shook his head as he responded. "That's not how we were raised. Idle hands and all that. Lexi wouldn't be happy without something to do."

From there the conversation died. It reminded me of how last night started off, but this time it was Missy asking questions and Darcy giving single syllable answers when possible. I felt a bit guilty for how Darcy must have felt last night, though I hadn't been able to formulate my thoughts under the circumstances.

I cut the silence. "As I traveled around the city this week, I noticed a Shop Rite and a BJs. I had thought I'd read that there was a food desert issue in urban environments. Is that not the case for Jersey City?"

Darcy set his piece down and gazed at me. "It's more complicated than that. Yes, the revitalization of the city has certainly helped, but imagine needing to take public transportation to the grocery store. It's time consuming, and you can only buy what you can carry. Canned goods are heavy."

"I suppose you can only buy a bag or two at a time." I nodded my head in understanding.

"Exactly, so you're going to need to go more frequently, which takes up even more time." Darcy's voice took on a higher pitch.

"If you have kids, you probably need to go more than once a week."

"Right, and if you're lower income and you rely on child care you're either paying longer hours for care or you're bringing children with you to the store." Darcy was getting more animated as he continued.

"Wow, such lively party talk." Missy scowled.

I ignored her. "That makes sense. I went on a weeklong leadership retreat with students from around the state. That was the time I told you about when I stayed here in college. That was the first time I really felt like I understood that not everyone grew up like I did. Things were a lot different here then. And that wasn't long ago. I believe strongly that God calls us to care for the poor and oppressed, the widow and orphan, prisoners. But I have struggled with how to live that out in a way that is actually helpful and keeps people's dignity intact. I mean, I've volunteered at the soup kitchen back home, and I'm not opposed to anything like that, but I want to be involved in something with longer term results. I guess that's why seeing the changes in Jersey City over these last years has been so impactful. It's more than painted murals. The lives of people here are improving."

Darcy grinned. "It's changed a lot. The addition of the farmer's market at Grove Street is a perfect example."

"Jane and I saw that. They had so much. Way more than just produce."

Darcy nodded. "It helps make fresh fruits and vegetables available for families in between grocery store trips, it builds community, and it connects the farmers and the consumers together in a more direct way, while also reducing the environmental impact."

I thought for a moment. "So where do you get your food? I assume someone takes care of that for you." Darcy was an enigma. But was he just a talk the talk kind of guy?

Missy lost no time. "I'm so busy that I pay someone to handle that for me. Darcy, I'd be more than happy to hook you up with them. I'd love to make sure you're taken care of."

Gag! I'm sure you would like to see that Darcy was taken care of.

Without even a sideways glance, Darcy spoke. "Oh, so you thought I was too aloof to care about the little people." Darcy put on a false British accent as he said the last words then laughed.

I am sure my face was red from embarrassment. He was calling me on my arrogance, but in a gentle manner.

"Honestly. I eat out quite a bit. The Farmer's Market was one of my dad's pet projects so I try to stop by when I can. You can buy a fully cooked meal." He lowered his voice as if telling me a secret. "Safer than a food truck."

I'm sure my mouth was open, but who was this man? I could enjoy a verbal sparring match with a man like this.

Darcy continued, "My favorite place to shop is just by the Grove Street PATH station. Sprove."

With my thoughts going wild, I tried to pull my head back into the conversation, "Sprove?"

"Uh, it's a mini, gourmet food market. Pre-made foods of all sorts, but groceries too. I might just grab dinner to go, or I might browse the aisles and find something interesting to whip up. They have a lot of unusual foods."

"You cook?" I covered my open mouth in feigned shock.

"Of course. I like a little adventure with dinner." *Was he flirting?* From the way Missy narrowed her eyes at me, that would be a yes.

Missy placed her hand on Darcy's arm and leaned a little closer. "Darcy, dear, I've always known how brilliant you were, but I am pretty sure you've never cooked for me." Missy put on an exaggerated pout.

All I wanted to know how was how Darcy could tolerate her.

"I only cook for Lexi and myself. If we have company, Lexi cooks. She's better than me. Cooking for a woman feels too much like a date, and I wouldn't want to give the wrong impression."

16: Darcy

Beth's phone began to ring. She startled and checked the number. "Sorry, it's my mother, I need to get this." The open floor plan didn't provide much privacy, but she stood and passed into the kitchen. I suspected Missy's ulterior motives when she followed right behind Beth to refill the barely touched snacks.

"Hi, Mom." I could hear her soft-spoken voice in the adjacent room. While I could see her attempt to cover her mouth with her hand, it did little to keep from hearing her side of the conversation, especially with the awkward silence. "We're coming home tomorrow...Jane's doing much better...We'll take the train. Mom...Please stop...No, we're coming home...Fine."

I could hear Mrs. Beckett's voice through the phone, but I couldn't make out what she was saying. Her voice was loud and shrill and it seemed from Beth's reaction that she was certainly getting an earful. Her mother didn't like the idea of the girls returning home. I had to admit, I felt the same way. I certainly didn't think I would ever be agreeing with Mrs. Beckett on an issue.

Beth seemed flustered when she hung up the phone. Her cheeks were red. It looked like she had sent off a text and waited for a reply before she returned to the table. She fiddled with her phone like she was anxiously waiting for a reply. Missy had returned to her seat before Beth, and her eyes followed Beth's entrance with a devious smile. *What was Missy up to this time?* I felt like rolling my eyes and wondered if she'd catch my disdain for her antics.

There was a knock at the door, and then Chad led Jane into the room. I watched as Beth stood and rushed over. She seemed to truly adore Jane. Chad's admiration was nearly as obvious. He was quick to move toward her, and he watched her carefully. Jane on the other hand never once looked him in the eyes. I'd begun to notice this pattern throughout the conference. It seemed that Beth was often setting the girls in our path, or Chad was drawing Jane into conversation. I never saw the opposite. Curious.

Jane greeted everyone warmly. "I just came to say my goodbyes and to thank you, Chad, and you, Darcy, for everything you've done for us."

Beth slipped her arm through Jane's and announced, "We'll be heading home tomorrow morning. We're truly grateful for everything you've done. We hope to be able to repay you somehow."

Chad rubbed his hand down his pant leg. "I'd really hoped you'd join us for church. It's a wonderful service. Lively worship music. Solid biblical teaching. I think it might be just the thing to strengthen you for the trip home. Perhaps you'll stay one more day."

Jane shook her head regretfully. "We've already been gone too long."

Chad looked like he was about to reach out for Jane's hand, but then he pulled his hand back. "How will you get home?"

"The same way we came. We'll take the PATH to Newark and the train to Princeton." Beth's smile seemed forced.

"You'll have all your luggage to navigate. Jane, will you have the energy for such a long trip?" Chad curled his fingers into a ball and glanced toward me.

I knew what his look was implying. "Chad's right. I'd prefer you to take my car. I can have my driver pick you up and take you home. There won't be any transfers or dragging bags or being on your feet for too long. It would be much easier for you, and I won't need the car. All I have tomorrow is church and I'll catch a ride with Chad." I intentionally kept my eyes focused on Jane. I wasn't sure how Beth would react. I didn't like the idea of Beth leaving, but a little distance between us would be much better. Beth appealed to me but the feelings were evidently not mutual. My heart wasn't as discerning as my mind, and it was beginning to betray me. This was for the best. I couldn't see how our lives would neatly fit together. They say to look at a woman's mother and you'll see what that woman will be like. When Beth had compared herself to her mother last night, the picture in my mind had soured our date.

A few minutes of back and forth with Chad urging the girls to accept the offer ended with plans for the driver to pick the girls up at ten in the morning and take them home. Chad asked the girls if we might pray for them. Jane's cheeks reddened and her head dropped. I couldn't hear what she said, but Chad's response indicated her assent.

"Father, we ask that you would be with Jane and Beth. Please be with them as they return home. Restore Jane's health and give her the strength she needs as she travels tomorrow. Amen"

Jane quietly thanked Chad, but Beth pulled him into a hug before they slipped out the door. My tension ramped up the moment the girls disappeared.

Missy stood and headed toward the kitchen, calling back as she went. "Honestly, I have no idea why you are being so generous unless you're trying to get rid of them. Beth Beckett is intolerable. Did you hear her with her mother on the phone? She might as well have had it on speaker phone with how loud that woman talks. The entire conversation she was asking Beth to stay a little longer in hopes of snagging a rich husband. Really, what day and age do we live in? Disgusting. And all that talk about grocery stores and economics? Who brings that up at a party? She has no social skills whatsoever."

I wasn't sure if Missy had actually heard the other side of the conversation or if she was making assumptions and treating them as fact. I wanted to ignore Missy, but I also knew that would only encourage her to keep talking. "Actually, I was impressed with her knowledge and understanding. But to be honest, I had some trouble focusing on the conversation every time I looked at those incredible hazel eyes. Gorgeous. And kind. She's quite a remarkable woman." With that, I gathered my coat. Chad's mouth was hanging open as I slapped him on the back. "I'm going to call it a night. Don't forget you're picking me up for church in the morning." I strode out the door without so much as a nod to the rest of Chad's family. I decided to walk home tonight. I needed to cool down.

17: Beth

Our return home the following morning was greatly improved by the offer of Darcy's car and driver. I already felt like I owed Darcy Williams too much. I hated to be any more in his debt, but this was for Jane. Our mother couldn't help but to fawn all over Jane and question us about every detail of the trip.

"Beth, please tell me that you helped Jane fix herself up each day so Chad would see her at her best," Mom pleaded.

"Actually, I figured that since he'd already seen Jane bowing to the porcelain god, it was a lost cause. I teased out her hair and used mascara to give her dark circles under her eyes. I figured it best to see where his interest in Jane really laid." I gave my entire speech with as serious a tone as I could fake.

My father reached over and squeezed my hand. In a quiet voice he said, "Oh Beth, I have certainly missed your sense of humor."

"Not that it would matter had she tried," Lydia chimed in. "It's not like Beth knows a thing about hair and make-up. You should have sent for me. I could have helped."

Still holding my hand, Dad squeezed it again and added, "And your sensible nature." I smiled to myself at his compliment.

"Honestly, being sick was such a small part of the trip," Jane said. "We had a wonderful time at the conference. I attended this amazing session on using music to teach math to young students." I could tell she wanted to move the conversation to something far removed from her dating life.

"We played chess at a mall. There were two-foot-tall pieces. Jane's better than me. I suspect it's because she's less impulsive and more thoughtful than I am."

"You went to a mall and you played chess?" Cat's voice dripped with disgust. "Do you even know how to have fun? Seriously, people go shopping at a mall. They grab coffee and meet up with friends. They don't play chess."

The rest of the conversation around the dinner table that evening was more drama than I cared to deal with. Mary remained virtually silent at the table. I wasn't surprised by this. I made a few attempts to engage her in conversation, but her curt responses kept me from pressing more. I wondered if anyone had bothered to speak to her the entire time Jane and I were away. I felt convicted that I needed to do more to draw her out. It must be lonely to be her, even if it was self-imposed.

After dinner, Dad mentioned again that he was grateful for the way I managed to make my sister's idle chat more sensible with my very presence. I was flooded with admiration and the warmth of being appreciated.

In the weeks that followed, Jane and Chad texted occasionally, but he hadn't returned to town. Our summer days passed by with reading, relaxing, and preparing for the coming school year. I never brought up Chad for fear of upsetting Jane's gentle spirit. Her smiles were just as bright, and she never wavered in passing out compliments and encouraging words to everyone. The lazy days of summer were typically filled with Jane playing the keyboard we had in the corner of our living room, but that wasn't the case this summer. She was quieter at Bible study. I also noticed she didn't hum her way through chores like usual. I had managed to drag her down to the shore a few times, a place Jane loved and I abhorred, but I desperately wanted to restore Jane's carefree nature. As summer gave way to autumn and the school year began, Jane seemed to fall into a steady rhythm of life. To most people, Jane was herself, but knowing her as intimately as I did, I sensed a falseness to her cheerful ways.

"Jane, it's Columbus Day. The first day we've had off this school year. We can't treat it like every other day. We need to seize the day."

I knew my pleading tone would get me what I wanted, but I hated that I had to resort to begging.

"Fine, but I don't want to be gone all day. I had hoped to get into my classroom and get a few more things done."

"Jane, you are more prepared than any teacher in the school. And it doesn't take all day to drive to the Water Gap and hike a few miles. Fresh air is just what we need. And hotdogs. You can't forget Hotdog Johnny's." I finished stuffing my backpack with water bottles, my wallet, and a sweatshirt.

As we drove, I was frustrated by the stilted conversation. This wasn't like Jane and me, so I did the only thing I could think of and brought up the obvious. "What's going on with you and Chad?"

I was met with silence, but continued to stare out the windshield in hopes that my patience would be rewarded.

As we pulled into the parking lot, Jane finally spoke. "He hasn't texted me in a while. Missy sent me a few texts, but nothing of importance. I guess he wasn't interested in me. Maybe Mom was right. It must have been my lack of make-up." Jane's forced smirk left me feeling deflated.

It wasn't like Jane to lighten a situation with humor. That was my MO, and I planned on whipping it out in full force. "Maybe you can test your make-up theory out soon. Did you hear Dad's got company coming?"

Jane looked at me warily.

Mom had called yesterday and held me hostage as she went on a lengthy rant about Dad's old business partner's son who was coming to visit. When their company had gone belly up and our home had been collateral on the loan, we had literally lost everything. Ed Johnson, on the other hand, was financially sound despite the failing business. He'd drawn up a financial settlement where he paid off the loan, but he gained ownership of the last portion of the Beckett estate that was still held by a Beckett. Due to the affection the two men held for one another, the contract stipulated that my father retain ownership for the remainder of his days and at that point the land defaulted to the Johnson family.

"Colin Johnson."

"Colin? We haven't seen him in years. The last time we saw him, he was in a Nerf gun phase. If I recall correctly, he was kind of an odd kid." Jane crinkled her nose, and I giggled.

"Well, maybe he's grown into his ears by now. I'm sure nothing would make mom happier than flirting with the enemy. She was pretty livid yesterday about his audacity to invite himself for a stay."

"When's he coming?"

I sighed as I responded to Jane. "Not for a few weeks. November, I think. We can all guess what every Friday night's dinner conversation will involve until then."

Jane nodded. We both felt for Dad. Mom's attitude had heaped insult on injury. In the end, it destroyed his friendship with Ed, a man we had once referred to as our uncle. I assumed this was partly because Dad was ashamed that his failure had cost his family's estate, though there was little left of it by the time he had taken ownership. More than that, I thought my father hoped the absence of Ed Johnson in their life would mean my mother wouldn't be reminded of the future of the estate and wouldn't complain as bitterly about their great misfortune. Dad knew that the terms of the agreement couldn't be changed, so he wasn't worried that Colin's visit was some form of threat to their way of life, but Mom was incensed by the audacity of this man who was planning on kicking her out of her home would dare ask to impose on their hospitality. Still, I could see the pain that crossed my father's face each time my mother went off on a tirade, but my father was firm that they all treat him with Christian charity.

"I hope he's given up on the Axe body spray." I shot Jane a smile.

"I would hope so. He isn't in middle school anymore." Jane's words were laced in a kindness that I never quite mastered.

"Maybe I shouldn't let him go so easily. I might need to fight you for him." I let out a burst of laughter, imagining me actually fighting Jane for a guy's attention.

"You better wait and see if he's worth the effort? I wouldn't want you to exert yourself needlessly."

Jane's teasing was a balm to my soul. I had missed our banter.

18: Beth

I snuck into Dad's study the day of Colin's arrival and found him reading his Bible.

"How are you doing?" I asked.

Dad looked up and a smile crossed his face. "If it was anyone but you interrupting me, I might have a different answer."

"That's not what I meant, and you know it." A smile tugged up my lips as I sat in the chair across from his recliner. "How are you feeling about Colin?"

I knew Mom's feelings on the matter. As predicted, Mom had spent weeks making comments like, "What kind of pastor throws a family out on the street?" and, "I hope he has a terrible visit and never wishes to step foot on our property again."

Dad's face was cheerful. "It's been ages since I've seen the boy. He was a quirky kid back in the day. I have to admit, I kind of hope he hasn't changed. I hate that I can't pass this home down to you or your sisters. You'd think if I couldn't give leave my home to you girls, I'd want my family home to pass on to a good man. Someone I knew would treat my legacy with reverence. But I don't. I'd rather dislike him, so I can resent him taking our home without any guilt."

"You know you can count on Mom to help you find his faults." I probably should speak more generously about my mother, especially to my father, but she had been on my nerves more than usual over Colin's visit, and the snide remark seemed to slip from my lips.

"Well, if we're lucky, Colin will provide us all with enough fodder for our family dinners for months to come."

We were both being petty and bitter, about different things of course, but it still left me with a greater sense of comradery with Dad. I would do what I could to ease Dad's guilty conscience and divert Mom's stinging barb aimed in his direction.

"You know you don't owe us anything, don't you? Your inheritance to us has been the life you provided for us, the education, the love, the family. It's enough. More than enough.

Dad stood, clearing the emotion from his throat. "It's about time we head to church. I suspect I have a few more things to repent of now." His grin was almost mischievous, but Dad was right. I had some repenting to do myself.

***

I could tell within moments that Colin was ridiculous enough to satisfy Dad's hopes. Dinner the first night of Colin's arrival should have been filmed for a reality TV show. Colin spent the entire evening sharing his every political and religious viewpoint. So much for the rules of civilized conversation to avoid those two contentious topics. Not that my family followed those rules in general, but they certainly attempted such when meeting practical strangers. Not that I was opposed to having intelligent political conversation with people from various viewpoints, and while I leaned more right than left, there was nothing resembling intelligence to be said for this conversation.

"Any thinking person, knows that you can't trust the mainstream media. It's so far to the left you'd fall off the face of the earth. The most liberal station I'll watch is FOX."

Silent nods were the only response. I was initially surprised by my younger sisters' restraint, but then I assumed they must have zoned out of the conversation ages ago.

"I tell my parishioners that the devil is traveling to and fro seeking whom he can devour, and he's using the news. And big government. I'm sure if C.S. Lewis wrote the Screwtape Letters today he'd be talking about CNN and the Democrats."

"C.S. Lewis wasn't even American." Mary's voice broke our family's unspoken resolve to not engage.

I had wondered if Mary, with her deep interest in theology, might get along with Colin, but the tone of her voice wasn't one of gentle chiding, She sounded exasperated. I certainly didn't blame her.

I was completely distracted by my analysis of my family's interactions until Jane's bump on my arm drew me back.

"What I asked, Beth, is if you prefer Philadelphia to New York?" Colin stared at me.

"Um, I haven't spent much time in either. Jane and I recently spent some time in Jersey City, but I prefer the country. The trees, the canal, the sounds of crickets."

Looking slightly offended, Colin's fork rattled as he dropped it to his plate. "I must assume your opinions are rooted in a lack of opportunity. I am certain, given time, you'll find Philadelphia far superior to everywhere else. Historically, we outshine any other place in the nation. The parsonage, so generously donated to the church by Mrs. Dee Burgh, is a few short blocks east of Independence Hall. There is so much culture in the city with restaurants, museums, and concerts. The Riverfront is spectacular. I think you will find the Delaware River vastly superior to your tiny canal. The life of a pastor is one of service, but even I have time to enjoy a smattering of what the city has to offer. I'm sure, if you ever visited, you'd find it far exceeds the charm of this quaint town."

I was going to do my best to be sociable and polite. While I didn't think hospitality was one of my spiritual gifts, all Christians needed to act that way, and I was feeling convicted of my attitude lately. "I certainly enjoy visiting historic homes and learning about our nation's history. I teach the Colonial Era to my 4th graders. I particularly enjoy seeing how faith played a part in the creation of our nation. I'm sure politics and religion were always tied together, but I like to think it was simpler back then, less divided than it is today. I like to think that my faith in Jesus makes me love others and care for them rather than fight with them over politics. Not that our beliefs don't guide our votes, but I prefer to discuss issues and not politicians. Rather than headlines, how about considering how the scriptures should transform our hearts."

"That's awfully naïve of you Beth. Christians need to be involved in politics. We were once a Christian nation, and we must make it that way again."

Lord, I'm trying to be patient and loving, but I'm going to need a little help here.

"I'm not at all opposed to a Christian being called into politics. Of course, we need men and women of God in the government. And certainly, Christians should vote according to their faith. Both political parties want to improve the nation, they just have different approaches to that. I think a Christian's primary purpose should be to transform their hearts to be more like Christ and to lead others in the same path. We wouldn't need so many laws telling everyone how to behave properly if more people lived a life of Christian charity."

"As a pastor, of course I agree with you. In the pulpit at least. The transforming power of Christ is most important. However, there are six other days of the week, and a world full of trouble that needs to be dealt with. I'm sure I could provide you with a few books to help you see the error of your ways."

I was at a loss for words, so I chose to honor myself by not pretending I had anything of value to add. I simply ate. Unfortunately, Colin needed no encouragement to continue monopolizing the evening. He spoke mostly to Jane who was too polite to ignore him like the rest of the family. However, the latter half of our dinner was nothing more than a list of his stances on every political and theological issue imaginable.

**

The autumn colors were reaching their peak, and Thanksgiving break approached. The weekend was unseasonably warm, a definite Indian summer. Colorful trees lined the entirety of the canal path and more sunlight was filtering through where leaves had already fallen to carpet the ground. Colin had been at the house for two days, mostly alone with Mom while everyone was at work or school. Normally, Jane and I enjoyed the solitude of our apartment. Yet, at the request of my father, whose tolerance for company was low, we had made the unfortunate decision to help play host to our guest. Jane suggested a bike ride into town. Mary declined as always. The younger girls would have preferred to take the car, but Dad had conveniently found someplace he needed to be all day. I could only guess why.

The ride down the canal was pleasant enough. Cat and Lydia complained of the heat and the distance, but they trailed so far behind I almost didn't mind that they had come. Heading from the canal path into town, Jane, Colin, and I bumped into Chad and Darcy crossing the university campus. The two gentlemen stopped. Chad seemed pleasantly surprised, but Darcy made little effort to look at anyone even when Jane introduced Colin to the two men. He was engaged on his phone, texting or emailing. *What is it with this man? One minute we're holding hands and praying over tacos and then next he's walking me to the door like I'm a disease. Last time I saw him we were discussing social issues over a puzzle and now he's blatantly ignoring my existence?*

Chad looked at Jane. "I'm so glad we bumped in to you. I just got back in town, and I was hoping to stop by this week but time got away from me. I'm hosting a fundraiser next weekend. It's at my sister and brother-in-law's house. Missy and I are staying with them doing some work for the Princeton branch. I'd love it you would join us."

Jane looked down. Maybe she was feeling some of the indignation that I was feeling. A fundraiser? Chad just shows up after practically ghosting her and wham, everything is fine? Oh, and he's trying to get money out of us?

Chad began to ramble. *Good he should feel awkward.* "It's a Farm-to-Table dinner party fundraiser to support the Educational Fund for The Agape Foundation. We hope to help a lot of kids. Support those programs you saw this summer." He briefly turned to me. "Jane, and you Beth, being teachers, could testify to the value of the work we're trying to do. And of course, Reverend Johnson, you're invited as well."

I knew Academic Success worked with Darcy's Foundation, but if this was a fundraiser for the foundation, shouldn't Darcy have been a little more invested in this conversation than in his phone?

I shot Jane a quick glance. A fancy fundraising event in Princeton probably had ticket prices far outside our budget. Jane stammered a moment. I wasn't sure if Chad noted the hesitancy, but he jumped back in. "Of course, your tickets would be complimentary. We've comped several of the guests and a few college students who we knew would be an asset to our event."

As if the mention of college students was enough to draw our younger sisters forward, they finally caught up and joined the party.

"College students. I hope they're boys." Lydia laughed.

"Hush," I said under my breath.

Jane brought the conversation back around. "I'm sure the three of us would love to attend." Jane had emphasized the word three.

"Three?" Cat whined.

I whispered in Cat's ear with the harshest tone I could still muster with a quiet voice. "Enough. You're being rude."

Chad appeared uncomfortable. Clearly, he couldn't include every person in the Beckett family to a fundraising event that they were not even buying tickets to. Looking from Lydia and Cat back to Jane, Chad nodded. "I'll send you the details for Saturday. See you then." He quickly spun, and he and Darcy hurried off across campus, the sound of crunching leaves under their feet made their exit all the more notable.

I was glad that Chad was so friendly, but a little peeved that he had disappeared for so long and then just picked up as if nothing had happened. Was it out of sight out of mind for him and Jane? I liked Chad, but how could be he so hot and cold? I wondered if he was taking lessons from Darcy.

19: Beth

The Monday before Thanksgiving, Joy's family joined mine for a small dinner party hosted by my Mom's sister, Pat, in downtown Princeton. They were the only family we had nearby. Mom's brother-in-law, Uncle Joe, worked in campus ministry at the University, and he and Aunt Pat often invited college students over to their home. It wasn't unusual for them to have one or more students renting a room or just staying the weekend. With Thanksgiving approaching, and several of the private high schools on break already, including ours, the gathering was a little more diverse. One particular guest caught my eye. He was older, closer to my age, perhaps a recent grad back to visit, or a master's student. Catching my eye, the gentleman crossed the room in my direction. I've never been one to get caught up in a pretty face or a charming smile, but there was something very likable about this man.

"Did you hurt yourself when you fell out of heaven?" He winked.

Seriously. Did he just use the worst pick up line in history? I stood in stunned silence.

"It was a joke. A cliché pickup line. I just thought I'd come introduce myself. Jonathan Wade. My friends call me Jon." He offered his hand.

"Beth Beckett. What brings you to my aunt and uncle's house tonight?"

"I was invited." A smile crossed his face.

I rolled my eyes. "I guess I should be more specific. How did you manage to get an invite?"

Jon pointed to a small group of guys near the kitchen counter. "See those guys? They invited me. I have a lot of friends around the university, and I was visiting. Not sure how much I fit in considering I don't go here, but they try to include me."

I laughed a little. "I understand that feeling, I feel intimidated all the time around here. I certainly wasn't Princeton material."

He shook his head. "No, it's not that. I'm not intimidated, I actually was accepted to Princeton, but some family issues got in the way. I ended up going to a community college for a stint. Being here reminds me of what I lost, but I don't want my friends to pity me, so I show up and smile."

I touched his arm briefly. "I'm sorry about that. It must take a lot of character to do that. It's admirable. How long will you be in the area?"

Jon waved his hand a little. "Not sure. I'll spend some time with friends who aren't going home for Thanksgiving, but sometimes when I visit I stay a little longer, rent a room, that sort of thing. It's nice here in the winter, the Christmas tree in Palmer Square, Small World Coffee, the quiet campus. I'm kind of in a transition phase now."

"I love walking around the square with hot chocolate and enjoying the lights." I said.

"Shopping?" Jon asked.

"Heavens no. I can't afford Princeton boutique prices. But it doesn't cost a dime to walk around."

Jon smiled appreciatively. "A woman after my own heart. I prefer the library to the bookstore and an actual park to a theme park."

"Exactly. I can stretch a dollar pretty far. I prefer a simple life." My thoughts drifted to Darcy. What did he prefer? Surely, I wouldn't have pegged him for tacos and ice cream, but I had been wrong.

"I lost you there for a minute. Where'd you go?"

Jon's word pulled me back. "Sorry. Just dreaming about the simple life." I smiled.

Jon and I passed the evening in each other's company. I couldn't recall a more easily flowing conversation with a stranger. Typically, I hated large gatherings of people, and talking to strangers made me uncomfortable. Jon had the gift of moving a conversation forward in a way that never seemed forced. He masterfully asked questions that drew me out.

Colin burst into our conversation for what seemed like the tenth time. "Beth, I was just talking to your Uncle Joe. Fascinating ministry he's doing at the university."

"Uh, yes. He's been doing it for a long time." I looked in the direction of my Uncle Joe who winked at me and smiled. I wondered if he had tired of Colin and sent him in my direction.

"I was telling him about the farm-to-table fundraiser for The Agape Foundation. He seemed interested. You should get your friends to give him a ticket."

Jon's expression hardened and his body stiffened.

"I don't think it would be much of a fundraiser if they gave away all the seats. Besides, the Educational Fund doesn't really work with universities." I glanced over at Jon who had lost his easygoing attitude. Taking my cue from this, I continued. "I just realized I'm getting hungry. I forgot that Aunt Pat had asked me to set out the desserts. Jon, would you mind helping me?"

Jon visibly relaxed. "I'd be delighted." He offered me his arm and my thoughts immediately flew to Darcy and our night out. We slipped off into the kitchen, leaving Colin behind.

"Are you alright? Your face dropped the minute Colin mentioned the fundraiser."

Jon let out a breath and turned to face me. "Have you ever met Darcy Williams? Because if you haven't, you'll likely meet him on Friday."

"Actually, I have met him, several times. I find him to be a contradiction or maybe an enigma. I can't get a good read on him. Honestly, the first time we met, I wasn't sure there was anyone I could like less than him. And from that face you just made, you have similar feelings."

Jon's face softened. "Indeed. There is no one I like less than Darcy Williams. You might be shocked to hear this, but we used to be practically family, like brothers. My parents passed away when I was fourteen. Mr. Williams, Darcy's father, was a close friend of my father, despite our obvious class differences. When my parents died and I had no near relatives, I was headed for the foster system. Mr. Williams, knowing what that system can be like, volunteered to become my legal guardian. I moved in with them. Darcy was a senior in high school and not thrilled with having another person in the house. I'm not really sure why, he barely came out of his room when he was home. I, on the other hand, craved family. I spent my nights with Mr. Williams. Mrs. Williams had passed a few years earlier. I only met her once or twice. But Mr. Williams was just as happy as I was to have the company in the evening. I adored him, and he felt the same about me, or so it seemed. Darcy hated it, but he could have joined us at any time. I would have loved to be his brother. Darcy went off to Princeton, like all Williams men, and I finished high school.

"The plan was for Mr. Williams to adopt me legally, and I would be the next Williams man to attend Princeton. It was my dream. Legally, it was easier to formalize an adoption after I turned eighteen, but before he began the legal proceedings, he died of a massive heart attack. Darcy was a senior at Princeton. He came home to help with his little sister, Lexi. He couldn't stand the sight of me. He kicked me out then and there. And if that wasn't enough, he somehow used his family's contacts with the university to have my admission to Princeton rescinded. I can't tell you how lucky I was that I didn't end up in foster care, but it isn't easy for an eighteen-year-old with no job to find a place to live. I couch surfed for a bit. It was too late at that point to try to find another college and get a scholarship. I got a job and put myself through community college. It was a hard time for me. I struggled to keep up my grades. It took longer for me to finish, but I was determined to make my foster father proud of me, so I never gave up."

"Wow! That's unbelievable. And I thought Darcy treating me like his valet was terrible. How could he? The man sounds like a real jerk. Did he ever give you a reason for what he did?"

"Oh, Darcy never apologizes, and he never explains himself. Most people are so blinded by his wealth that they fawn all over him. It's actually quite refreshing to find someone else who can see him for who he really is." Jon smiled, but his eyes looked past mine to some place far away. "However, if it makes you feel any better, I don't think Darcy will have the charmed life. His mother's good friend has a daughter, Anne. Ever since they were kids, the moms dreamed of Anne and Darcy marrying. Anne is weak and pale and sickly." He gave an exaggerated shudder. "Never went to college and has been too sick to hold a job. Darcy would never go against his mother's wishes, especially now that she's gone. Sounds like a boring marriage if you ask me. Loveless and miserable. But what else does marrying for status and money get you? And that's what the rich always do."

I couldn't hold my snicker back. "Well that would serve him just fine. For all his interference in your happiness, I hope he gets a taste of his own medicine."

"Now, more about you being Darcy's valet. This sounds good." Jon laughed.

I felt my pulse pounding. I put my hands on my hips and balled them into fists. "How can you joke about this? Don't you want to expose him for who he is? People around here know him, and I must say, from the little I've heard, most of them think he's arrogant. You'd find friends here."

Jon leaned over and gently pulled my hand towards him, carefully uncurling my fingers from their tensed state. He held my opened hands in his. "Friends in town might help me decide what my future might hold. Friends like you." I felt the thrill of his touch as his hand warmed mine.

I continued to fume the entire evening. *How could Darcy be so heartless? What kind of person throws an orphan out on the street? Who could be so vindictive as to get someone disinvited to a college, especially a prestigious one like Princeton?* My thoughts kept coming back to the conversation all night. I could hardly wait until we returned home to talk to Jane.

Lying in bed, I told her the entire story just as Jon had told me.

"I can't believe it. Darcy is such a nice man, and Chad is so close to him. Chad could never be friends with someone who was as terrible as all that. There must be more to the story."

I looked at my sister, and I can only assume the shock I felt at her justifying Darcy must have been visible on my face "You have such a good heart, and you could never believe anyone to be wicked. But in this case, either Jon has told an enormous lie, or Darcy is a horrible person. I don't think even you can come up with a way to make them both good people."

Jane pushed up on her elbow and looked at me "That's not true. We can't be so hasty to judge. Maybe there was a misunderstanding. We just can't know until we learn more." She flopped back down on her bed, and I did the same.

20: Beth

A nor'easter blew in the following day, with more fury than would have been expected for a storm this early in the year. Ice coated the power lines, and made branches still laden with leaves too heavy to hold their own weight. While the view out the window was that of a winter wonderland, the downed trees and branches knocked out power to homes all across the central region of the state. Chad texted Jane a few times to check in on her. His house, being closer to town, hadn't lost power. He asked if there was anything he could do for us, but sweet Jane graciously turned down his offers.

Jane and I decided to spend a few days at home where there was at least a fireplace. That meant enduring not only our sisters, but the dreaded Colin. I had felt Colin following me around the previous night, but I had hoped it was simply that he was shy and was searching for a familiar face. However now, I realized he was still hovering. If I sat on the couch, he sat down as well, and often a tad too close. If I was washing dishes, he was puttering around in the kitchen. It was beginning to get ridiculous. I wasn't sure how to gracefully extract myself from the situation. Not one to be overly sweet, I tried to make it clear that I needed some space, but I also wasn't cruel, and I had been raised to be a good hostess. I wondered how I could be both welcoming and polite while hiding in my old bedroom until Colin left.

By the time the fundraiser arrived that weekend, I was more than ready to get out of the house. Even considering that Colin and now Cat and Lydia were joining us, my general dislike for large gatherings, and my distaste for high society, I was sufficiently miserable at home that I could endure almost anything a change of pace allowed. The Hurst home was situated on the northern outskirts of town, a comfortable stroll away from the downtown area, but on a property that was far larger than anything downtown.

Pulling up to the front of Nick and Heather Hurst's house, we had to pass through a gated entrance. The circular drive led us to the front of a midcentury modern home where a valet met us. I immediately realized that he was dressed very much like I had been the day I first met Darcy. I hoped no one was looking at my face just now. Turning over the keys, our party of five entered the Hurst's home. This house was a far cry from the 70s TV sitcoms I had watched in reruns. The straight lines of dark wood and light grey fieldstone walls. The flat roof was one of several "layers" that laid one upon another, and almost drew you up the steps and through the front door. I was never a fan of more modern architecture, but I couldn't deny that this house, or more accurately mansion, was gorgeous.

"We're not in Kansas anymore, Toto," I whispered under my breath.

Jane, who I figured would be more uneasy than myself, considering she'd be seeing Chad tonight, seemed unaffected by the opulence of the place. "Don't be like that, Beth. You've lived in Princeton long enough that you've seen plenty of big homes."

"Sure, but usually helping Joy catering a party."

A greeter took our coats and pointed towards a set of sliding glass doors leading to the backyard. Natural gas lanterns that looked like open bowls of flame were burning along a stone wall that surrounded the pool and patio. They gave off a beautiful light, but the air hadn't fully lost the chill from the recent storm. Around the patio were boards highlighting the educational programs The Agape Foundation sponsored both here and abroad. The backyard contained several large white tents. White Christmas lights were strung throughout them. Clear plastic sides covered in sheer white curtains cast a warm glow.

"This place is amazing!" Cat's voice could undoubtedly be heard by the people around us.

"Forget the place, check out the guys." Lydia was shamelessly pointing at a few college age men standing under the nearest of the four tents.

"Try to be discreet," I admonished my sisters whose only response was to head straight for their prey.

Colin looked over the house and yard. "This home is lovely, but not to my taste. I much prefer Mrs. Dee Burgh's home. It's a stately apartment overlooking Independence Hall. She has me over quite regularly."

For the number of times he'd brought that woman up in conversation, I was wondering if Colin didn't harbor some romantic feelings for the older woman. Either that, or it was idol worship. I could do without either.

We found several long rectangular tables arranged end to end which were covered in white linen table clothes with dark wooden folding chairs more elegant than the dining room chairs my parents had in their home. The tables were set with crystal stemware, white china plates with golden edges, and real silverware. The autumn inspired centerpieces were set low as to not impede people's vision as they chatted throughout the dinner. My breath caught as I took in the vision. This was clearly nothing like I had expected when Chad had spoken of a backyard dinner.

"I see Chad and Darcy near the sound system. I would like to let them know we've arrived, but I don't want to interrupt them while they're talking to the real guests," Jane said.

"We are real guests, even if we didn't pay $500 a plate to be here. We just need to contribute to the cause with our conversation. Though, I never thought my mouth would be worth that much." I laughed as I bumped Jane's shoulder.

"I am sure it's worth far more than that. After all, you do talk for a living."

I glanced around at the nameplates, recognizing that our family was split up. Jane was seated near Chad and Missy at the end of one table. At the opposite end not too far from Darcy were Lydia and Cat. Colin and I were seated more towards the middle. I was disappointed to not be near Jane, but took my seat beside Colin and introduced myself to the woman next to me.

"Hi. I'm Beth Beckett. I teach at the Asbury Christian Academy."

"Dana Carter. I live in the neighborhood. I run an advertising firm in New York."

"New York? Have you seen the work Agape Foundation is doing there?" Best to start earning my dinner sooner rather than later.

Our conversation was interrupted by Chad welcoming everyone and explaining the way the dinner would work. Several local farms provided the ingredients for the seven courses. A local vineyard supplied the wine. Chefs from three different restaurants were hired to prepare the food and explain the dishes to the attendees. With four tents, I wasn't sure, but I suspected that the meals were being served at slightly different times as the chefs to circulate through and provide the same spiel for each group of 30-40 people. Salad, soup, sorbet, pasta, meat, and two desserts. While each course was small, I was stuffed by the time I ate the pumpkin cheesecake torte at the end of the meal.

"The food is wonderful, but I can't help but think that the money spent on this evening could have been put to better use by simply donating it to the cause," Colin stated.

"The dinner is so much more than that. It's an opportunity to share the mission of the Foundation, learn about the programs they support, make connections between businesses, build community. Heck, it even supports the local farms and restaurants." I kept my voice low, but loud enough that the nearby guest who heard Colin's statement wouldn't get bent out of shape. And here I was worried about my sisters.

"I suppose you're right. I mean, handouts really aren't the way to go anyway. People need to earn what they have and not expect charity. Of course, as Christians we should give generously, but we don't want to make people lazy." Colin's words dripped with condescension.

"Colin, these are educational programs. For children. Certainly, you don't expect kids to get jobs and pay for their own school." I was getting ticked.

"Of course not, but they have parents. These people are all educated people. Princeton folks. I'm sure they agree with me that a society can't function with some people working and others taking handouts."

I heard Dana mumbling to her neighbor. "For $500 a plate I didn't expect to be subjected to such ignorance."

I turned so I could whisper directly in Colin's ear. "If you didn't want to support this cause, you should have stayed home. Chad was generous with his invitations, please don't insult his generosity."

I spoke up. "I understand Mr. Johnson's hesitancy about handouts. I've read some about how charitable organizations providing services for free have unintentionally hurt communities economically. Businesses lose customers and people become dependent on handouts. The very thing they were trying to help they created. However, I am pretty sure I have never read anything that indicates providing more education to children does anything but help communities. Free or otherwise. Watching those kids build bridges, I could almost see them dreaming about become architects and engineers. It was a beautiful thing. A worthy thing."

The few heads nearby nodded in agreement or at least in polite acceptance. Those people surrounding us who made any effort to engage me in conversation seemed interested in my perspective as a teacher in the local community as well as what I had experienced while visiting the different educational programs in Jersey City.

I saw the brilliance in Chad's invitation to the event and wondered whether getting Jane and me last minute seats on the tour was pre-meditated with this event in mind. I was pleased that I could speak so well of the way The Agape Foundation was using its resources. I felt like I was contributing something to their work even if it wasn't financial.

"I loved the idea of using volunteers for the summer programs, especially education majors on summer breaks. Providing housing options for them and even a small stipend would widen the potential candidates."

"I imagine that would significantly increase the expense of these programs." A man nearby looked at me and leaned closer. His attention demonstrated his honest interest.

"Probably. But there are probably ways to do so without as great of a cost. There must be rental companies who have open units willing to donate the space for the tax write off. Maybe college dorms not used over the summer would partner with the program. I considered it myself, but as a teacher I can't afford to not only volunteer my time but also pay for the transportation and living expenses. If I could volunteer for a few weeks, not my entire summer break, and it not cost me anything, I would be all in."

I felt Darcy's eyes on me. I didn't even need to turn my head. I could literally feel him staring at me. The hairs on the back of my neck were on end. Maybe I shouldn't have been troubleshooting out loud. Was he irritated? I'd have to look over at him to gage his reaction better, but I was not going to look at Darcy Williams.

Colin burst into the conversation. "Are we screening these kids to make sure they're American? If we keep educating immigrants and then they take their education back to their countries we're only hurting ourselves."

I couldn't resist any longer. I turned to Darcy only to see a frown firmly planted on his face. Then he turned his face from me. I know violence wasn't the answer, but smacking Colin might just be the exception. *Grr!*

By the time the plates were being cleared, I could hear the voices of my younger sisters at the end of the table. They were seated near what appeared to be two university students, both male. I suspected that they might have managed to get served wine despite their age. While my sisters didn't need any help to be catty and loud, wine would certainly make things worse. I could no longer resist my urge to usher my sisters away from the table.

When I reached their end of the table, I leaned down to whisper in Lydia's ear. "Could you please help me? I'm heading to the ladies' room."

Lydia, with no discretion or volume control responded, "Why should I chaperone you to the bathroom?"

I was sure my face turned red, partially from embarrassment as every eye in the room turned to me, and partially in outrage over my sister's horrendous behavior. "Lydia, please. I'm not feeling well, and I think I might need a little make-up to freshen myself up." It was a pathetic excuse, but one I hoped would spark my sister's interest. My red face might help to prove my point.

Lydia eyed me, sighed, then dramatically dropped her napkin on the table and stood up. Once I had Lydia on the move, I looked at Cat and asked her if she wanted to join us. There was nothing Cat hated more than being left out, so even a trip to the bathroom was reason enough to follow. I let out a slow steadying breath as we moved into the house. Once inside, I ushered the girls down the hallway and toward the restroom that the staff had pointed out to us. I wasn't sure if I would be able to talk any sense into them, so I allowed my sister to apply make-up to my face, which I hoped I could mute before going back outside. I persuaded them to wait while I used the restroom, and then before returning to our table, I guided them into a side room out of the view of the staff. Before I could begin my lecture, my eye caught several beautiful pieces of art on the wall. The landscapes had an almost medieval feel to them with dark pastels, if such a thing existed. I drew my sisters' attentions to the paintings, buying myself a little more time before confronting them.

Finally, unable to think of anything else to keep them from the party, I asked my question. "Are you two drinking?"

Lydia glowered at me. "So what if we are? We're plenty mature to handle a glass or two of wine. It's a stupid law."

I clenched my fists. "Well, perhaps you might be wondering why I'm asking. I can assure you it wasn't because I could see what you were drinking. I'm asking because I could hear your conversation from all the way down the table. I'm not sure you can handle your *drinks* quite as well as you think. You're embarrassing our family and our host."

Lydia raised her voice. "Like you care. I'm just enjoying the party. This is a party. Just because you're lame doesn't mean that the rest of us should follow your pathetic lead." Lydia turned to storm off, but before she had the chance, Darcy stepped through the doorway.

His throat clearing drew all eyes toward himself. "I don't believe this room was intended for use this evening." *This is the first thing he has to say to me all night?*

Surely, he had to know that I was only trying to help, and this was my attempt to discreetly deal with my sisters' behavior. How could he possibly be chastising me for this? I stood to my full five-foot, two inches and tilted my chin up as I locked my gaze on him. "We were just leaving." At those words, Lydia and Cat both pushed past Darcy, nearly knocking him over. When I began to leave, he leaned down and whispered in my ear, "Perhaps you might want to check yourself in the mirror before you head back out."

My face burned again. Was he mocking me? I growled. I hate to admit I was so childish, but I actually growled. I followed up my mature behavior by stomping into the bathroom for the second time in only a few minutes and began to remove most of the makeup I had just allowed Lydia to paint all over my face.

By the time I stepped outside, the backyard had been transformed. The tables cleared and the area set up for mingling. I spotted Joy across the way removing the remnants of the dinnerware. I hadn't realized I'd see Joy here, and I hurried to her side. "What on earth are you doing here?"

"As you can see, I'm working." Joy laughed. "I got a call just tonight asking me to come help out because they were understaffed. There are a few of us from the café here. I couldn't resist the chance to see inside one of these crazy expensive homes. You should see the kitchen. Ah-mazing!"

"I'm so glad to see another friendly face. Tonight has definitely tested my patience. I can't take one more minute of Colin or my little sisters." As if on cue, Colin approached.

Joy looked at him. "Oh Colin, I was wondering if you might give me a hand. I certainly don't want to interrupt your evening, but I was asked to move a few of these tables closer to the edge of the tent, and I'm just not sure I have the strength to handle it myself. Would you mind?"

Stroking Colin's male ego would be enough to get him to do just about anything. Joy was pretty savvy that way. I mouthed the words, "Thank you" as I snuck away. I was still looking at Joy as I moved backward and crashed into something. As I spun around, I nearly lost my footing. I righted myself and looked up at Darcy.

"Beth, I must say you're looking better than the last time we spoke."

Feeling the weight of another insult, I abruptly pulled back and lashed out. "And each time we meet, Mr. Williams, I try to figure out just what kind of man you are? You're like Jekyll and Hyde. "

His smile disappeared. "And why exactly is that?"

I glared at him. "I have tried to figure you out since the very first time you insulted me." Darcy smiled, and I hoped he wasn't thinking about the valets out front this very minute.

"So you think about me? Nice."

Shaking my head a little, I continued. "Just when I think I know who you are, something comes along and changes my mind. Most recently it was making the acquaintance of a Mr. Jonathan Wade. I'm sure you remember him. He certainly remembers you."

I was shocked enough by the look of rage on Darcy's face that I had to take a step back. I had clearly kicked the hive now. I wasn't sure what to make of his response, but I started to think his reaction implied guilt.

It took Darcy a few moments to unclench his fists and speak. "I have no doubt that Jon Wade remembers me, and I very much hope that he will never forget me. He may make friends with his charm and good looks, but it has been my experience that he doesn't retain them for very long."

"That sounds a lot like jealousy to me."

Darcy gritted his teeth. "I feel many things toward Mr. Wade, but jealousy is not one of them." And with that, he turned on his heels and stormed off.

I stomped my foot. When would I learn to control my stupid tongue? This was not the time or the place to lash out at Darcy, if there ever could be such a situation. Once again, I had let my embarrassment and frustration about the evening cloud my judgment. I was starting to act no better than my younger sisters.

I had had enough of this evening. I strolled over to where Jane was speaking to Missy and her sister, Heather, and politely interrupted. "Jane, I'm sorry to interrupt you. I really think it's time to go." I knew Jane would never say no to such a request no matter how desperate she was to stay. She hugged the two women goodbye amidst their insistence that she stay a while longer. I gathered Colin and my other sisters, who made their protests known to the entire gathering, and our party exited the home.

I had hoped the agony of the evening was over, but the fifteen-minute car ride was nothing but Colin's overdone praises on the home, the food, the company, and anything else he could think of mingled with the gossipy chatter of Lydia and Cat commenting on how cute the college boys were and criticizing every adult in the room. By the time I slumped into my own bed in my apartment, I had nothing left inside myself. Jane went to bed in silence as if she knew that was exactly what I needed.

21: Beth

Saturday morning Jane and I slept in, but with Colin leaving the following day, we were expected over at our parents' house for brunch. Mom had planned this because she thought it would make us sound fancy and leave Colin with a favorable impression of us all. When I arrived, I could tell something was off with Mom. First off, Mom was scrambling the eggs like they had personally offended her. And she was sort of bouncing on the balls of feet. Nervous energy, perhaps? Mom was not known for her energetic nature.

"Mom, are you alright? You seem jittery? Too much coffee?

"Don't be ridiculous. You know I hate coffee. I'm perfectly fine."

"I'm not sure the eggs would agree with you. I think they are plenty scrambled."

"Stop pestering me and go and set the dining room table."

When I entered, I found Colin sitting at the head seat. He leapt to his feet as I approached. I slowed my steps in confusion. *Was he doing something he wasn't supposed to be doing?* Colin moved toward me with an intensity that startled me.

"I've been waiting for you." He took my hand.

I tried to pull away, but he gripped me hand tighter. "Uh. Why?"

"You must know. Surely, you can see how I feel?"

"Feel?" My voice cracked as the word came out.

"You know I'm leaving tomorrow, and I couldn't go without telling you that I've decided that we should get married."

This time, I pulled with enough force to release me hand from his grasp. "You've decided what?" I couldn't decide if I was more offended by the idea of marrying Colin or that fact that he felt he could decide something about my future without my consent.

I backed toward the kitchen, but Colin cut off my retreat, blocking my only exit.

"I have already spoken with your mother, and she couldn't be happier. It's a perfect situation. As I am the owner of your family's property, marrying you would keep the property in your family. Or at least keep the inheritance, as I of course intend to sell to the Williams family once I acquire the deed, but I'm a patient man."

I made no attempt to hide my disgust. "You spoke with my mother before speaking with me? Why would you do that? You obviously don't know me at all."

With each step I took backward, Colin stepped closer until I was nearly pinned against the wall. "Beth, that's not true. I've watched you these past two weeks. You're beautiful and good in the kitchen. You cook and wash dishes and like children. Dee Burgh, the wonderful woman who heads the pastor parish committee at my church, has encouraged me to find a Proverbs 31 wife. I am certain you meet the requirements and would make an excellent pastor's wife. I can give you not only the financial security that your father obviously couldn't provide, but you will get to live in a spectacular historic city and dine with Mrs. Burgh regularly in her luxurious home. I can't imagine a good Christian woman of your economic condition and age could want anything more."

I pushed against Colin's chest to free myself from the cage he was forming around me. "I don't wish to insult your offer, but no. Just no. Please excuse me." I tried to move away when Colin reached out his hand to stop me.

"The highest calling for a godly woman is marriage and child bearing. How can you in good faith turn down my offer? Your biological clock won't wait much longer and you won't likely get a better offer. You're not just rejecting me, but God's call on your life." He leaned forward in an attempt to seal his offer with a kiss, but was met with the sting of my palm across his cheek. I pushed away. I didn't wait to see his reaction as I darted from the room.

I rushed past my mother in the kitchen. The look on Mom's face went from jubilation to shock as I raced past her in a flurry. I bundled up against the cold air and slammed the front door behind me. I took the scenic trail through the grounds and down toward the canal. The flowers had long since dropped off and withered up. The bright colors of autumn had turned to the browns of winter in all the places where the trees were not already bare.

"I could never be persuaded to marry Colin. He's a ridiculous bore." I verbalized my thoughts with conviction, but his words had hit their mark. Not the part about a women's highest calling being to marry and raise kids, I'd heard that before and rejected it outright. But many of my friends had fallen in love and married right out of college, and I was no closer to finding love than I was in middle school.

His mention of "no better offer" had stung even if it had come out of the mouth of that donkey. I wasn't like those girls who were boy crazy, but I would still have liked to find someone who would appreciate me. Definitely not Colin, but someone. I ranted a little out loud, seeing my breath as I spoke. It was almost like watching my prayers rising up to God. "God, I am certain my destiny is not to marry Colin Johnson, but I sure would like to know what my future holds. I know I don't need a man to be happy, and I love my work. But is it wrong to want to find a man who will love me as an equal? A man who wants to partner with me in serving you? Could you help a girl out?"

I texted Jane before I came home just to make sure the coast was clear. *Is it safe?*

Jane: *Depends on your definition. Colin went to the café for now, but he's still planning to stay until after church tomorrow.*

Jane's response didn't bring me much comfort.

Me: *Guess I better get this over with while he's out. What did he say to Mom?*

Jane: *Are you sure you want to know?*

I wasn't sure, but better to rip it off like a Band-Aid. Me*: Spill.*

My phone rang a moment later. Jane.

Without even a hello, I said, "Spill."

"He said he wouldn't cut his vacation short for someone of such little significance. He said he tried to be the gentleman and help the family retain their inheritance, but he could find better marriage material elsewhere. Said his father had mentioned once that he couldn't do better than one of Henry Beckett's girls. He disagreed."

"I can only imagine how Mom took that."

"Mom practically begged him to marry Mary. I'm glad she was in her room as always. It was embarrassing. Colin said he'd never marry a Beckett and stormed out of the house. Mom went straight to Dad's office. I haven't heard anything more than raised voices. I can't make out what's being said. I'm in the kitchen packing up the uneaten brunch."

My parents were waiting for me in the kitchen when I crossed the threshold. My father was calm, but my mother was pacing the floor. Mom began railing at me immediately.

"How could you do this to me? To the entire family? You are such a foolish, selfish girl. You could have saved the family's inheritance, but no, you insult our guest and ruin all hopes for your sisters' futures. When your father's gone we'll all be piss poor. Go to the café this very minute and take it back. Fix this, Beth, and marry that man!"

"Mom, you can't possibly be serious. I would be miserable married to Colin. Dad?" I looked to Dad with pleading eyes.

"I'm not kidding. You marry him or I will never speak to you again." Mom's voice was shrill. Looking at my dad for confirmation she continued. "Tell her. Tell her I won't speak to her."

My father stood and took my hands in his. "You have a big decision to make. Your mother won't speak to you if you don't marry Colin, and I won't speak to you if you do."

I broke into a smile and threw my arms around my father. A few tears rolled down my cheek as I let the stress from the day roll off my shoulders.

My mother's irritated cry from behind my father didn't even cause me to tense up again.

Jane agreed to accompany me back to our apartment and not return until after Colin had departed for home on Sunday. I noticed Colin sitting with the Douglas family in church, but was fortunate enough to avoid even eye contact. As Jane's beautiful soprano voice rang out next to me, I sent off a prayer of thanks. *Lord, thank you for Joy for keeping Colin away from me today. She is a good friend. And thank you for giving me such a loving and supportive father. It has certainly made this easier. And for Jane who makes everything better.*

22: Beth

The first week of December was nothing but gloom. The snow had all but melted from the nor'easter, leaving behind nothing but quagmire. The trees were barren of their beauty and life. The sun rose so late and set so early that I only saw it briefly through my classroom windows or while bundled up for recess duty. The approaching Christmas season held little charm. It was already dark most days by the time I finished up in my classroom. I'd had a parent teacher conference today, so it was even later than usual. The cold wind whipped through the grounds as I dragged my tired body back to my apartment only to find Jane crying on the couch.

"What's the matter? What's happened?"

Jane didn't look up from her laptop. She just passed it over to me where I sat beside her on the couch. I quickly scanned to the signature line at the top of the email to discover the author of Jane's brokenness. Missy Woods.

Jane,

I am so sorry that I didn't get the chance to see you before we left. I had such a wonderful time with you at the fundraiser the other night. I was certain we would be seeing each other quite often. Unfortunately, some business issues came up for Chad that have forced us back to Jersey City. Things in the Princeton office were going so well, Heather and Nick will be just fine holding down the fort once again. I'm sure they are thrilled to have the house to themselves finally. Chad is just so busy heading up the entire company, flitting from one office to the next. It's always best when he is back at headquarters.

I hadn't mentioned this earlier, but as we have become fast friends, I thought I could share my secret with you. Lexi Williams will be home from college shorty, and I'm certain that this has motivated Chad's return. He does all he can to be in the area whenever she's home. I am hopeful that I'll be getting to call her my sister soon. Chad and Lexi have always shared a sweet bond. The months apart are hard on him, and he tries to find comfort and distraction when possible, but soon I feel there will be no need for such things.

Please look me up if you are ever in the area.

- Missy

My mouth had dropped open, and my thoughts were swimming around untamed. What on earth was this about? It was ludicrous. Chad dating Lexi? He was looking for a distraction while she was away at school? Exactly how old was this woman? Girl? I pulled my attention back to Jane. I gazed off hoping to find the right words to say. "Oh, Jane. I'm so sorry. I can't believe this. I can't believe a word of it. Chad Woods is too kind a man to be a player. I don't believe it."

I set the laptop down on the coffee table and pulled Jane to my side. As I held her, Jane's tears fell. I tried to process this information. I had pretty strong feelings about Missy, and they were the opposite of my feelings for her brother. How could Chad leave without even mentioning it to Jane? He had her number. They texted. It didn't make sense.

"Jane, did Chad say anything to you? Text you?"

Jane fumbled around to retrieve her phone from her pocket, used her thumb to unlock it up, and handed it off.

Chad: *Business called me to Jersey City. Sorry. Hopefully we can catch up the next time I'm in town. Have a great Christmas.*

Jane: *Merry Christmas to you as well.*

I read the texts a few times. Merry Christmas? That's weeks away. I guess that meant he had no intention of being back before the holidays. I was fuming at him. That was all he gave her? But Jane's response was almost as bad.

"Jane, don't you want to talk to him again before Christmas?"

Her sobs answered my questions, but I waited for the words she needed to say. "Of course, I do. I think I love him. I know we haven't spent much time together, and we've never even talked about dating, but it's true. Not like I'd ever say that to him. Chad is so much better than me, I didn't want to get my hopes up or look so pathetic around him. But clearly, he doesn't want to talk to me, and I think Missy's email explains why." Jane continued to weep. For all Jane's sweetness, she was not overly emotional. Jane crying was as unlikely as Darcy Williams being warm and friendly. Jane had never had her heart broken this deeply, and that broke my heart. I felt the tears of compassion filling my eyes, but I shoved them away.

"I don't think that at all. Something isn't right in the text or the email. Chad seemed to adore you. It was obvious to everyone. Don't believe any of this. Least of all that Chad doesn't want to see you."

"All evidence to the contrary."

My heart was heavy. Sweet Jane. Had this been me, I probably would have shot off at the mouth at both Missy and Chad. There'd be no question how I felt about this slight, but Jane was my opposite in nearly every way. Jane would suffer in silence the same as she had the end of summer and fall. No, Jane's hurt ran deeper this time. There was nothing to do but comfort her through this.

I announced, "Chinese take-out, copious amounts of ice cream, and a musical."

Jane nodded. I pulled my phone out to place our order.

23: Beth

Palmer Square was lit up for the holidays, and I was sure that getting out of the house would make Jane feel better. I hatched a plan with my Aunt Pat. She would host a small gathering of people for a light dinner, some window-shopping, and hot chocolate. The party would include the entire Beckett clan, the Douglases, Jon Wade, and the three college students that lived with Aunt Pat and Uncle Joe. When the day arrived, we all met at my aunt's house just after six. My aunt had made a huge pot of potato leek soup, Jane's favorite. The Douglases had brought a couple of loaves of the fresh bread the café had shipped in daily. My mom had brought cookies for later when we'd have the hot chocolate I had made. Our group ate dinner, and then we wandered downtown to enjoy the lights strung around town and especially throughout Palmer Square. The party meandered around talking and looking.

Joy sidled up next to me and brought her voice down low. "Let's hang back a bit. I want to talk to you."

I offered my arm out to my best friend and slowed my pace. My smile fell on Joy, giving her an invitation to open up.

"I wanted to tell you that I got engaged."

I halted in my tracks. I looked at my friend, searching for sign of this being a joke. I saw none.

Joy continued, staring directly in my eyes. "Colin Johnson."

With those words, I did laugh. I had never thought of Joy as being one to have a dry sense of humor, but she couldn't possibly be serious. The look on Joy's face as I laughed stopped me immediately.

"It's not funny. Not at all. Just because you turned him down, doesn't mean everyone should. You think it impossible that someone wants to marry me? It's insulting."

I shook my head. "No. Of course not, I just hadn't realized that you were even friends with Colin." I pinched my lips tight and tried to force a slight smile. "When did you start dating him?"

"We've been texting since he was here in November. We sort of skipped the dating part. I'm not like you. I don't have your constitution. You're incredibly independent. If the perfect man doesn't come along to sweep you off your feet, you'd be perfectly happy teaching and serving God on your own. But I'm lonely, Beth. All I ever wanted to be when I grew up was a mom. I know compared to your feminist views that's practically Neanderthal. I don't need Prince Charming. Colin is a pastor. He's a good man, even if he isn't a prince. He's kind. He can offer me a good life. A life that I don't have here. Plenty of people have arranged marriages, and they learn to love each other. I already know more about Colin than that, and I'm sure we can learn to love each other. I need a different life, Beth, and Colin might be my only chance for that." She waited, and when I didn't speak she continued. "Don't look at me like that. I can see the disappointment in your eyes."

I shook my head and then found my words. "No. I could never be disappointed in you. I love you, and if this is what you want, I'll support you. But you're wrong. I don't think being a wife and mother is anti-feminist. Not at all. I just don't think it's the only thing women were made to be. You know I want to get married someday. And have kids. I just don't think it's where a woman's value lies, but it certainly can be what God calls you to do. I just want you to be happy. I'm surprised, not disappointed. Please know how much I care about you. Oh, Congratulations, Joy!" I forced myself to hold my smile.

We embraced then continued down the street to catch up with the rest of our party. I wasn't sure if my heart would recover from the shock of Joy's news. I certainly hoped this outing was helping Jane, because it certainly wasn't helping me.

When we arrived back at Aunt Pat and Uncle Joe's house, Jane helped our aunt serve the hot chocolate that was being kept warm in the crock-pot while I unwrapped the plates of Christmas cookies. My mother had many flaws, but she made the world's most amazing cookies, and plenty of them.

The entire month of December the kitchen turned into a cookie factory to rival the Keebler elves. My mother made several batches each of a dozen different kinds of cookies. Mom started the tradition years ago as a way to make inexpensive gifts for friends and family, but as the years went on, the operation grew and now she made cookies not only as gifts, but she donated them to local charities and froze them to eat year-round.

If Mom had wanted to sell them, I was sure she'd be able to make a pretty penny, but if she sold even a single cookie, she would be a working mother, and in her mind, the highest calling of a woman of God was being a mother, therefore taking on a job after having children was a disgrace. She wouldn't go as far as to say it was a sin for the "poor unfortunate" women who had been forced back to work due to divorce or widowhood, but I wondered if deep down my mother thought those women must have sinned for God to put them in such circumstances. From my side, I couldn't understand how she could justify this view considering the ideal Proverbs 31 woman clearly had a job, but bringing that up to Mom always ended poorly.

Once everyone was settled into the living room with cookies and cocoa, Mrs. Douglas cleared her throat. "I wanted to make an announcement." The room slowed to a hush. "Our dear Joy is engaged to be married to the Reverend Colin Johnson. She's going to be a pastor's wife in Philadelphia."

There were several gasps, then the room fell eerily silent. Jane looked at me. I clapped my hands and almost shouted out my congratulations. I felt the need to encourage the entire room to join in the festive spirit, even if it was as fake as Santa Claus. I jumped to my feet, hugged Joy, and moved to hug her mother and her father. My actions had just the reaction I had anticipated. Jon, Jane, Dad, Aunt Pat, and Uncle Joe quickly followed suit. Joy's sisters didn't react much, but clearly this wasn't news to them. Mom was uncharacteristically silent, her lips pinched shut like she was holding back a tirade of epic proportion, and her eyes focused on me were telling me exactly on whom her ire was aimed. She was the only one to remain in her seat as the hugs and well wishes were exchanged with a hesitance that spoke not only of the suddenness of the engagement, but also the oddity of the match. Mom was holding her tongue until later. I was certain there would be a later, and I would never hear the end of how I had been the ruination of my entire family.

Before the gathering dispersed, Joy pulled me aside and gave me a hug. "Thank you so much. I appreciate what you did to cut the tension after my mother's announcement. Having seen the look on your mother's face, I know what this is costing you. You're the best friend ever."

The ride home was exactly as I had imagined. My mother ranted non-stop about how ridiculous it was for Joy to get married to a man she had only know a few weeks, totally ignoring her own double standard. She criticized her friend on the timing of her announcement and topped it off with less than wonderful predictions regarding the impending marriage.

When I could no longer take another word, I asked my mother to please stop.

The result was the redirection of all of her rage onto me. "You want me to stop? This is all your fault. You had the chance to save our family from financial ruin, but no, you couldn't be bothered. Well, I hope you'll be happy when Joy Douglas is living in your house, living the life you couldn't be bothered to live. Tell me to stop!" But finally, she did stop, much to my relief.

When my dad dropped Jane and I off at our apartment rather than heading directly to their home, I knew he had done so as an apology of sorts. Perhaps on behalf of Mom, or possibly because he never stopped his wife from speaking to his children the way she did. He didn't like her behavior, but he was either too weak or too lazy a man to do anything to curtail it. I had always adored my father, but I was ticked. This wasn't the first time he had silently witnessed his wife berate one of his children.

24: Beth

December crept along like Narnia under the White Witch; always winter, but never Christmas. In the classroom, I had hung snowflakes and set up white Christmas lights. Each morning we started our day with a different Christmas hymn. I had even worn a Santa hat all day on Friday, but still, everything seemed glum. I watched Jane wander through her days without the typical joy she ordinarily exhibited. She had promised herself she wouldn't text Chad, who hadn't sent another message since the day of his departure. The ball was clearly in his court. She determined that she wouldn't be one of those girls who couldn't take a hint. She said it was better to rip the Band-Aid off quickly and move on, but I suspected Jane had no intentions of moving on. Time to bring in the big guns.

"Hi Aunt Erica, how are you?"

"Beth! I'm fine. Kids are great. I've got dinner simmering on the stove, and Bert will be home in a little while. And now that you've called, life is bliss." Erica let out a soft sigh.

I couldn't help but smile. Erica was the poster child for familial bliss. Her strong faith in Jesus and her love for Bert and her kids made her exactly the kind of woman I wanted to be. "You have a minute?"

"Of course. Always for you."

"I've been dreaming up another scheme."

"It this the kind of scheme I'm going to have to repent of on Sunday morning?" Erica laughed. She knew me better than that.

"Absolutely. Probably for a few weeks running."

"I'm listening."

"I was thinking maybe you could invite Jane up to spend Christmas break with you and Uncle Bert. Nothing is more joyful than kids at Christmas. You know that would cheer Jane up. Maybe doing some touristy things might help. See the tree in Rockefeller Center. Hot chocolate. Ice skating in Bryant Park. The perfect medicine for the soul."

"That sounds like a sweet idea. But am I missing something? Where's the scheme in all this?"

Sheepishly, I added, "I thought maybe, being so close to Jersey City, maybe Jane could meet up with Missy and see Chad."

"What? That Missy woman is trouble. Why would you want to have anything to do with her?" Erica's indignation wasn't uncalled for. It was definitely the most questionable part of my plan.

"Yes, but maybe all Chad needs is to see Jane again. And Missy and Jane were friendly enough that I doubt Missy would suspect anything. Jane was pretty hurt, so it might be a hard sell. I might have to steal her phone and set up on her behalf."

"BETH!"

"Last resort. I promise." I waited for Erica to respond. The jury was definitely out on this one.

"I'd be more than happy to have Jane here. And I agree it'd do her some good. If she happens to make plans while she's up here to visit friends or do anything else, that'd be fine with me. But I won't get involved in anything else, and I advise you not to either. Let me run this by Bert after dinner."

"And that's why you're my favorite aunt." I couldn't keep the smile off my face.

Erica laughed out loud. "I've met your relatives. I'm related to most of them. I am certain the bar was pretty low for getting the favorite aunt status."

"Aunt Erica, how unkind of you. Shame." We both giggled that time.

"Now I will have to repent. You're right, even if you said it in jest."

With that, our call ended, but my plan continued to run through my mind.

25: Beth

This afternoon, Mom had asked me to come and help her with another round of Christmas cookie baking. I stepped into the kitchen and the sight of Jon Wade made me smile.

"Your mom just went up to grab your sisters."

I grabbed an apron from the pantry door. "Seems like every time I come over, you're here."

"I can leave if you want."

"Heaven forbid. You are just the thing to brighten these dreary December days." I shot him a smirk.

"Funny, that's almost exactly what Lydia said yesterday when I stopped by."

I wrinkled my nose. Not what I wanted to hear. It wasn't jealousy, it was just that Lydia was in high school for heaven's sake. I hope Jon wasn't encouraging her. "The girls never help in the kitchen. Hence Mom calling me over. If I need to deal with all this," I motioned to the baking sheets, racks, bowls, and tins, "it will be nice to have some eye candy, too."

Jon grabbed at his chest like he was pained. "I see how it is. I'm just a pretty face to you."

"You, my friend, are more like the eye of the storm. In a few minutes, this kitchen is going to be a baking hurricane and you will be my calm." I wove my fingers together and held them under my chin. I knew it was flirtatious, but Jon really did make me feel at ease.

"Then I shall turn over my man card and put on this frilly apron and earn my keep. I bet Darcy would never be seen in a kitchen. He probably orders his cooks around sending back his dinner because his food isn't cooked to perfection."

This wasn't the first time Jon had thrown out derogatory comments about Darcy. I guess I had opened Pandora's box and now he felt he had an ally. My sisters always agreed with him when he went off on Darcy. The sound of my youngest sisters racing down the stairs pulled me from my thoughts. I rolled my eyes. "I guess you are more like gravity, having the power to pull even the laziest teens from their rooms to work."

Mary was unsurprisingly absent.

The girls raced in and immediately hugged Jon. Lydia for longer than seemed appropriate. I would have felt better if Jon had seemed in anyway bothered.

"Jon, I'm so glad you're here. Are we going to be able to go to your friend's party tonight?" Lydia was practically bouncing as she asked.

"Sadly, no. He changed his plans. I called a few of my other friends, but most of them are busy this weekend." Jon put on a fake pout.

For someone who should have graduated college a couple of years ago, he seemed to have an awful lot of college age friends on a campus he didn't attend. Sure, Jon may just be one of those people who oozed flirtation, but I felt slightly uncomfortable with the flirtatious manner he spoke with my not yet eighteen-year-old sister. Just then, my mother walked into the kitchen.

"Mrs. Beckett, I am here to serve your cookie baking needs. Put me to work." Jon hooked his thumbs behind the neck strap on both sides of his apron and then did a little twirl so the apron rose up.

My mother giggled like a schoolgirl.

Then again, I thought, Jon flirts with my mother just like he does with my sisters.

We worked side by side into the evening. I had been on my feet teaching all day and ready to call it quits, but there were still a few more cookie sheets ready to go in the sink. My sisters had long ago headed out with the excuse of homework I doubted was getting done. Even Mom had taken a break in the other room. I began washing the mound of dishes by the sink. "Who taught you to make cookies? You seemed fairly decent with a rolling pin."

"My mom wasn't too bad in the kitchen. I helped her out occasionally, but it was actually the cook at the Williams' that taught me the most. I spent quite a few afternoons with her. School would let out, and I'd find myself watching her make dinner while I ate a snack and procrastinated getting to my homework."

I looked over at Jon who sat at our kitchen island. "Sounds nice."

"It was. Darcy was never around. Too below him. His sister Lexi would sit with me sometimes. She used to be sweet, but I hear she's just as bad as her brother. Stuck up. Stepping on the little people."

I was tiring of the negativity even if it was directed at a man I enjoyed disliking.

"Well, however you learned, it's a good skill to have. Girls like guys who can cook. It means they can share the load together. Equal. I enjoy cooking, but if I ever get married, I'd like to know that we could take turns or even cook together."

Jon looked up from the plate of cookies he was snacking on and spoke. "Oh, you'll get married someday. I predict a handsome man will come along and snatch you up. Not as competent in the kitchen as me, definitely not as good looking, and he won't be able to pull off a frilly apron, but a good catch. And you will run off into the sunset and live happily ever after. Well, at least moderately happy because, you know, no frilly apron." Jon smiled at me.

It was hard to stay irritated at him.

Christmas Eve Day arrived without snow and without its usual charm. I couldn't pinpoint the cause of the spiritless holiday. I considered Jane's broken heart and the news of Joy's approaching wedding, but nothing felt quite right. I was feeling lonely, which didn't really make sense because between teaching and family, I was rarely ever alone.

I assisted Mom and Jane in the kitchen and set the table. I was in the dining room when my Aunt Erica approached.

"Beth dear, I've noticed you with that Jon fellow. What's his deal? It seems to me that his entire life is aimed solely at bad mouthing Darcy Williams. Does he have no other occupation?"

I continued placing utensils at each place setting. "That's actually a good question. I have no idea what he does. He's mentioned looking for a job, and he talked a little about checking on his investments, but now that you mention it, he certainly seems to have a little too much free time. And while his gripe with Darcy seems valid, I have to admit I'm tiring of his talk. It's like a broken record."

Aunt Erica placed her hand on my shoulder to garner my full attention. "Please be careful around him. I've seen the way he flirts with you, and I worry that he's not who he seems to be. You can do far better than a man like that."

I smiled at my aunt, but turned back toward the task at hand. "You're showing your age." I smirked. "You sound very old fashioned. For no good reason, you think I should keep Jon at arms' length simply because he hasn't found a job yet? Or rather because you have a feeling? I'm a little shocked by you." Despite my teasing tone, I wasn't being completely facetious.

"Don't confuse a woman's intuition with out of date rules on marriage based upon status. I'm not as concerned with his bank account as with his character, and something tells me that you're not seeing as clearly as you ought. Don't confuse charm with Godly qualities. Do you know anything about his faith in Christ? That should be the number one thing you're looking for in a partner."

My tone softened with her rebuke. "You're right. Perhaps I'm being unfair to you. I appreciate your candor. I just kind of assumed that Jon must have some faith because I met him at Aunt Pat and Uncle Jon's. Surprisingly, we haven't really talked about it. I assume he goes to church."

"You know better than that. Even if he did go to church, that doesn't mean anything about his commitment to God. You aren't shy about talking about Jesus. It makes me wonder why it hasn't already come up between the two of you. I wonder what's gotten in the way of the more serious talk." Aunt Erica's pointed look was not one of general curiosity, but the knowing look you give a naughty child.

Sheepishly I replied, "I do love flirting with him. I guess I justified it as meaning nothing because he flirts with everyone. I'm sure I could use a little more discretion. I promise to guard my heart and pay better attention so that I can judge more clearly."

My aunt hugged me. "That's all I'm asking of you, my dear."

**

I tried to console myself on my solitary Christmas break with visions of Jane happily married to Chad Woods. I had been working my way through every Christmas movie available on Netflix and Amazon Prime over the break. I was pretty sure I'd gained five pounds in Christmas cookies alone. My new ritual included a nightly phone call from my mother.

"Are you coming over tonight? It's not good to sit all alone in that tiny cramped apartment when you have a house and family next door."

"No, Mom. I'm happy having the place to myself. I'm trying to rest up."

"It'd be different if you had a date or something. You can watch movies here. Why don't you have a date?"

"Mom, we've been through this every day this week. I'm an introvert. This is how I reenergize."

My mother's exasperated sigh punctuated my sentence. "Well, all the good ones are getting snatched up. You're running out of time. And if you aren't going to at least try to find a man, you ought to spend more time with your sisters. They'll be all the family you have one day."

I missed Jane, but worse than that, it seemed that my mother believed spending more time with me could compensate for Jane's absence. She tried to lure me over to the house for dinner every night, and I had completely run out of excuses.

"Mom, I'll come over tomorrow. I'll even spend the night so I don't have to drive home drunk."

"Not funny. You better not bring alcohol into my house. You might be old enough now, but not in my house."

This might be the only area where Mom put her foot down. She was a teetotaler. She didn't ever say why, but we all knew the rule. I shouldn't have poked her. I knew it'd bug her and that's why I said it. It seemed I could never just give my mother what she wanted without a tiny dig. I suppose I was no better than her, but I suspect her digs at me about marriage and kids had a better motivation than mine. Ugh! When would I grow up? *Lord, help me control my tongue. After so many years of following You, I don't know why I can't be more kind to my own mother. I'm not going to make anyone a very good wife if I can't be a thoughtful and loving daughter. Please transform my heart. I want to be more like You.*

The next night, the wind stung my face with each step closer to my parent's home, and Mom's tongue stung just at bitterly once I arrived.

"I can't believe you left your house like that." She shook her head in disapproval.

"Pjs are all the rage. Besides, if I wore them here, I didn't need to pack an overnight bag."

"What if we had company coming over?"

"Oooo, do we? I am so glad I picked out this cute matching set with the snowmen. It even has this formal collared shirt." My teasing tone did nothing to change my mother's stern face.

"It's inappropriate to be waltzing around in mixed company in your bedroom attire," she huffed.

"Bedroom attire? It's not a negligee. It's comfort wear. And will there be mixed company?" I shot her a questioning look.

"No, but you didn't know that. What if one of your sisters brought a boy over. Just because you never do, doesn't mean they don't,"

That was certainly the truth. "I'm sorry, Mom. I didn't mean to embarrass you. I can run home if you'd like.

Relief was not to be found, so I counted the days until Jane's return, and I texted her each night. Sitting on the couch beside Cat and Lydia, I pulled out my phone.

Jane: *I texted Missy and let her know I was in the city. She invited me for coffee Friday*

Me: *Yay! Anything fun on the agenda for tomorrow?* I asked Jane this same question every day, hoping she'd be seeing Chad soon. So far it was all fun with the kids.

I popped some popcorn in my mouth as I waited for her response. The vibration pulled my eyes from the Hallmark movie we were watching.

Jane: *Skating in Bryant Park.*

Me: *Not Rockefeller Center?*

Jane: *It's cheaper. Shorter lines. Better for the kids. This is a bucket list item for me.*

Me: *You have a bucket list? I thought that was just me.*

Jane: *Of course, I just won't tell you what else is on it. ;)*

Me: *Well, mine is so long I could never tell you it all. Skating at Rockefeller makes the cut. Go big or go home. Seeing the ball drop in Time Square. Not from the street. Too cold, too crowded. I need like box seats or something. Definitely a bathroom.*

Jane: *I had no idea you were so high maintenance. No ball drop for me.*

Me: *Are you enjoying yourself?*

Jane: *Yes. I suppose this was just the distraction I needed. Your plot succeeded.*

Me: *What plot? I never plot.*

Jane: *Seriously?*

Me: *Who told you?* ☺

Jane: *No one. I overheard Aunt Erica talking to Uncle Bert. I love how much you care about me. That's why I figured I better text Missy. I hated to see all your scheming go to waste.*

Me: *Thanks for tossing me a bone.*

**

Friday evening after family dinner I rushed home to call Jane. No texting tonight. I'd pinned a lot of hope on coffee with Chad, and I wanted all the details. Jane would never spill them over text.

"So, how was Chad?"

"Missy, not Chad. I met Missy for coffee."

"What? Are you telling me Chad wasn't home?"

"No, we met at a coffee shop. Chad was working. Missy and I chatted. It wasn't as friendly as it'd been in the past. She didn't suggest getting together again. It felt more like a blind date or a job interview than coffee with a friend."

I tapped my finger on the arm of the couch. "Well, what did you talk about?"

I could hear the sadness in Jane's voice. "Well, Missy talked about Lexi Williams and how wonderful her and Chad look together, and how hard Chad is working to become a successful business man so he doesn't have time to meet up for coffee."

"You've got to be kidding."

"Nope. She talked about how much she disliked being so far away from things when they lived in Princeton and how she never wanted to move back. Oh, and she said Chad was on the same page as her when it came to that."

I let out a tiny scream. "Are you kidding me? That woman gets under my skin. Don't believe a word she says, I don't trust her at all. Text Chad yourself and let him know you're in town."

Jane gasped. "I can't do that. I texted him last. If he wants to see me, he needs to text me. I'm not going to chase a man around who clearly doesn't care."

"Even if it breaks your heart?"

And with that Jane did start to cry. "He already broke my heart. This is my attempt to keep him from breaking it again."

My eyes teared up as well. "I'm sorry. I shouldn't have pushed you. You're right. I don't want to see you hurting any more. Please, stay away from Missy. She's bad news."

"I absolutely agree. I don't intend to ever see her again."

"Jane, that's the most unforgiving thing I have ever heard you say about another person. Bravo!"

**

Jon Wade returned from his Christmas holiday with a girl on his arm. I watched the couple with great interest. We were at my Aunt Pat's and Uncle Joe's when I first saw him.

"Beth, I'd love you to meet my fiancé, Susan."

Jon looked at me with a bright smile on his face, but the crinkle on his forehead made me think he worried about my reaction. I had no trouble responding with joyful exuberance. "I'm so happy to meet you. I am sure there is a story here dying to be told."

Susan tightened her grip on Jon's arm and gazed up at him adoringly. "Jon stepped into the party my parents were hosting, and it was love at first sight." Susan let out a dramatic sigh.

She actually sighed. I almost laughed, but held it together. Jon returned her gaze, but the lightness of his voice wasn't quite what I was used to in him. "Absolutely. When you know, you know." Jon returned his gaze to me.

He'd been away a week. A week. Who was I to pass judgment? *Okay, being so judgmental was something I was praying to do better on. Here was my test.* "I'm happy for you." I'd promised my aunt I'd keep my eyes open and my heart guarded. I was pleased to find that I wasn't jealous of this new woman in Jon's life. I was merely intrigued.

"May I see the ring?" My curiosity couldn't be abated.

"Oh. I haven't gotten her a ring yet. It was such a whirlwind romance. I couldn't contain myself and just had to propose."

"It was so romantic." And then she sighed again.

"What are your plans?"

"Daddy owns Oakview Health Insurance Company. Jon's going to work for him."

"Do you work there also?" I asked.

"Heavens no. I'm still in school. And I want to be a proper wife, anyway."

I looked at Jon, my eyebrow raised in question. How old was this girl? "I hope you won't be too far away?" I don't recall where Jon said he was visiting.

Jon was so serious as he spoke. "Connecticut. We'll live in my in-law's guest house until we find a place of our own."

My attention was dragged away by my Aunt Pat carrying a heavy platter in from the kitchen. I was almost relieved to make my exit. I had some thinking to do. Was he using Susan for money?

To be honest, making decisions based on money wasn't all that terrible. If Joy could marry a man for stability, there was no reason Jon couldn't do the same. Certainly, when you looked at the marriages in the Bible, you saw all sorts of arranged marriages based on little more than money and status. Isaac married Rebekah the day they met; Rebekah agreed after being given gold jewelry. Abraham and Jacob both took concubines for the purpose of making babies.

Kings did it for political connections. Certainly, this was not a sin, even if in my own heart I knew that I couldn't be persuaded to marry for any reason other than love. But then again, I was used to being relatively poor. Or at least poor by Princeton standards. It might be a more tempting option if I had gotten a taste of wealth and risked losing it. I didn't know what I was missing.

Susan seemed to be friendly and easy going. She sat with Lydia and Cat for a while, deep in a discussion that included lots of hand gestures all around. Jon, I noticed, seemed content to be back in this familiar home. He was his typical charming self.

I was occupied in the kitchen the next time I saw Jon. I hadn't even heard him approach.

"I hope your concern about where I shall live has something to do with the fact that you'll miss me, at least a little."

I turned toward Jon, but continued to train my eyes on the arranging the cookies on a tray. "Of course, I'll miss you. Perhaps not as much as Lydia and Cat, but I'll miss having someone to tease."

"Good. Because I would hate to think I could leave without notice. Yours was the opinion I was most concerned about. Do you like her?"

I looked through the doorway to see her still chatting with my sisters. "I like her just fine. But the only question that matters is whether you like her?"

Jon's response was slower in coming than it was during introductions. "I like her just fine. She has some great attributes."

I wasn't going to play dumb. "I'm not sure if you're talking about her body or her bank account, but I'm sure both will make for a pleasant marriage."

Jon laughed. "Your candor always has been refreshing. I suppose you're right. She isn't as intellectually stimulating as you are, but you and I are both practical people. I would have liked things to have been different. Truly."

I looked up at Jon and met his eyes. His confession bordered on inappropriate, but I wasn't heartbroken, and I wanted him to see the truth of that.

The Saturday after the New Year, Jane returned home. Lydia had heard the car pull into the driveway, or perhaps she had been watching from Cat's bedroom window.

"They're here! They're here!" Her yells were followed by the sound of her feet racing down the steps. Not just hers, but another set as well, I could only assume belonging to Cat. Mary would certainly tear herself from her room begrudgingly, but even Mary couldn't act entirely indifferent to our two little cousins who had come with their parents.

"Jane, I never thought you'd come home. You've missed so much." Lydia practically screamed as she raced down into the foyer.

"Don't you dare tell her everything," Cat demanded.

"Oh, look how adorable you two look. Let me help you with your coat, Sadie. Give yours here, Miles." Lydia stooped down to help our cousins. Cat followed her lead.

Mary came down the stairs slowly, carrying a book in her hand. "Hi Aunt Erica, Uncle Bert. Hi Miles. Hi Sadie." I was glad to see Mary interacting a bit.

I enveloped Jane in a hug, followed by hugs to Aunt Erica and Uncle Bert.

The peace wouldn't last long. Cat and Lydia were determined to fill Jane in on two weeks worth of events in the first hour she was home. If there was any verse in the Bible whose truth I questioned, it's the one that says the ears do not tire of hearing. Oh, they do. Of that I am certain.

Of all the stories that the girls most wanted to share with Jane, the news of Jon's engagement to Susan topped the list. While Cat and Lydia pouted and cried as they told of the great loss to them personally, Aunt Erica caught my eye. I could read the knowing look that came across her face. Jon, who was flirting with me the day before Christmas, was now engaged to someone else? I blushed as I thought about how foolish I had been with him. Still, I smiled at my aunt and nodded my head to convey my thanks for helping keep my heart intact.

Over dinner, Aunt Erica proposed an idea. "Beth dear, we've had such a lovely time with your sister this past week, I was thinking it might be nice to do something similar with you over summer break. There is an amazing day camp down here for two weeks in July. Jane has agreed to drive the kids to and from camp and watch them for the remaining time. I'd love for you to come with your uncle and me to Maine. The kids are still too young for any serious hiking, and I'd love to visit Acadia National Park. Do some more challenging hikes, that sort of thing. Would you come along?"

I nearly knocked my glass over when I threw my hands up and caught the edge of the table in my exuberance. "Yes! I would love that!"

"Perfect!" She laughed. "That was easy."

I loved my aunt and uncle more than anyone else in the family save Jane and my father. Perhaps it was because so many of my family members were nearly as ridiculous as Colin, but I knew it went beyond that. We enjoyed nature walks and hiking. We shared a love of literature and history, and we shared a deep love for Christ. I respected the wisdom of my aunt and my uncle, and the thought of two weeks with them might be just what I needed to help figure out the next step in my life. Not career related, I loved that part of my life, but the rest of my life. I felt unsettled; I needed this.

26: Beth

Joy and Colin were married on Valentine's Day at his church in Philadelphia. Because I'm a teacher, I could only take two days off from work, so I wasn't able to spend any additional time with my friend in the days leading up to the wedding. I arrived Friday morning to help set up for that evening's rehearsal dinner and then help Joy on Saturday with the final wedding preparations for the wedding which was to be held Sunday evening. Colin insisted on preaching on Sunday morning so he expected to be preoccupied with church business most of my stay. That was fine with me.

I climbed the few concrete steps to the sturdy, old wooden doors painted bright red. They stood out against the brick structure. A blue plaque claimed the building had been erected in 1837, so too new for Revolutionary, but old enough to deserve some reverence. As I entered, I was hit with a mixture of furniture polish and old books. I stilled as my eyes focused on the stained-glass window directly in front of me, behind the pulpit. The morning light was casting a rainbow upon the golden cross that sat upon the altar. It was breathtaking. It was holy.

Just then, Joy bumped into my back with the box of centerpieces she was holding, almost knocking the bags in my hand out of my grasp. "Beth!"

"Sorry." I hurried out of her path. "It's just so... so spectacular. I hadn't really thought what your new home church would be like, but I guess I hadn't imagined it would be a work of art."

I could see the pride in Joy's eyes. "It really is, isn't it?"

Jane came in carrying a second box of centerpieces and we followed Joy down the stairs into the fellowship hall where both the rehearsal dinner and reception would take place. On my way, I couldn't help myself, but to run my fingers along the back row of pews as I passed by. What had these pews witnessed? I just might need to ask Colin if he knew much about its history. Maybe my curiosity could be an olive branch.

The infamous Dee Burgh was already downstairs when we arrived. Joy's pinched lips clued me in to the fact that she was less than pleased. For the past two months, I had heard all about Mrs. Burgh's hand in this affair. She had instructed the couple as to the florist, the music, the caterer, and the color scheme. Perhaps having only one daughter who was still unmarried, she felt the need to plan a wedding.

"Good. You're finally here. I was wondering if I was going to have to do everything myself." Dee's soft voice didn't hide the chastisement she directed at Joy.

"Yes, we arrived a few minutes early, but I was so taken by the sight of that magnificent stained-glass window in the sanctuary, that I couldn't tear myself away." If I knew anything from the many praises Colin had espoused and the laments of Joy, Dee prided herself in this church.

Dee set the glass she was holding down on the circular table she was setting, and she focused all of her attention directly on me. "It's original to the building. My great great grandfather was on the committee that commissioned the window. It almost wasn't in place when they christened the church. It was made in London, but there was some delay in the shipment. Apparently, arriving late to church has been a theme since the church's beginning."

And so much for a distraction.

Jane came through the door holding another box.

"Joy, where would you like the centerpieces for the reception?" She held up the box in her arms just a bit higher.

"Put them in the pantry behind you." Dee didn't even give Joy the chance to speak. "Where are the centerpieces for tonight? You didn't forget them, did you?"

"No, Dee, I have them right here." Joy carefully reached into the box she had placed on the counter at the pass-through window that led to the kitchen.

Without even taking a moment to appreciate all the hard work Joy had put into making each globe of red and pink roses, Dee began dictating. "Well, set them on the tables. And make sure you don't knock the glasses over."

I sidled up next to Joy, and began removing the top layer of her beautiful work out of the box and placing them gently on the countertop. Today was going to test the Jesus in me.

Joy told me that she endured Dee's demanding ways because she feared resisting her could negatively impact her future husband's favor with such a prominent member of the congregation. I had only just met the woman, but already several times I had wanted to put her in her place, and that place was back in her home and far away from the wedding.

Sunday's worship service was far different from the one Joy and I attended in Princeton. It went beyond the more traditional pews, organ, and hymnals. While I preferred the more lively music and less formal dress of my own church, I still enjoyed this more formal experience. It had been a long time since I had recited the Lord's Prayer and the Apostles' Creed. There is something beautiful about the community of believers that is sometimes lost in the more relaxed church service I attended. Knowing that believers all around the world were reciting the same thing, confessing their common faith moved me. I had been so judgmental about Joy's decision to marry Colin, I had failed to see that her choice, while different from mine, wasn't necessarily wrong. I was glad I had come to realize this now. I still had my hesitations, but I was feeling better about Joy's big day.

During the reception held in the church basement, Joy approached me. Her face was lit up like a woman in love, but I had difficulty imagining that was actually the case. Perhaps the love Joy was feeling was for the freedom her new life was offering her. I wanted to smack myself for my own thoughts. I couldn't seem to be gracious when it came to Colin. And telling myself to shut up didn't seem to be enough. *Lord, help me take my thoughts captive. Give me a gracious and kind heart.*

"I'm going to miss you so very much. Please say you'll come and visit me," she pleaded.

"Of course, I will. Why would you even ask such a thing? We've been friends since we were little girls. Nothing will ever change that."

Joy squeezed my hand. "Come for spring break. My father and sister are coming up. Dad is only staying for the weekend. He can't leave Mom running the café all by herself for long, but you and Izzy could stay the whole week. I love my sister, but it would be so much nicer to have you here as well. Please come."

Jane, who was sitting next to me, slipped her hand into mine and gave it a gentle squeeze. "You should go. It'll make the separation easier knowing that you'll be here again in another few weeks. You should say yes."

Joy nodded her agreement. I could see in Jane's eyes that she was thinking more of Joy than she was of me, and with that sweet spirit, how could she be refused? "I'd be thrilled to come."

**

Easter and with it Spring Break came later than usual. The daffodils and tulips had both burst forth with their bright colors. Clusters of bright yellow daffodils dotted the landscape even in the shade cast by the copses that scattered the Beckett grounds. I enjoyed taking my class outside whenever possible searching for signs of spring. Animal footprints in the mud along the canal path, buds forming on the maple and oak branches, new growth on the pine trees, and the sounds of birds that had returned from their winter roosting all spoke of newness and life. I wouldn't say I was excited about the prospect of spending my entire spring break with Colin, but I did love Joy, and I loved the idea of a week in such a beautiful, historic city.

Mr. Douglas, Izzy, and I had driven to Philadelphia, but the return trip home without Mr. Douglas was going to involve navigating the SEPTA trains, which included transfers. I was already feeling anxious about that and hoped that my time in the city would include some experience with public transit to prepare me for escorting Izzy home. We parked in the public lot only two blocks from Joy's house that Joy's father had prepaid for. We wheeled our suitcases down the sidewalk and stopped in front of an old brick row home. The houses in the area all looked relatively the same, but I could see the personal touches that adorned each home. Joy had always loved flowers, so I wasn't surprised when the flower boxes hanging on the lower level windows were bursting with bright colored flowers and ivy flowing down like a waterfall. On the door, a wreath with pastel colored Easter eggs and a soft white bunny welcomed us. Joy answered our knock and ushered us in with an exuberance that made me wonder if she was putting on a show. All my concerns for her happiness melted away when she wrapped me in a tight hug. I'd missed her, and I fully intended to enjoy this trip as much as possible.

The invitation for dinner the following evening at Mrs. Burgh's home came the day we arrived. Mrs. Burgh was hosting a small gathering of people. She had company coming in for Easter Sunday and wanted to welcome them with a celebration. Colin was ecstatic about the invite and talked about it the entire evening. I wanted to roll my eyes for Joy to see, much the way we had done back home whenever my mother went on one of her tirades. Fortunately, I caught myself when I realized this was Joy's husband now. I'd need to be on my best behavior and try to think before I spoke or acted.

Joy must have sensed the time to switch subjects had passed long ago, and turned the talk to our Saturday plans. "I reserved tickets for us for Independence Hall, save for Colin who will be preparing for a busy day of Easter Services and won't be able to take the time out and still attend the party at the Burgh's. So the four of us will go. The weather looks perfect. We can walk the few blocks; visit Independence Hall, the Liberty Bell, and several other sites. Let's skip the Constitution Center. That's a good thing to do on a rainy day. I don't want to waste this weather."

"You know how much I love to be outside on a beautiful day and how much I love history. It's been years since I've toured either of those places. Perhaps we can have a picnic lunch on the lawn."

Joy turned her head to the side of the table where her father and Izzy sat. "How does that sound to you?"

Izzy nodded her head. "I'm game."

Mr. Douglas smiled and placed his hand on Joy's. "Anything that involves spending time with my little girl is just fine with me."

The weather report was spot on for Saturday. Joy led the way to Independence National Historic Park. Hundreds of tulips in various shades were in full bloom. The park was crowded with families, many likely on spring break. I almost hated to enter Independence Hall for love of sunshine, but my desire to revisit the historic building and the timed tickets Joy reserved pushed me on. I was glad she had encouraged us to start out early, because the security line to enter for our tour was longer than I expected. Once inside, I was in awe of the surroundings. So much had taken place in this building that shaped the Nation. I took a few pictures, but mostly committed all I could to memory to share with my students next year. I always made them memorize the Preamble to the Constitution, and we discussed the impact the Revolutionary War had all around the world. Next year, I'd show them a picture of The Rising Sun Chair I'd taken. The day continued in the same manner it began, perfect in every way.

We found a place on the grass to enjoy our picnic. The opposite end of the grounds held a traveling exhibit that took up a significant portion of the open space. The Doctors Without Borders event, free and open to the public, was designed to educate the community about the challenges refugees faced and how they could support relief efforts. Once I saw that the dates of operation continued for the length of our stay, I determined I'd visit that later in the week.

"How do you liking living here? You were never as big a fan of history as I was, but the city is gorgeous." I turned to look at Joy as she responded.

"Honestly, I don't really think much about the city itself. I've been really focused on the church congregation. I started teaching a women's Bible study. I was worried I would miss our Bible study group so much when I left, but the women here have embraced me. It feels so good to teach the Bible. I've made a number of friends. I started a hospitality ministry as well. Bringing food to new mothers, visiting people in the hospital. That sort of thing. It keeps me almost as busy as Colin."

"He works a lot?" I wasn't too surprised. Pastors were like teachers, but without the summers off.

"Yes. I know he can come off strong, but he really loves his job and the church. I think he's sort of insecure. He talks too much when he's nervous. Once he's more at ease with someone, he's a very different person. He listens to me. We talk. Well, when he's not working."

I took a moment to think before I responded to her. "You know, I think you're right. When we were kids, Colin really wanted to be liked. Not in a bad way, more in a friendly way. Sometimes he went about making friends in a sort of awkward way. Like the time he told Mary that he really liked fat girls." I shook my head at the memory. "He hated that she never played with us, and he thought maybe she was self-conscious of her weight. Mary stormed off, leaving Colin behind in shock. His dad had to explain to him how his comments might have been taken as offensive. Honestly, I hadn't thought of that incident in a long time."

"Oh, wow. I can see that happening. Poor Colin. He really does try." I could hear the sincerity in Joy's tone.

"Yes, he does." Joy was right. I was going to look at him with new eyes.

As the dinner hour approached, Colin's exuberance skyrocketed. "Just wear the nicest thing you brought. No need to worry if it's fancy enough for the Burghs. But, Beth, try to put some effort into your appearance. I know you don't like to be bothered, but perhaps you can put aside that foolishness for one night. I'm sure Izzy could help you do something."

For Joy's sake, I bit my tongue. My resolve was already fading. Colin was her husband. I could respect her by respecting him, but I was absolutely not putting make-up on for this. I figured I could blow out my hair and use a clip or something to give the appearance of effort. Jewelry would help. Big earrings and a brightly colored necklace ought to do the trick. I didn't bring more than one dress. With Easter tomorrow, I didn't want to waste it on tonight nor did I want to wear it two days in a row. I settled on navy slacks, a cream-colored blouse, and a blue and purple necklace that jingled with each step. The matching earrings would make the outfit seem more complete. I hoped that would be enough to satisfy Colin.

Dee Burgh's place was nothing short of spectacular. Black metal gates that allowed visitors to park in a secured underground lot had the feel of wealth but fit the ground level brick siding. We had walked, but the entrance to the building was situated adjacent to the parking entrance. The metal and glass exterior of the upper floors seemed out of place against the backdrop of the numerous older structures in the area. My idea of an apartment in Center City was completely thrown out the minute we stepped through the front door. One look at the ostentatious open floor plan, and I needed to consciously keep my mouth from hanging wide open. Seeing even Mr. Douglas agape assured me that I was not alone in my thoughts, just in my outward reaction. From the entryway, guests could see a wall of floor to ceiling windows that looked out over Independence Hall, which now sat lit up. The room was decorated with a modern flair, white furniture, light grey cabinets and countertops, and minimal color. Straight lines, lots of lighting, and enough art on the walls and shelves to scream lavish but not gaudy.

I wondered why people had homes that dripped of showcase. Homes should be warm and lived in. White should never be a couch color. I handed off my coat to the woman who'd greeted us and followed our party into the living space. Joy made introductions being thoughtful enough to share a few details about each person and their relationship to her. Mrs. Burgh's daughter, Anne, remained silent. Dee on the other hand took the information in and then began questioning each member of the party about their life and stay so far. Some might call her bold, but I thought her rather presumptuous.

"And you, Beth. How old are you? You can't be much younger than Joy here. And still unmarried?"

I clenched the fabric of my pants. "Yes, ma'am, still unmarried. Having been raised in this century, I was assured that it wasn't necessary for a woman to marry in order to be happy in life."

Mrs. Burgh gasped. "Well, if you keep wearing the pants, I'm sure you won't be attracting any eyes on yourself. These feministic ideals are what's destroying the church."

I smoothed down my pants to remove the crinkles I had undoubtedly created. "I am not interested in any man who is more concerned about my legs than my mind."

At that moment, two men entered the room from a hallway I assumed led to the bedrooms. I turned my head to see their approach, but at the sight of Darcy Williams, my body responded before my mind could temper my reaction. I shot to my feet.

Darcy's eyes widened, and a grin appeared.

"Darcy? What on earth are you doing here?" I asked.

He chuckled. "What am I doing at my aunt's house? I've come for Easter just as I do every year. I think the better question is what are you doing here?"

Aunt? Did I forget that being mentioned? Could this really be happening?

Dee Burgh gave me a disapproving look while Darcy introduced his friend Jeff all around and clarified that Aunt Dee was not actually his aunt, but his late mother's best friend. Darcy had been calling her Aunt Dee since childhood. After losing his mother years ago, Dee had made Darcy promise to continue his visits, especially on Easter. To honor his mother's memory and the love the two women had for each other and for him, Darcy had always complied.

I thought the night couldn't have been more awkward. Every topic of the night so far had my hackles rising. We went from one politically charged topic to the next like being shoved off the ski lift only to have your head cracked by each subsequent chair gliding by.

"Honestly, I don't understand all this talk of teachers wanting to be paid more. They barely work. Summers off and weeks at a time throughout the year. Case in point, a week for Easter. And it doesn't take a rocket scientist to teach adding and subtracting." Mrs. Burgh waved her fork towards me as she spoke.

"Most of the people I work with have master's degrees. And the hours they work during the weeks that school is in session average more than 40 hours a week even when spread out across a full year." I was gripping my utensils a little too tightly, so I eased my grip and forced myself to slowly ease out my breath.

"Psht. Everyone works more than 40 hours a week. If teachers wanted to make more money, they should have picked a better career."

I bit my tongue to keep my thoughts from spilling out, but I continue the conversation in my mind. *Well, the trophy wife major at my college was all filled up when I applied, so I guess I shall have to content myself with a meaningful pursuit rather than a life of material things.*

"Free market economy works. Salaries rise based on supply and demand. People pay for what they need." Colin's voice grated on my last nerve.

Like the way we pay pastors? UGH! If that wasn't enough, Darcy continued to glance at me from the far side of the table.

"Perhaps the most meaningful positions are undervalued in a market economy because there are so many good people who chose meaningful pursuits that the economy can get away with lower than usual compensation." Darcy's words were unexpectedly kind. He didn't leave room for additional comment by quickly moving the conversation on.

"Aunt Dee, perhaps tonight we could watch a movie. I know it's not the normal thing for us, but you have such a great setup. It seems a waste if no one gets to enjoy it. With Easter tomorrow, I think *The Passion of the Christ* movie would be appropriate, but if that is too deep for a dinner party, I'm sure we can find something else."

"A movie? With all the company we have? One can watch a movie when they've nothing better to do. No. Perhaps a game," Mrs. Burgh suggested.

"You forget how much I dislike games, but I suppose we could break into groups," Darcy said. "Inside for a game, and out on the deck for conversation."

Mrs. Burgh nodded her consent. I wondered if Darcy recalled my own aversion to the games at Chad's house in Jersey City. What was his deal?

When dinner was over, Darcy, Jeff, and I retired to the deck, while the remaining six began to play Apples to Apples. Occasionally the noise and laughter from the game drifted out to the deck and would catch our attention. Most of the conversation outside was between Jeff and I. I marveled at how easy it was to talk with Jeff and how little Darcy said the entire night. Jeff had asked about our plans for their visit.

"Oh, today, while at Independence Hall, I noticed the Doctors Without Borders exhibit. I'd love to check that out. I've always been intrigued by their work. I also hope to visit the waterfront. I'm sure we'll do some touristy things for Izzy's sake, but mostly, I came here to see Joy."

"And yet, you're out here with us, while Joy is in there with them," Jeff noted.

"Well, I can't spend all of my time with her." I laughed. "Everyone needs some variety in their day." The conversation moved to Jeff. "So Jeff, what are you vacating from this week?"

"Oh, my sister has a new baby, and was a little worried about germs. I typically go there for Easter, so I jumped at the chance to spend time with my old friend here rather than sitting at home in front of a game console like a teenager."

"And when you aren't in front of a game console you?"

"Oh, you mean like work? Yes, sometimes I'm forced to work. I'm a vice president at the family business. Shipping and exports. Nothing exciting or terribly noble. Just a job."

Darcy practically interrupted. "I'd very much like to see what MSF is doing. Would you like to go together? Jeff, would you like to come along?"

"MSF?"

"*Médecins Sans Frontières.* Doctors Without Borders." Darcy said.

How pretentious could this man be? "Well, that was delayed. I thought we'd moved on from that topic. While I'd love to see the exhibit, wouldn't you rather go with your aunt and Anne?"

Jeff slapped his knee. "I cannot imagine Aunt Dee or Anne having any interest in such an exhibit." In a voice like Mrs. Burgh Jeff said, "It's such an eye sore. It's ruining my view. Don't I pay enough in taxes? I shouldn't have to deal with this nonsense. They'll not get any of my money."

Darcy laughed at his friend. "Jeff is quite right. While my foundation doesn't work directly with Doctors Without Borders, I've connected with them over the years. We fund several programs in the same areas. I like to see what they're doing with their display. So, if you'd like to go, how about Monday morning at ten-thirty?"

I nodded my head seemingly without my own consent. *Did I just agree to see Darcy yet again?* Trying to regain a little bit of the upper hand, I looked at Darcy. "Jane spent Christmas in New York City with my aunt and uncle. Did you happen to see her while you were there?"

He clenched his jaw. "No, I never saw her."

"Funny, she met up with Missy Woods, but never mentioned seeing anyone else the entire time she was there. I was at home and spent most of my time with my family and Jon Wade." The look on Darcy's face told me I'd gone too far. Perhaps if I had started out with this conversation I wouldn't have plans to see him again Monday morning. I was certain I'd see him at church tomorrow. Three days in a row was a bit much.

27: Beth

I stepped into the kitchen early Sunday morning. Joy was bustling around preparing

for the Easter luncheon. She had clearly been up for hours already. The oven was on, and the kitchen was warm. Joy hummed as she stirred a pot of boiling potatoes. She turned towards the doorway when I spoke.

"Is there anything I can do to help?"

"Grab a seat, and I'll get you breakfast. After you eat, perhaps you can set the dining room table. We're expecting eight people for lunch."

"Eight? Isn't your dad leaving right after service to be with your mom? Who else will be coming?" *Please don't say Darcy.*

Joy began to count on her fingers as she rattled off the names of church members. "They're just a few people without any close friends or family in the area. Everyone was so welcoming to me when I arrived, and I wanted to make sure our home was always open to others."

Joy's cheeks were flushed from exertion and most likely the warm stove, but her eyes sparkled with true happiness. Joy had the gift of hospitality. She always had. This life really did suit her.

As I placed Joy's wedding china around the table, I surveyed the room. Joy had created a centerpiece of candles and flowers. She used to make them for catering events back home. Pictures adorned the walls that hadn't been there when I came for the wedding. Curtains on every window. It felt like a home. A home filled with love and warmth. While my apartment was lived in and Jane and I loved each other, for a brief moment I longed for the hominess of a place like this. My regrets washed over me. How judgmental I had been about Joy's choice. I hadn't even taken the chance to get to know the real Colin. The man behind the strong opinions. And while I didn't regret turning Colin down, for the first time, I understood Joy. She had chosen well. I felt ashamed.

I crossed back into the kitchen where Joy was arranging deviled eggs on a tray and sprinkling them with paprika. "You're a lucky woman, Joy. You've made a beautiful home, and you're using the gifts that God has given you to bless other people. I don't believe there is anything more one could want for in life." I heard the emotion in my own voice as I drew her into a hug.

The whispered, "Thank you," that escaped Joy's lips revealed their emotion.

Not one to stay in such a state, I stepped away and asked Joy to put me to work. "We still have some time before service starts."

*****

I spent the better part of Monday morning pacing around the house. Having voiced my plans to visit the exhibit this morning, Joy and Izzy had made plans for some sister bonding, and Colin had gone off on church business, leaving me alone to make the most of my regret.

At ten-thirty sharp there was a knock at the door, and I hurried to answer it. Darcy and Jeff stood outside. I grabbed my jacket from the hook and the spare key Joy had left for me. I fumbled as I tried to lock the door and needed to consciously remind myself to settle down. What on earth was the matter with me? The walk from 3rd Street to the National Park didn't take long. Darcy remained his usual reserved self, and Jeff carried the conversation like he had the previous Saturday evening. I enjoyed Jeff's company and marveled at how Darcy could have two such outgoing, fun-loving friends and yet be so different in character and disposition. In short order, we were standing in a rather lengthy line outside the chain link fence that enclosed the outdoor exhibit.

I turned to Jeff. "I've been interested in some of the mental health work being done for refugees. I'm sure physical needs come first, but so many of the people being served must have been through trauma."

"No doubt. It's probably hard enough to get permission from government organizations to even set up a facility in many of these locations. I imagine metal health care probably adds a dimension to their services that could create a bigger headache."

"What do you mean?" I asked.

Jeff paused as he thought. "Some of the things that cause trauma are related to war or the way governments treat people. While often people have left their home country, it doesn't mean their place of refuge is welcoming them with open arms. Some cultures take a different view of women than we do. Or of mental health care. I imagine governments might worry that therapeutic care could be politicized."

"I hadn't thought of that. Have you done any travel to places like that?

"Me. Heaven's no. I like 5-star hotels and all-inclusive resorts. I'm no Darcy." Turning to his friend Jeff continued. "I'd think you'd have some input into this discussion, considering your work with your father's foundation. It's not like you to be so quiet, especially on topics of a serious nature." Jeff slapped his old friend on the shoulder.

Darcy gave a half-hearted smile to his friend. "It's my foundation. And I do have opinions. I just enjoyed hearing yours. I like to have all the facts before I pass judgment on your intelligence."

Jeff's laughter burst forth. "I'm sure you do, old friend. I'm sure you do."

I straightened my shoulders and faced Darcy. "So, you think your opinions are the only right opinions? Anyone who disagrees with you is ignorant or unintelligent?"

Darcy tilted his head to look down at me. "Of course, I think my opinions are correct. Isn't that the very definition of an opinion?"

I drew my hands tightly together in front of myself, holding them closed as if willing them not to strike out at this man. "But you pass judgment on anyone who disagrees? Have you never changed your mind on an issue?"

"Certainly. I gather more information, and then I am less ignorant than before and therefore I consider my new opinion to be the correct one. Hence, I always believe my opinion to be right. But I'm open to new information. Do you have some new information to share with me, Beth?"

"No, I don't because I don't even know your opinion on these issues. I somehow imagine they involve small government and people learning to solve their own problems rather than giving them handouts." With that, I turned my back to Darcy.

"You're a lot of work, Beth. Do you know that?" Darcy laughed.

I stomped my foot and let out a tiny scream. "That's ironic coming from you. I'm here hoping to learn something new. I don't assume my opinions are always right. I'm trying to become a more informed person. I'm not sure why that makes me somehow difficult." Sure my eyes were ablaze, I glared at him.

Jeff stepped forward and placed his hand on my back. He leaned in and spoke quietly in my ear. "Darcy's just trying to rile you up. Don't let him. He's just having a little fun."

"Whatever. I'm not sure Darcy even knows how to have fun."
Jeff chuckled.

The line moved quickly despite its length. Groups were let in around thirty at a time. The tour guides gave each person an identity that included their country of origin and the reason they were fleeing their home. We were given three minutes to "pack our bags." We were allowed to take only five items with us from a selection of cards labeled such things as cell phone, medication, money, and warm clothes.

I glanced over the board. Medicine. Yes, I needed that. And money. Of course, my identifying papers like a passport. That was already three things. What else would I take? Food. But how long would that last? I grabbed my final card. A coat. I already felt anxious as I followed my fellow travelers into the inflatable motorboat for the next stop on our tour.

I listened to our guide describe the dangers we'd face on our journey, the rights we did and did not have, and the struggles of life in a camp. No employment. No education for the kids. Limited sanitation, medical care, and counseling services. There was little talking from anyone other than the tour guides.

We exited the boat, walked through a pathway marked by security dividers and entered the camp. The tour guide continued the spiel about local markets and water collection. I was shocked at the weight of the water containers. How did the women and children carry these, day in and day out? Stepping into a mockup of a family home is where my breath caught. An entire family living in a tent. Rustic conditions. And not for a few weeks. Years. When our tour guide said that the average length of time a family spends in a refugee camp was seventeen years I nearly cried. I reached out and grabbed for Jeff's arm. But it wasn't Jeff standing beside me. It was Darcy. I realized my error when his hand closed over mine and stayed there. He seemed to understand the depth of my emotion and offered me his strength without the judgment I would have expected from him. I stood rooted in my spot as the tent emptied out. My emotions were raw. Silently, Darcy's hand on my lower back guided me through the remainder of the tour.

At the end of the tour, we found ourselves in a tent where we were able to see short videos with real refugees, make a donation, or write a note of encouragement to an aid worker. I selected a note card and a pen.

Dear MSF worker,

Thank you for the work you are doing. I am sure you see the most broken parts of our world, and perhaps you wonder if you are making a big enough difference considering how vast the problems that surround you appear. You are. You are making a difference for every life you save, for every mother whose child is healed, for every person who has hope just knowing there are people who care. Don't lose heart. Don't give up. Your work matters.

I hesitated before I added my final line. Doctors Without Borders wasn't a Christian organization. Still, my heart needed to be true as I poured out my thoughts.

I am praying for you.

Sincerely, Beth

Completely engrossed in what I was doing, I hadn't realized Darcy and Jeff had left the tent. I looked around for a bit, and assuming they had finished up already, I rushed to turn in my note. Just as I was turning to exit the exhibit, I heard my name called.

Darcy's voice called out to me. "Beth, I'd like to introduce you to someone. This is Dr. Simmons. We worked together on a project in Haiti a few years back. He's with MSF now and just happens to be here today."

I extended my hand. "It's nice to meet you. I'm very impressed with the work you're doing. I hope this exhibit does all you are hoping in order to bring more support to your organization."

"Well, with Darcy here today, I'm sure it was all worth it."

What had he meant? Did Darcy's foundation support MSF? Wouldn't he have mentioned that earlier? Maybe he just meant it was worth it to him to see his friend. I continued to ponder that until a hand on my shoulder brought me back to the moment.

"Are you ready to go?" Darcy looked at me quizzically. "You look like you have a lot on your mind."

"It's just the exhibit. It was very thought provoking. Yes, I'm ready." I nodded to Dr. Simmons. "It was nice to meet you."

"Likewise. And Darcy, I'll be in touch. Jeff, nice to meet you." Dr. Simmons strode away. The two gentlemen escorted me toward the exit.

28: Darcy

Jeff returned to his self-appointed task of keeping the flow of conversation going. "Is there anything specific that you'd like to do before we drop you off? It's a lovely day."

I was grateful for my friend's easygoing nature. I wished I wasn't so tongue tied around Beth. I'd never been great at small talk, but it was so much worse with Beth. It wasn't her appearance. I hadn't really considered her to be beautiful at first. My opinion on that had changed the more I got to know her. Her inner beauty truly began to alter my view of her outer self. Beth unsettled me. In a boardroom, I was sure. I did my research and came in with confidence. I had been studying Beth now for months, and I never felt like I really knew. She'd accused me of being Dr. Jekyll and Mr. Hyde, but I felt the same way about her. I wasn't sure which Beth I would be getting from moment to moment. I needed to work so much harder in her presence, and the harder I thought, the less I knew what to say. And what I did say came out with the snark I was known for with my closest friends but had effectively hidden from my business companions. Besides, did I even want to figure Beth out? That was the real question.

"Actually, I am kind of worried about something. Perhaps you might be able to help."

My ears perked up at her words and I spoke without thinking. "What's bothering you?"

"It's kind of embarrassing to admit this, but I'm not really very good with public transportation. I've taken the train from Princeton into New York enough times that I hardly get nervous at all, but even my trip to Jersey City with Jane last summer, I had to transfer to the PATH and find the right platform and get off at the right stop. I was a wreck. It's my job to get Izzy back home on Sunday. We drove here with Mr. Douglas, and I assured him we'd be fine, but honestly I was hoping I'd be able to pick up some understanding of SEPTA this week, but we've literally walked everywhere we've gone so far."

I had no idea. I'm glad I offered her my car last summer. She was anxious about getting home and still was willing to turn down my offer. Was she that stubborn or that brave? Probably both.

Jeff stepped up and offered Beth his arm. "I'm sure I can help you with that. Darcy here uses his driver so much, I'm not sure he remembers how us peasants travel. Come along now Darcy, perhaps you can learn a thing or two as well."

I laughed. God bless, Jeff. Of course, I remembered how it was done. I'd just taken Jeff with me on the PATH to New York City last week before I had driven us down to Philly. Jeff was always teasing me about how I didn't understand how peasants lived even though Jeff's family was wealthy, and I had spent more nights in third world countries sleeping in pretty basic conditions than Jeff had spent in a hotel with less than four stars. I kept that to myself. I'd enjoy spending some more time with Beth, and if we could allay some of her worries that was all the better to me.

Jeff steered Beth over to a bench and had pulled out his phone. First, he helped her set up the SEPTA app. Then he pulled up a transit map using the app on her phone. He pointed out where we were and where she would be going. "You'll get on at this stop here." Jeff pointed to the map. "Then you'll follow it up here, and transfer to the Trenton line. Once you get to Trenton you'll be on the NJ Transit line that will take you to Princeton Junction. I assume you already have that app on your phone, and you can buy your tickets right through the app. SEPTA hasn't caught up with that technology yet. When we get to the station, we'll buy single use passes today, because it's more cost effective. If we were riding around all week it'd make more sense to buy a weekly pass."

Beth nodded. "So, how will I know which train to take once I get to the station? It looks like there are a lot of ways to make a mistake."

"Don't worry; we'll take you through it in a minute. I just wanted to give you the big picture. We'll head to the station now and show you firsthand."

"It probably seems silly to be so anxious about this."

"Of course not," Jeff replied. "Mastering public transportation is a valuable skill, but it's not silly to be worried about something that's new and unfamiliar. I admire your courage to commit to doing this before you were confident you had the skills. It says a lot about you."

"Indeed it does," I said. Beth was a spitfire. I loved her audacity and her adventurous spirit. I felt like I'd lost mine when my Dad had passed away. I had taken on the responsibility of Lexi and took control of the family real estate holdings as well as leadership for the foundation and creating my own company. I used to spend summer breaks during high school and college visiting the sites the Foundation supported. Now I squeezed in a short trip to one or two sites a year. I lost my passion and sense of adventure. I'd become just another suit. Beth's desire to do what scared her was reminding me of a part of me that I missed in myself.

Smiling, I looked towards Beth. Her glare caused shivers to run up my spine. Was she angry with me? She must have taken it the wrong way. I was admiring her, and she must have thought I was mocking her. Could I ever say the right thing to her? She really was a lot of work. As frustrating as that was to me, I didn't tire. I wanted to know more. I wanted to discover every aspect of her. She was a mystery worth getting lost in, and I definitely enjoyed being lost in a good book.

I trailed behind Jeff and Beth as they headed to the train station. I couldn't complain about the view, but I'd rather Beth was holding my arm instead of Jeff's. With that thought, I released a sigh. What was I thinking? There was no way that a relationship with Beth could work. Beth seemed to despise everything about me and my life. There was just no logical explanation for the attraction I felt for her. She had nothing but disdain for me. She was an elementary teacher. Our worlds didn't exactly coincide much. And her mother, heck, her entire family was uncouth, except maybe Jane. Thoughts of a woman becoming her mother in twenty years had turned my head from quite a few women over the years. Missy and Anne being two perfect examples. My thoughts were fickle. It was out of character for me, and it made me feel unsettled.

The lesson on public transportation took us through several stations. Beth took notes on her phone. I found it rather adorable. She was like a kid studying for a test. I figured she wanted to make sure she didn't end up in Delaware with Izzy in tow. I'd remained silent for most of the trip. I'd have felt like a third wheel if I suspected that Jeff had any romantic interest in Beth, but knowing my friend's firm belief in marrying a woman with as much money as he had, I knew his interest in Beth was purely one of friendship. However, Beth was making me second guess my own convictions about marrying a woman from a family like my own.

Giving Beth additional practice with her subway skills, the three of us opted to stop for lunch at both Pat's and Geno's to compare the rival cheesesteak restaurants. Once again Beth was shocked when she saw the sign at Pat's that said "cash only," but I had assured her that treating her to some real authentic Philadelphia culture had to be my treat considering this was her first real stay in the city. Sitting in the grass at the adjacent park we divided the cheesesteaks and fries and dug in. Beth couldn't decide which one she enjoyed more, but her smile told me she wasn't disappointed.

Beth spoke, "Next time you're in Princeton, I'll treat you to Hoagie Haven. That's our specialty. And they do take credit cards."

I winked at her. "You know I went to Princeton, right? I love Hoagie Haven, but I haven't been there in a long time. Next time I'm in town. I'm holding you to that."

I noticed the pink rising to her cheeks. I liked that I could make her react like that, but what was I thinking? I was just flirting with her right after I had given myself a pep talk about keeping my distance. I was definitely having trouble keeping my resolve.

After lunch, we returned Beth to Joy's house and made our farewells. I was surprised it took Jeff a full minute before broaching the topic of Beth. "So. You like her, huh?"

"I like her just fine, but not enough to date her. It's a terrible match. And in case you hadn't noticed, she doesn't like me at all."

"I can't say how she feels about you, but I haven't seen you so quiet since you lost that huge deal right after your company started to turn a profit. Perhaps your interest in her is because you can't have something. Most girls are more than happy to date a guy like you." That sure was one way Beth differed from her mother. I have no doubt Beth's mom was pushing for wealthy in-laws.

I wondered if Jeff was right. Maybe it was the thrill of the chase and nothing more. That would certainly make parting from Beth easier. Yes. Beth wasn't special. I was simply reacting to her rejection by trying to win her over. Jeff had just given me the answer to my problem. But deep down I didn't believe my competitive nature was truly the cause of this dilemma.

**

Aunt Dee decided to invite the Johnsons and their company for dinner on Saturday evening. I wondered if Jeff had anything to do with that. Jeff had encouraged me to take a walk on Tuesday down by the riverfront only to find Beth doing the same thing. He didn't seem surprised at all to be running into her. I suspected Jeff had dragged me out of the house knowing exactly where she would be. On Wednesday, it was raining, and Jeff was certain that a trip to the Constitution Center was absolutely necessary. I had never known him to be much of a history buff, but with Anne on my arm, the three of us headed into the museum only to bump directly into Joy, Izzy, and Beth. Again, he didn't seem surprised. On Thursday, when he insisted we once again take a riverfront stroll, I refused to go. Jeff had never been so interested in getting out of the house as he was this week. So, when he returned mentioning that he'd seen Beth once again, I was surprised only by the tinge of jealousy I felt.

I considered I might be wrong about Jeff's lack of interest in women without a trust fund. Certainly, Beth could make any man forgo their reservations. I didn't like how it felt thinking about Jeff dating Beth, kissing Beth. I wondered if Joy was the one feeding Jeff their itinerary, and was she encouraging the relationship? Joy had been giving Beth strange looks whenever I was around, and several times she had brought up the conference in Jersey City. Was it all a matchmaking game to find a wealthy man for her friend? I was irked by my reaction to the situation. Having money had tainted my view on dating. So many women were more interested in my status than my person.

"Seriously, Darcy. Beth is an intriguing creature. I can't figure out for the life of me why you avoid her. You're less civil to her than you are with Anne. Another relationship of yours I can't figure out." Jeff pulled two mugs from the kitchen cabinet and began pouring coffee into them. I sat in at the kitchen island certain a long talk was coming.

I better start with the easier of the two. "You know how I feel about Anne. She's sweet and kind, but I just don't have a lick of chemistry with her. Conversations with someone shouldn't require so much work. I couldn't possibly spend my life married to a woman I couldn't talk the night away with."

Jeff sipped his coffee and eyed me. "I've never had any trouble talking with Anne."

"Then maybe you should marry her. She's got the trust fund and all."

Jeff's nervous laugh drew my attention. "You seem to have trouble conversing with Beth, but I don't think a lack of chemistry is the issue there." He smirked.

I broke eye contact. "Chemistry might very well be the issue there. She riles me up like no one ever has. One minute I'm tongue tied and the next we're arguing over tax laws. I actually love making her mad. It's insane. I can't marry a woman who makes me crazy."

The burst of laughter coming from Jeff startled my attention back to him. "That's exactly the kind of woman you should marry. The rest of the world calls it passion." Jeff shook his head while I sat there, my forehead resting on my hands as I gazed into my coffee mug. "Darcy, the tension you feel is you fighting this. Besides. I never mentioned marriage. You did. I know you've been talking that way since the day we met. I get that you see dating as merely a means to a goal. I'm not saying you should become some playboy, but maybe if you got out of your head a little and focused on enjoying a woman's company for no other reason than to enjoy her company, you would be able to figure out who the right woman really is. Real life isn't like real estate where you make a list of what you're looking for and evaluate the prospects before deciding."

Of course Jeff was right. Maybe. "Are you interested in Beth?" I couldn't meet his eye. We'd been friends for too long.

Again with the laughter. "Darcy, I have never once gone after a girl you've liked. There's a bro code."

"But all week." I didn't even finish my question. I just let my words stay there.

"I don't think I've had a more enjoyable vacation in a long time. Figuring out how to keep forcing you and Beth together to watch your reaction has been like dinner and a show. And I got orchestra seats."

"Jerk." I couldn't force a convincing scowl.

"Doubt you'll think that when I tell you that all we talked about today was you." And with that Jeff rose and stepped out of the kitchen.

"Great."

When the guests arrived Saturday evening, I was more than a little surprised to find that Beth wasn't with them. Aunt Dee wasted no time with her inquiries.

Joy spoke on behalf of her friend. "I'm so sorry Beth didn't make it tonight. She had a headache all day, but it wasn't until shortly before we were leaving to come that it got worse, and Beth decided to stay home. I figured it was too late to call at that point."

Aunt Dee expressed her dissatisfaction at Beth's poor timing at having a headache. She ushered everyone directly to the table, telling them that her plans were to eat first as to allow for more time to play games later if we so desired.

29: Beth

I hated lying and felt terribly guilty about the fib I'd told Joy. The thought of spending another night being judged by Aunt Dee and seeing Darcy Williams one more time this week was really where the pain came from. It wasn't exactly in my head. I needed some distance. I'd thought of nothing else since my walk with Jeff the other day.

"How long have you been friends with Darcy?" I had asked him.

"Since freshman year in college. Roommates. Stayed roommates until Darcy left senior year. Finally had the whole place to myself." Jeff's smile let me know that he was teasing.

"Why'd he leave?"

"His Dad died. His mom had already been gone a few years, breast cancer. Lexi was only sixteen and still in high school. He commuted his last semester and then put Lexi in boarding school in Lawrenceville."

"Seems kind of harsh. She just lost her only parent and then he ships her off?"

Jeff stopped in his tracks and faced me. "No, not at all. Darcy didn't even want to do it. And it wasn't exactly right away. Sure, it made it easier for him to travel once his business took off after graduation, but Lexi pushed him. She thought it would be easier to handle the loss if she was in a new environment. Darcy made sure she was close enough they could see each other often. They were always close, and the grief only strengthened their bond.

"I must say, I'm shocked. I hadn't thought of compassion as one of Darcy's qualities."

Jeff laughed. "Well, he certainly doesn't go around with his heart on his sleeve, that's for sure. But Darcy's a good man. He was raised with money, a whole lot more than my family had, and no one ever said my family was poor, but his parents were different. Every summer, he traveled to some of the most Godforsaken places on the planet checking on the Foundation's partner sites. And not just photo shoots. Darcy helped build things with his own hands. Heck, Darcy was just about the only guy I knew in college who went to church faithfully every Sunday morning. He dragged me there a number of times, but I liked to stay out a little too late on a Saturday night to be convinced too often. Despite the hard times, he never lost his faith. Always impressed me."

"I hear such different opinions of Darcy that I must say I don't know what to believe. Some people seem to think him nearly a devil and yet others seem to think he could do no wrong. How am I to decide? You're obviously biased. You seem to like him a lot."

"I am biased, but with good reason. Darcy is loyal to those he loves, and quite frankly he's loyal to those he hardly knows. Let me give you another example. I recently learned that he convinced a good friend to cut off a relationship that was bound to ruin the man. Most people will shy away from the confrontation and watch while a friend makes a grave error just to keep the peace. It takes a strong person to risk their friendship to speak truth into someone's life."

I pinched my lips closed for a moment. "What was so bad about the relationship?"

"He didn't mention specifically, something about the mother being a gold digger and the family being horrific. You know, when you marry someone, you marry the entire family. It's not just a saying; it's true. Girls marry their fathers and turn into their mothers. Darcy believes in the Christian covenant of marriage. There's no divorce when you find out your mother-in-law is intolerable."

I gravely nodded. "Indeed." We had only taken a few more steps before I made an excuse about needing to be back home, and we parted ways.

I had thought about little else since Thursday. The solitude of the house would finally give me time to digest it all. The entire time I had known Darcy he'd been an enigma. One minute he's inviting me to dinner then next minute he's cold and silent. Sometimes he seemed to almost be flirting with me, and the next he was insulting me for not knowing how to use the subway system. His friends called him loyal, but not everyone was his friend. I was furious about Jane and Chad. I knew that was who Jeff had been talking about even though he never mentioned it. I wanted to punch Darcy Williams in the face.

A knock at the door startled me from my inner-turmoil. When I opened the door, I was face-to-face with Darcy Williams. He looked distressed. Without asking permission, he pushed past me into the house.

"I heard you were sick. I came to check on you."

"That was kind, but there was no need for that. It's only a headache." *One that is increasing in size each moment I am in your presence.*

Darcy stammered, "I needed to know you were alright. I needed to see you. I needed to see you alone. Oh, I'm messing this all up." Taking a deep breath, he captured my hand in his and guided me to the kitchen table and gestured for me to have a seat. He, however, didn't sit. He paced back and forth across the kitchen. "I can't stop thinking about you. It's driving me crazy. All logic and reason would say that we would make a terrible couple. Our lives are so different. But despite all those obstacles, I'm finding it incredibly hard to continue ignoring my feelings for you. I've fallen in love with you despite this. I am sure I can learn to tolerate your family. I hate the thought of you leaving and me not seeing you. Marry me. Please Beth. Marry me."

I couldn't wrap my mind around what Darcy had just said. Did he just propose to me? Impossible. He hated me. He was barely civil toward me. He just said he didn't even want to think about me. And how dare he come here and propose like this. The nerve! "Mr. Williams, I am both flattered and repulsed by your proposal. I must say it was the very last thing I thought I would ever hear come from your mouth. But I wonder if you've surprised yourself just as much by the words that just fell from your lips. It's customary for a man to propose with a ring. It requires forethought. You don't seem to have thought this idea through or there would be a ring. I suspect that tomorrow when you have thought through your rash outburst from tonight you'll regret asking the question. Let me spare you that pain and decline your offer."

Darcy stopped his pacing and looked in my eyes. "It's only because you're worried I am being too impulsive that you're rejecting me? I could change your mind."

I cleared my throat and took in a deep breath. The pressure inside me was building up and the dam was about to burst. "No, you can't change my mind. It's not just that. While I suspect one day you'll regret this choice, my decision has more to do with your character than the pathetic delivery of your proposal. Marriage is hard enough without going into it actively trying to not love your wife. It would be illogical, and you are a logical man. You said you tried to forget me, and I assure you that if we were married, you won't forget me even for a second. But it's more than that. I've heard the stories of Jon Wade. They gave me pause about your character. Jane wanted me to give you the benefit of the doubt, but I wonder if she'd be so gracious if she knew what you did to her." I could hear the tremble in my voice, but my emotions were raw and too powerful to stop me from continuing.

"The final straw was when I found out that your meddling was the reason for her broken heart. How you could turn Chad away from her is beyond comprehension. I've dried her tears for months, and knowing that you are the cause of them, my outrage lands squarely on your shoulders. I know you said you can't tolerate my family, but if you can't see the goodness in Jane than the problem lies in you and not her. I wouldn't marry you if you were the last man on earth." Even though it wasn't my intent, I was practically shouting by the end of my tirade.

Darcy's fists were clenched. He stood erect, shifting his shoulders back and forcing his chest out. With his broad shoulders and over six-foot-tall frame, Darcy was imposing in every way. I wasn't fearful for my safety, because I knew him better than that, but the rage in his eyes still made me hold my breath. "Thank you for so clearly sharing your opinion of me. I am sorry I offended you. I'll let myself out." And with that, he spun on his heel, trudged through the kitchen, and out the door, slamming it behind him.

I dropped my head on the table and sobbed harder than I had ever cried in my entire life. I was sure I was grieving for every broken dream I had ever had, for Jane's broken heart, for my embarrassment of my mother and my sisters, and even for the pain I had caused Darcy despite being firm in my resolution. I wasn't sure what was to become of my life, but I was certain that tonight was not a sign of good things to come. That insulting proposal felt more like an omen that my life was falling apart, and I was sick with anxiety and sadness.

30: Beth

I finished as much packing as possible on Saturday evening before Joy's family returned. I wanted to already be in bed so no one would talk to me, but I wasn't foolish enough to believe I'd be sleeping tonight. I sank into the mattress at the first sound of the door opening, and rolled so my back was facing the bedroom door. If I could focus on slow steady breaths, I thought I'd be able to pull off my ploy. When Joy peeked in the room and then quietly shut the door, I let out a sigh. My troubles weren't over yet; I knew I'd see Darcy at church tomorrow. It was too small of a congregation to miss someone you were trying to avoid. All night I tossed and turned, alternating between anger and grief. My pillow, wet with tears, muted the soft sobs I couldn't contain.

I kept my head down throughout the service. I was acutely aware of Darcy's presence, and was grateful to find that I was seated several rows behind him, knowing that he was too self-controlled to be turning around to glance at me during the sermon. I possessed far less fortitude, but at least my stolen glances went unnoticed. At the conclusion of the service, I had hoped to rush out the doors, but I found myself trapped in the pew and unable to exit gracefully.

As I waited, I heard the most dreaded of voices beside me. "Excuse me, Beth?"

I turned slowly around to face Darcy. I did my best to hide my anxiety and hoped he didn't notice the dark circles under my eyes. Upon turning my eyes up to his, I saw in him the same haunted eyes reflected in my own mirror this morning. I couldn't bring myself to say a single word, so I continued to stare until he broke the contact.

He held out an envelope. "I've written you a letter. Please read it. And when you are done, I hope you'll destroy it."

I didn't want to accept it, but my hand acted of its own accord. I felt my grip tighten on the envelope and then the weight of his grip release. I nodded my consent, and then he was gone.

Joy turned to me. "Whatever is the matter? Are you still ill?"

I could barely move my head to look my friend in the face. "I'm not feeling well. I think I need some fresh air. Don't wait lunch on me. I'll be back and grab some leftovers before Izzy and I need to leave for the station." Without waiting for an answer, I pushed past her into the aisle and slipped out the door.

I rushed down to the waterfront. A small festival of sorts was being held near the arena; so, most of the crowd was further down from where I sat. I opened the envelope.

Dear Beth,

I am not in the habit of writing letters, but I find there is no better way to communicate to you my response to the accusations you made last night. I hope you will give me the courtesy of reading this letter with an open mind and will destroy it once you have read it. It has been my general opinion that one should not make an effort to defend one's own character. If one lives a life above reproach, the Bible tells us that others will not believe it when they hear ill spoken of you. I usually let people believe what they want, yet I find myself compelled to share the truth with you.

As it relates to Jane and Chad, I admit that what you heard is true. I did encourage Chad to break ties with your sister, but my motivation was pure. I watched him and Jane on several occasions, and it always appeared to me that Jane was far less interested in a relationship than Chad was. Having heard your mother talk of her hopes of an engagement between the two of them based entirely on Chad's money rather than character, I cautioned Chad that I thought your sister was acting the part of a dutiful daughter following her mother's wishes rather than as a woman in love. If I was wrong on that account, I am very sorry. I never meant to cause either of them harm. When Chad pulled back and Jane made no indication that she wished to see Chad further, Chad agreed with my assessment. I did so out of devotion for a friend and nothing more.

The issue with Jonathan Wade will be slightly harder to address, as I am not sure what rumors you have heard. However, as this is not a new rift between us, I can only imagine what he's told you based on previous rumors. Jon was the son of one of my father's employees. His father was a good man, and our families occasionally did things together. When Jon's parents passed away, my dad took him in. My father paid for his private education and saw that he had the right contacts and the same connections that my sister and I had. I was a senior in high school at the time, Jon in 8th grade, and Lexi was in 6th. Due to the legalities of adoption, my father intended to wait until after Jon became a legal adult before pursuing adoption. It made little difference, as my father was already covering all his expenses; it was more a symbolic connection. Jon turned eighteen his senior year, but there was no rush in my father's mind. He'd already written his recommendation to Princeton University on Jon's behalf and declared him a legal dependent. When my father died the spring of Jon's senior year, things changed for him. No longer would he become a legal heir. The law makes no provision for eighteen-year-olds who are family in name only. While I knew my father would want Jon to be included, my dad hadn't updated his will since shortly after my mother passed. As executor of the estate, I had to find a legal way to provide for Jon, which ultimately meant using my personal accounts.

In looking into what could be done for Jon, I discovered several things. One was that he had been cheating in order to get the grades necessary for admission to a top college. Another was that he was spending a lot of time partying and including Lexi in his escapades. I found out that Jon had concocted a plan to assure his inheritance from my father by marrying my sister. Because Lexi was a minor, he had discovered that if she was pregnant the State would allow an underage marriage. He began his plan of seducing my sister, plying her with alcohol and had convinced her to elope. Fortunately, there is no proof required of pregnancy, so the plan was to claim pregnancy and petition the court to allow them to marry. Lexi was so wracked with guilt over all the sneaking around that she finally came to me and confessed the entire thing. I was furious that he would take advantage of Lexi's vulnerable grief-stricken state. In addition to kicking Jon out of our home, I contacted the admissions office at Princeton to inform them of the cheating. That was enough to have his offer of admissions revoked. With no money for college and cheating on his record, Jon was left with few options.

I offered to pay for him to go to community college and earn his way with further promises of a four-year college if he made better choices. He took the initial sum of money I paid to the college, but refused to submit to any of my requirements to earn additional financial support. It sounds like after that he mostly moved from place to place mooching off old friends from high school, hanging around in college towns where there are lots of girls, parties, and cheap booze. He'd run up debts and then move on. He often finds wealthy girls to date so he can play on their sympathies. While I know my father intended for Jon to receive an inheritance, I am confident that had he truly known Jon's character, he would have agreed with the choices I have made.

Please keep this matter confidential, especially the part regarding my sister. She was both heartbroken and humiliated when she learned of Jon's true motivation. I have kept the truth of his actions as quiet as possible for her sake, and hers alone.

I hope this explanation serves its purpose. You mentioned that you couldn't quite understand my character because of such differing accounts of me. This is my story, and I hope you will see it for truth. Please let me add one additional note. While I know my appraisal of your family's behavior was hurtful, and though I feel it is a fair evaluation, I want to clarify that I exclude you and Jane from such an unkind assessment. I believe you both to be Godly women of great character, and I have nothing but respect for you both.

Yours truly,

Darcy Williams

I read the letter several times and then began pacing up and down the waterfront. My emotions flitted between outrage at the lines the letter held to remorse for my terse words to shame for my family's behavior to sorrow for having believed Jon's lies. It took me a while to come to the conclusion that of all the stories I had heard, Darcy's version seemed the most valid.

Jon seemed to test the waters to see if people favored Darcy before sharing his stories, and those stories became more extreme once Darcy had left the area. Jon was evasive about his job and how he afforded his lifestyle. I had always thought it odd that someone old enough to have graduated college would still spend so much time on a college campus. If he was looking for a wealthy woman, it was no surprise that he hadn't moved our friendship beyond that casual talk we had had these past months.

I found it harder to understand Darcy's explanation about Jane and Chad, but I did have to agree with him that from outward appearances, if you didn't know how shy and reserved Jane was, it might appear that she didn't feel much affection toward Chad. Besides, I had been there the night that our mother had made the inappropriate comments about marrying her daughters off to rich men and speaking specifically of Jane and Chad. Embarrassment and shame were the emotions that filled me the most as I folded up the letter and finally headed back to Joy's house. Looking at the time on my phone, I couldn't believe how long I had been gone. I noticed several texts from Joy, so I responded as I headed back. We'd have to take a later train than I had planned. I couldn't even feel bad about the delay because I was already so upset with myself over Darcy that there was nothing left to give to my other regrets.

**

Izzy and I headed into the subway station. I was trying to recall Jeff's instructions to me that day, but thoughts of Jeff turned to Darcy. Izzy's chatter was just the distraction I needed to bring my focus back to the present. Which train did we need? Where did we need to transfer? As we swiped our cards and passed through the turnstiles, Izzy's prattling held my thoughts in check. We crossed to the correct platform and awaited our train's arrival.

Once on the train from Trenton to Princeton Junction, I was more relaxed and my thoughts drifted back to Darcy Williams. I'd always appreciated his good looks, his broad shoulders, and his strong arms. I momentarily slipped into thoughts of visiting his Aunt Dee next Easter as a guest in her home. Aunt Dee would likely despise the idea. What would it be like to marry a man like Darcy: confident, strong, intelligent, but most importantly Godly? I had to hold back the tears at the realization that I would never know. I had let my temper and my pride get in the way. In the same way that so many people look down on the homeless, I was looking down on the wealthy. My prejudices were no less dishonoring to God because the object of my scorn were people that society doted on. I offered up a prayer of repentance. *Lord, I am so sorry for giving preference to everyone except the wealthy, for treating Darcy with disdain and speaking such hurtful words to him without first seeking the truth. Please forgive me, and help me make amends if possible. Give me the strength to do better.*

31: Beth

I was utterly exhausted by the time I stepped into my apartment. I had turned down an offer to eat dinner with my family, claiming I needed to rest before school started back up in the morning. Jane made dinner and the two of us had a quiet evening. I had so much scrambling my mind that I wasn't ready to share my troubles with anyone, not even sweet Jane. Especially not Jane. I was sure with Jane's keen observation skills that she knew I was working through something, but she was sensitive enough to know when to push and when to wait. I loved that trait about my sister.

The time finally arrived on Thursday evening. I approached Jane who'd been softly singing along to worship songs while cutting out laminated pictures of farm animals for an activity for the following day.

"Mind if we talk? Can I help you cut those out?"

Jane looked up at me. "I've been waiting for you to feel ready. What's going on?"

I rummaged through the end table drawer and pulled out a pair of scissors and grabbed a sheet of cows. I needed to tell Jane, but not everything. There was no way I could tell her about Darcy's role in Chad's sudden exit from Jane's life. I needed to tell her just enough to help me work through this without hurting Jane in any way. I couldn't bear to add an ounce of pain to her life.

"I guess I'll just start big. Darcy Williams proposed."

Jane's eyes widened and her mouth fell open a touch. She stared at me in silence long enough to make me question my own story. "To you? Are you serious? That doesn't seem possible. You said he hated you. WAIT! What did you say?"

My eyes began to fill with tears. "Yes, to me, and I said no. And while I don't think it was the wrong thing to say, he's gotten me so confused I'm not even sure any more."

Jane put her scissors down and drew me into her embrace. Tears flowed down my face, but I didn't sob. It was almost as if I wasn't crying and the tears were simply carrying away my sorrow on a river of emotion. I pulled back and looked up at Jane. "It was the worst proposal in history. He told me how much he didn't want to like me, but despite all his effort he had fallen in love with me. He said we'd make a terrible couple, but he didn't want to be apart from me. Who says things like that? He didn't even bother to bring a ring, like it was some half-baked idea he'd come up with in a moment of indecision about his feelings. It was worse than Colin's proposal and that was terrible. What's the matter with me? And as terrible as it was, what if I never get another proposal? What if Joy's right and love grows, and I just turned down the only man who will ever love me, even if he hates the fact that he loves me?" With that admission, I bawled.

Jane pushed my shoulders back to force me to look in her eyes. "Do you love him? It matters of course if he loves you, but only if you love him. Do you?"

I closed my eyes and rolled them up ever so slightly as if I could look inside my mind to see my own thoughts. "I don't know. I mean, I thought I hated him, and then I was confused, but after we spent all that time together in Philly, I started to like him maybe a little. But Jane, there's more."

I looked to Jane to see if she was ready to hear the rest. She nodded. "Go on. I'm listening."

"I was terrible to him afterward. Horrible. I accused him of being cruel to Jon. I told him I wouldn't marry him if he were the last person on earth. I told him his proposal was awful but his character was worse." I didn't need to look at Jane's expression to know she was appalled by my confession. Jane would never have done such a thing. "But then, he gave me a letter at church the next morning. He was cool and detached. He just asked me to read it and then destroy it. Oh, Jane. He told me everything about Jon. And while I've heard so many conflicting things, the more I thought them through, Darcy's explanation makes the most sense. I think Darcy was the good guy in the story and Jon's the villain. I hate to say it, but it's hard to come to any other conclusion."

Jane tilted her head as she looked at me. "What was his explanation? Couldn't it just be a difference of opinion or something?"

"Oh, Jane. I love the goodness in your heart, always wanting to give everyone the benefit of the doubt, but no. They can't both be honest and loyal and good. I think those traits must all be attributed to Darcy and Darcy alone in this story."

I spent the next few minutes filling Jane in on all the letter had said about Jon and explaining why I felt it was most likely the truest version of the events that had transpired.

"I have to agree with you, Beth. It does seem that Jon has played us all the fool. I want so badly for that not to be so, but I think you're right."

I laughed for the first time possibly that week. "Who are you and what have you done with my ever gracious, forgiving sister?"

Jane laughed a little as well.

I continued, "But now that I know the truth, and I know how hurtful my words were to Darcy, and I see his character to be good, no, not good, Godly. I sort of regret my horrible behavior, and I've possibly lost my chance to see if Darcy and I could have been happy together. I wish I were more like you Jane. Sweet and kind and always in control. I'm rash and opinionated, and I never think before I speak. I might have just ruined my life this time. I can't undo what I've just done." I could feel the tears welling up in my eyes while I gazed off, looking not so much out the window as into the future or the could-have-beens. Unable to shake off my remorse, I closed my eyes tightly while my stomach stormed. "Jane, I know I talk a great deal about being an independent woman and equality, but that doesn't mean I don't believe in love and marriage. I do want a husband, but one who would see me as an equal partner. I want to be swept off my feet and treasured. I want strong arms around me to make me feel safe. And kids. I want kids. I know it's a lot to dream, but I want all of that, and maybe Darcy Williams was the only man who could ever love me."

Jane rested her head on mine and kissed my hair. "I don't think that. All I ever wanted was the husband and kids. You know that. But there are strong men who aren't intimidated by strong women. There are smart men who are looking for an intellectual equal."

I nodded my assent, but not truly believing Jane's words. She might as well have just said there were other fish in the sea, but I'd been deep sea diving long enough to know that in the sea of Christian men, the fishing wasn't very good. "I'm going to have to apologize to Darcy, but I just don't know how that's going to be possible."

Jane clasped my hand. "Could you text him and tell him you wanted to talk? Just to let him know that the letter impacted you some. Make the first move towards reconciliation?"

I grunted. "I don't have his number."

"What?"

"Look, I never needed it. It's not like I considered him a friend. There was never a moment where that would happen. And, yes, I could go all stalker and contact him at work, but that would be so humiliating, like I was setting up a business meeting. And I'm not asking anyone else. I don't want anyone else to know about this."

"There must be another way."

I looked at Jane. "Why, do you want to ask Chad for it?"

Jane's face fell. "No."

I felt terrible for my insensitive words. "I'm sorry. That was thoughtless. I didn't mean to upset you."

"It's fine. Let's just finish this work and call it a night."

Jane packed her things away and headed to our room. I followed in silence.

I'm such a jerk. I can't believe I went there. So much for not hurting Jane. I shouldn't have ever brought this up. I felt nauseated by my own selfishness. The tears rolled down my face into my pillow.

**

At the Friday family dinner, I was subjected to a summary of all the gossip my sisters had heard for the past two weeks. I could tell that my father was more annoyed than I was, possibly because he was hearing most of it for the second or third time.

"Did you hear about Jon?" Lydia said. "He broke things off with that girl. I never liked her anyway. He's better off without her."

At the mention of Jon's name, I shot Jane a look. I wondered what the story with that was, but I was certainly not going to ask. Maybe for the first time ever, I was grateful to be listening to Lydia prattle on. "They say that she had a lot of money. I heard that her daddy didn't like Jon. He like fired him right after he hired him, but I don't believe it. Jon was too good for her. He needs a woman like me."

I might not be at liberty to reveal Jon's true character to Lydia, but I could at least try and reason with her. "Jon is at least twenty-five years old. He's old enough to be out of college. You're still in high school, and just turned eighteen."

Lydia scoffed. "I'm a grown adult, and I'll be in college in the fall. We're like six years apart, and since girls mature faster than boys, we're practically peers. Besides, I've always been mature for my age. I've never wanted to settle for a high school boy. Too childish."

I shook my head. There was no point in continuing. While I couldn't very well say that Lydia was one of the least mature eighteen-year-olds I had ever met, I dropped the fruitless conversation. Unfortunately, I was feeling less relieved when the next topic arose.

Lydia announced with far more exuberance than was necessary that she was going to spend the summer at a shore house in Seaside Heights with her friend Amy and Amy's family. Lydia had seen every episode of Jersey Shore, and I knew her plans would certainly include parties, bikinis, and college boys.

I looked from Lydia to my father. "Dad, you can't seriously be letting her go. Shouldn't she be home getting a job?"

My father stopped eating and looked up at me. "We've decided to let her go. There'll be plenty of time to get a job when she's grown. The Fosters are sensible people. It's not like she'd be living in a house with a bunch of teenagers. It'll be fine. Maybe burn off some of that youthful energy."

Before I could respond, Cat burst out, "It's not fair. I want to go. I never get invited to do things like this. Lydia's like two years younger than me. I should be the one to go." With that, Cat threw her napkin down and stormed out of the room. Lydia's smug face indicated just how pleased she was with not only her summer plans but with tormenting our sister as well.

I wasn't one of Lydia's parents, so it wasn't my job to get involved. The entire thing had been decided before I had returned from Philly, so the best thing I could do now was pray. And pray I would.

The dinner conversation was effectively ended by Cat's removal. Mary closed her book and headed upstairs. I don't believe she'd spoken a single word the entire meal. Jane and I cleared the table and washed the dishes with no help from anyone else. For all that had happened inside my own heart, it was almost surreal that so little seemed to change in my home. I turned my worries over and over as we worked in silence. Lydia spending the summer down the shore, with or without a family to watch her, sounded like a disaster waiting to happen. At dinner, Mom seemed pleased by the prospect, and Dad was more resigned than approving. It would be worthless to continue to argue my point. It was no secret that my mother often frustrated me, but thinking about my father's response, I found myself unusually disappointed.

Darcy's letter had made me think more critically of my family. I'd elevated my father on a pedestal for years, and perhaps I had laid too much blame on my mother. My father had chosen the path of least resistance at every turn. I wanted him to lead his family, not simply co-exist with it. The idea of a man leading his family seemed counter to my views on equality, but in this one case I tended toward the conservative. A man should be the spiritual leader of his home. If I believed this, then I also needed to look more closely at myself. Could I relinquish some of my independence to a husband? That dreaded word submission. Did I resist relationships because I wanted control? What would it mean to submit to someone who loved you like Christ loved the church? Someone who put you above themselves? Not a dictator, but a loving partner. A husband like Darcy Williams?

My other problem was that I wanted a husband that met the requirements of my list of the perfect man, but what was I doing to become the kind of woman that would complement such a man?

**

In the final weeks of the school year, I was busier than usual with report cards and field day and the million other things necessary for a teacher wrapping up the semester.

I just closed our read aloud book. I loved *Caddie Woodlawn*. I still had a few chapters left and needed to make enough time before the year ended. "What can we learn from our main character? How has she changed so far in this book?"

"She learned that mending clocks and quilting are similar with their tiny bits."

"Good. Michael?"

"She learned that being a girl isn't just about wearing dresses and cooking"

"Good. Anyone else? Sarah, what do you think?"

"She learned that God made girls and boys different because he had all these different jobs he needed done and needed people with different gifts to do them all."

"Yes. Yes he did. He does."

Once again, God was using my students to refine me even more.

I hadn't stopped by my family's house in the recent weeks, save for Friday dinners. The past few Fridays, Jon Wade was at the house when I arrived. He was his usual self. He didn't seem heartbroken by his lost job or girlfriend. He was charming and witty just as I remembered him, but I made a greater effort to sidestep his approaches and shorten our conversations. I remained cool in our interactions, but I wasn't sure that Jon had noticed. I was highly aware of how vague his responses were to questions about his work and life. At one point, he made a comment about Darcy, and I'd had enough.

"I spent a great deal of time with Darcy over spring break. His aunt lives in Philadelphia near Joy. I also met his old friend Jeff, do you know him also?"

I noticed a bit of shock in Jon's expression, but he quickly regained his composure and faced me. "Jeff? Not really. That must have put a damper on your vacation."

"Surprisingly, no. It was rather pleasant getting to know them both, and hearing stories of Lexi. I must say my opinion of Darcy was vastly improved by the time I returned. I think I may have misjudged him."

Jon said nothing for a few moments and then turned his face from me. "Well, I'm glad your trip was pleasant."

I looked toward Jane who simply nodded.

**

Aunt Erica and Uncle Bert came down for Lydia's graduation. I was pleased to see them as always, but I was less thrilled with the news they brought. Uncle Bert's law firm had taken on a large case, and he wouldn't be able to take off much time. Our plans for Acadia National Park would have to be put on hold. Aunt Erica had come up with an alternative. With the kids staying in Princeton with Jane for their camp, I could come to NYC and stay with them. They'd make it a staycation of sorts. Uncle Bert would have some time off. Some of the trip would be just us ladies, and other days it would be all three of us. But even with Uncle Bert working at times, we'd be able to have dinner, take in a Broadway show, and enjoy time together.

While not the peaceful vacation that I had hoped to have hiking through God's beautiful creation, I still thought it would be a nice break from the pit I had dug myself into. I did, however, mention my reservations to Jane about bumping into Darcy, but she brushed them off. The chances of bumping into him in a city of eight million people was unlikely, especially since Darcy lived and worked in Jersey City where his tech company's headquarters were located. She assured me that I had nothing to be anxious about.

32: Beth

By the end of June, I had wrapped up all the required tasks to close up my classroom for the summer and was busy packing for my trip. Without work to occupy my thoughts, my anxiety about Darcy seemed to kick up a notch. By the time my aunt and my uncle arrived to drop their kids off to camp, I was more nervous than my young cousins who had never been away from home for such a long time. At least Aunt Erica and Uncle Bert had rented a car and driven down for the day as it kept me from dealing with luggage on the train while keeping my nerves in check.

The drive into New York City afforded us time to make plans in regards to some of the activities we might be able to experience. Aunt Erica turned toward the back seat and looked over at me where I sat on the driver's side. "I would love to visit The Agape Foundation building for their display."

I tried to hide my horror at the suggestion. "Oh, I don't know about that. Won't it be odd to go to the foundation's headquarters?"

"Of course not," my aunt shook her head, "The first floor is open to the public. There are displays highlighting their work at home and abroad. I believe it is much like the museum at the National Geographic building we visited a few years ago when we stayed in DC."

I had enjoyed that exhibit. "Perhaps a tour of the UN Building would be even nicer. Remember when we went before and saw that giant Norman Rockwell with the mosaics, and the exquisite ivory carving from China? The images of the nuclear bombs dropped on Japan will be forever seared in my mind. Oh, and the display on the land mines, amazing work they're doing."

Aunt Erica shook her head again. "I just chaperoned Miles' class trip there this year. I'd much rather visit something new. It's gotten excellent press."

I couldn't tell her that my true fear was bumping into Darcy Williams, but I could beat around the bush. "After everything that happened with Jane and Chad, I wonder if we might bump into Chad. The Agape Foundation and Academic Success both support some of the inner-city initiatives in the city."

"Nonsense. The chance of that is nearly zero."

I reasoned to myself that Darcy's real job was his cyber security business, and he was merely a figurehead at his father's foundation anyway. He would likely be traveling or working in Jersey City, not in Manhattan at the foundation. "You're right. I'd love to go. I was impressed with the work I learned about at the conference last year. Jane and I even toured some of the school sites they worked with in Jersey City. I'm just being silly. Even if Chad were there, that's no reason for us to miss out." I spoke with more confidence than I felt. Satisfied with my answer, my aunt faced forward.

"We should do that tomorrow morning while your uncle is at work and then meet him over at the 9/11 Memorial. The foundation is close to the memorial. We'll just need to reserve the 9/11 tickets online tonight."

With everything settled, I was left to mull my worries over in the privacy of my own mind.

33: Darcy

I stepped into the front lobby of The Agape Foundation building. I was headed to a board meeting, and the traffic this morning had put me behind schedule. Lexi had already been waiting for me in my office for the past fifteen minutes. We were supposed to discuss a grant proposal she was working on, and then I was taking her out to lunch after the meeting adjourned. I rushed through the glass door and began striding towards the elevator when a familiar sight caught my attention. I paused mid-step and hesitated before turning back. Could that be Beth standing just inside the gallery entrance? Was I so preoccupied with her that now I was imagining things? It's been weeks since that terrible evening, and I'd not seen nor heard from her, but that wasn't surprising. It's not like I was about to follow her to Princeton. *Pull yourself together!*

I purposefully turned back around. There was no question. That was Beth, and she had seen me as well. The look on her face spoke of fear. Did she still despise me? My letter might have had the opposite impact I had intended. Steeling my nerves, I forced myself forward. Beth stared at me, her hands wringing together. She was clearly nervous.

"Beth, what a surprise to see you here." I tried to sound casual and relaxed.

She looked down, unable to hold my gaze. "I am so sorry. I didn't expect you to be here. What are the chances? I thought you'd be in Jersey City. I mean this is your office as well, but..."

She was talking so quickly and quietly that I felt the need to assure her it was fine. I gently placed my hand on her shoulder. "It's fine that you're here. I hope you're enjoying the displays. The work we are doing in Jersey City and New York are further back. But perhaps you won't be as interested in those because you already saw some of that close up."

Beth tilted her head up a little, but still didn't look at my face. "No, I'm sure it will be just as interesting. Thank you."

"Are you here alone?"

She shook her head. "No, I'm staying with my aunt and uncle this week. It's not too far from here, and my aunt wanted to come. She's just over there." Beth pointed in the direction of a woman older than herself, but younger than her own parents.

I smiled. "I hope you'll enjoy your stay. I'm sorry to cut this short. I have a meeting to get to, but could you wait here for just a few minutes? I'd really like you to meet someone if that'd be alright."

As soon as Beth nodded her consent, I quickly turned. The Board meeting wouldn't start without me, and Lexi could talk to me about the grant proposal over lunch. I hurried to my office and found Lexi sitting at my desk writing something. "Darcy, you're late. The meeting is about to start."

"I know, but we've something to do first. Come with me." On our way back to the lobby, I explained the situation to my sister. I asked her if she might be willing to invite them all to dinner at our house tonight. I promised to pay her back, buy her a pony or something, but Lexi only laughed and swatted my arm playfully.

Back in the lobby, I spotted Beth quietly talking to the woman she had pointed out earlier. "Ah, Beth. I wanted to introduce you to my sister, Lexi. She's just graduated and is taking her place at the helm of our family's real estate business. We both just happened to be in the office today for that meeting I mentioned."

Beth's nervous facial expressions turned warm, and she took Lexi's hand in both of hers. With a huge smile, she told her how happy she was to meet her and how she had heard such wonderful things about her from Chad and Jeff and me. Lexi blushed under the compliment but returned a genuine smile. I knew that my sister was shy, but I also knew she would do what I asked because she was a truly wonderful sister.

Beth motioned to her aunt. "And may I introduce my aunt, Erica Vaughn, to you? This is Darcy and Lexi Williams."

After hands were shaken all around, Lexi looked at Beth and then to her Aunt. "Would you come to dinner tonight? It would be so nice to have some company. Darcy is terribly boring, and I've been home over a month now without a single woman to talk to. We're just over the river. A PATH ride away. Please say you'll come."

Just like Lexi to throw me under the bus. She must be laughing inside. She'd done exactly as I'd asked and managed to do so while getting a dig in. I loved that about her. Now the question was whether or not it worked.

Beth stammered, "Um, well, we have plans to go to dinner with my uncle. He's at work right now."

Without missing a beat, Lexi interrupted. "Oh, perfect. Bring him along. Then the men will be able to talk as well. It would do Darcy some good to have some fresh conversation. Is seven okay?"

Beth looked to her aunt who was beaming. "It's perfect. Thank you so very much. It would be an honor," Erica said.

"Wonderful. Darcy can text you the address."

Suddenly I realized just how clever my sister really was. I could kiss her about now. "I don't have your number. Would you mind?" I pulled out my phone, opened the screen to a new contact, and handed it over.

Beth's face was all flushed. I had to smile. I sent up a silent prayer that this wasn't a terrible idea. *Lord, this might be the worst idea I have ever had, but I'd sure appreciate a chance to close this gap between Beth and I.* Beth looked at me for the first time. She seemed to be studying me. Slowly and quietly, she reached for the phone and typed in her information. As she handed it over, I tried to school my expression. "Thank you. I'll send you a text in a few minutes. Unfortunately, Lexi and I are late for a meeting. We'll see you tonight."

34: Beth

My head was still swimming as Aunt Erica placed her hands on both of my shoulders and turned me to face her. "What on earth was that about?"

I was silent for a moment. "I have no idea."

"I suspect there is a lot more to this story than you're letting on, and I intend to hear it before seven tonight. Let's start off with, how well do you know Darcy Williams?"

I took a deep breath. "How about we tour the displays like we intended to do this morning, then we head to meet Uncle Bert at the 9/11 Memorial? I'll answer your questions over lunch."

I knew my aunt wouldn't push the issues in the lobby of The Agape Foundation. She was discreet enough. When my aunt smiled and took my arm leading me back into the display area, I released my breath. I had bought myself a little more time. I needed to think about what I was going to say, and what I wasn't going to say. Aunt Erica and Uncle Bert were no fools. I definitely couldn't mention the proposal, nor could I mention what I knew of Jon Wade or Jane and Chad. I needed to downplay the amount of time we had spent together. Not having exchanged cell phone numbers before now would definitely work in my favor. As if on key, my cell buzzed with a text. Aunt Erica didn't even try to hold back the laughter.

I pulled my phone from my pocket and immediately switched it to vibrate. Turning back, I saw the text with the map location for Darcy's house. I shot off a quick thank you and asked what we could bring. No response. Aunt Erica and I turned to begin our tour of the exhibit. I paused at each area, looked at the pictures, and feigned reading, but my thoughts were elsewhere. I had told Jane I needed to apologize, but couldn't text him because I didn't have his number. Now not only did I have his number, but I was going to be eating dinner at his house. Then my thoughts changed. Perhaps I could use this surreal twist of events for Jane's benefit. I just might be able to learn of Chad's interest in Lexi. Would Chad be there as well? I hoped he would, as he might be able to reduce the awkwardness of the evening, but that was unlikely considering Lexi's comment about my uncle providing conversation for Darcy.

**

The day passed more slowly than I could have imagined possible. My anxiety about the evening was growing. Over lunch I tried to frame the entire conversation so it would seem that my aunt and uncle were already privy to all the necessary information.

"Remember how we met Darcy when he came down to Princeton with Chad? We barely spoke." And, "Remember how we saw them again at the conference, and Jane was so sick? Chad was so attentive, but Darcy was around at times as well." And, "Remember how I bumped into him in Philly this past spring when I visited Joy? Oh, didn't I mention that?" I did my best to act as if these were all just casual encounters. I left out tacos in Jersey City, dinner at his Aunt Dee's, and of course the proposal. Throughout the conversation Aunt Erica and Uncle Bert continued to eye each other with knowing grins. I pretended I didn't notice anything and concluded the story with, "I'm just as surprised as anyone that Lexi would invite us over. Obviously, we aren't that close, I didn't even have his number until today."

Uncle Bert clapped his hands together. "Well, I for one am tickled by this. Darcy Williams is a very important man in this area, really in any area, and while we don't work in the same business, a little networking is always good. Businesses need contract lawyers, and Darcy works with lots of businesses. He's a decent fellow from all I've heard. Gives away a lot of money through that foundation, one of the largest philanthropic organizations in the world. Never heard a bad word spoken of him by anyone in business. And with real estate holdings, tenants, and such, there's always somebody up in arms about something. I think this ought to be a fine evening."

I wasn't shooting for fine. I had set my hopes on survival and would count the night a huge success if I could manage to end the evening without making things worse between Darcy and myself. I'd have to apologize, but I doubted there would be time or place to do that tonight, not under the watchful and seriously suspicious gaze of my aunt.

35: Beth

We arrived at Darcy's home to find the building attendant awaiting our arrival. He provided the passcode for the elevator to reach the top floor and then stepped from the elevator car. Upon exiting at the top floor, I took in my surroundings. It appeared as if the entire floor of the building was a singular unit. Could Darcy have purchased an entire floor and renovated it into one home, or was it possible that he had built this building and his home to spec? The elevator led us into a large entryway, and after we rang the bell, Lexi welcomed us inside their residence.

Their home was warm and cozy, nothing like the sleek modern lines of the home in Princeton that Chad's sister owned. There were tall windows that overlooked the marina, and you could see the Statue of Liberty from his great room. Of course, you could. I actually laughed at this revelation and drew the attention of my aunt and uncle. Surprisingly, the furniture was more provincial than I'd have expected. A dark leather sofa, a love seat, and a couple of chairs created a comfortable seating area that faced a stone fireplace with a wooden mantle. And this was a real fireplace for wood, which was stacked neatly inside a built-in storage space.

The hardwood floors were light in color, and along the wall were a series of dark cherry barrister bookshelves. I loved those bookcases and the way the glass doors slid open into the unit. I was sure I could get lost trying to read through a library of this size. Despite the vast number of books on display in this room, I suspected that the house held additional shelves. I imagined that each room held its own treasure trove of books, which I yearned to discover. Thinking of what I had so cruelly turned down pricked my heart and tears threatened to spill over. I needed to take my thoughts captive. I ran my fingertips across the upper edge of the shelf, and then faced our hosts. Darcy's eyes were on me, but he glanced away as soon as we made eye contact. I followed everyone into the kitchen.

The kitchen was more modern, but still had a country feel with the white farmhouse sink nestled into dark granite countertops. The stainless-steel appliances and the grey cabinets were gorgeous, but what really caught my attention was how Darcy circled the island and then resumed cooking dinner. He was stirring the sauce and adding the finishing touches to a salad and what appeared to be chicken parmesan with pasta.

"Lexi, would you handle the drinks while I get this all served up?"

Lexi hadn't actually needed to be asked, because when I looked over, she had already pulled out several glasses from the cabinet. "Before I get your drinks, can I take your things?"

I handed her my light jacket with my wallet and phone tucked in its pocket, while my aunt handed over her purse.

Darcy looked at me with a smirk. "If you get chilly, you can grab your jacket from this closet at any time."

While Lexi saw to the drinks, I scooted closer to Darcy and offered to help with dinner. Lexi answered for Darcy with instructions as to where to find the serving dishes. As Darcy added the food to the serving dishes, Lexi and I placed the food on the table. Surprisingly, we ate in the kitchen rather than at the spacious dining room table just beyond the doorway. Lexi had pulled me closer, essentially separating me from Darcy. I felt both relief and disappointment at this.

Throughout the night, Lexi spoke quietly with me. The conversation was easy, despite Lexi's admission that she was incredibly shy.

"What did you study in college? Darcy said you just finished?"

"Business. Five-year MBA program. I'm taking over Williams Holdings. Darcy's thrilled to have time to focus on his own business.

Okay, that's an exaggeration. He's a little worried about overwhelming me with the handover, but he has faith in me. He didn't want to have to sell off the business when Dad died. He always wanted me to have it, but I was too young at the time. So he did his best to juggle them both for a while."

"Wow. He must have been busy."

"No kidding. Darcy's the best." Lexi looked at Darcy and smiled. Darcy didn't even notice as he was chatting with Uncle Bert. "Darcy said you're a teacher. What do you teach?"

"I teach fourth grade. It's the perfect age. Old enough for good conversations, young enough that I can get away with doing some pretty silly things and still call it 'work.'"

Lexi smiled. "Like what?"

I thought for a moment. "I have an entire trunk of costumes in my tiny apartment. I dress up whenever possible for a lesson. Cooking shows in math. Colonial dresses for history. No costumes involved, but we act out the way different single cell organisms move and eat. It's a riot to see a group of students playing an amoeba eat a chair or another student." I felt my eyes crinkled when I smiled, calling the memory up in my mind.

When I looked up, all eyes were on me. I guess I had gotten louder in my excited state.

"Sorry. I love my job. Sometimes I get carried away."

Aunt Erica was aglow. Darcy nodded and turned his attention back to Uncle Bert and resumed their conversation. I was sure my cheeks were red with embarrassment.

"Lexi, dear, are you involved with The Agape Foundation much?" Aunt Erica's question moved the conversation on from my embarrassment.

"Not as much as I'd like, but yes. Darcy and I will eventually split the leadership. It's something we're both very passionate about. I've done a lot of traveling over school breaks to visit the sites and work on grant proposals. Our work focuses mostly on Christian charities that help children, but I'd like to see more work done with micro loans for women to help them begin businesses. Research shows the incredibly positive ripple effect that can have on a community."

"Does a lot of your work deal with fundraising?" Aunt Erica asked.

"Not me personally. I mean I occasionally need to go to an event, but Darcy knows how much I hate large gatherings. I'm shy and an introvert. Nothing is worse than a big loud party." Lexi laughed.

"Nonsense. You just met us, and you seem perfectly at ease." Aunt Erica patted Lexi's hand with motherly affection.

"Well, there are only five people here, and I already know Darcy. And I feel as if I almost know Beth from all the stories I've heard."

At that, I choked a little on my drink. Lexi was going to blow my cover. "I feel the same way about crowded events. I never know who to talk to and for how long. Dinner with a few people, even strangers is far easier than mingling. But give me a book and a quiet space and I'm in heaven."

"Exactly!" Lexi exclaimed, once again drawing Darcy's attention and a huge smile.

The dinner continued much the same. While Lexi and I talked, Darcy and Uncle Bert seemed to be engaged in a fascinating conversation. All I could discern from the tidbits I'd overheard, it had something to do with business law and finance. It didn't sound like work, but if I were honest, it didn't sound the least bit interesting. Aunt Erica seemed happy to flit between both conversations. I could read my aunt's contented expression and was confident that coming here had been a good decision. Lexi was exactly as I had imagined her. Visions of the story Darcy had shared with me about Jon's seduction of Lexi made me queasy. Who could treat such a lovely girl in such a fashion?

With dinner over, Lexi laid out dessert and set up coffee and tea on the kitchen island. She encouraged everyone to enjoy it in the seating area of the great room. As I was settling myself into the love seat next to Lexi, I heard Darcy's voice rise up. "Well, that settles it. Tomorrow we'll have to take my boat out. You can't let your vacation get spoiled. We can kill two birds with one stone. We'll head over to Ellis Island and drop the women off like they planned, and then you and I can take the boat out into the open water and do a little fishing. Chad is actually the one who convinced me to join the yacht club, and I don't take advantage of it nearly enough. It's wasteful, so you'd be doing me a favor."

The expression on my uncle's face was that of pure delight, like a child who had just opened the very Christmas gift he had begged for and had been assured Santa wouldn't be bringing. Once I recovered from the shock of everything, I had to ask. "Um, are you allowed to bring a private boat up to Ellis Island? Aren't there rules for those kinds of places?"

Darcy smiled. "Probably, but I'm sure we can get permission." *Did he just wink?* Realizing my mouth was hanging open, I quickly clamped it shut.

I had little to say while we ate dessert. I felt so dumbfounded by the entire surreal experience. My uncle was going fishing with Darcy Williams. They were taking his boat out. I was sitting in a room that looked out at the Statue of Liberty. Whose life was I living here? I tried to be polite, I tried to engage, but I couldn't. Lexi was quiet as well, but a few quick glances at her indicated that she was in awe of her brother. Unlike me, she seemed comfortable in her own silence. By the time Darcy handed my coat back to me, and we were headed out the door, I felt like the last bit of my energy had been drained away. I hoped my brain would allow me the necessary rest, because apparently, I'd be up early tomorrow heading to the Jersey City marina.

36: Darcy

Once the door closed on our guests, I gave my sister a quick kiss on her forehead and pulled out my phone. "I need to make a few phone calls, but then I'm cleaning up. Don't touch a thing. Get a book and relax. I appreciate everything you did tonight."

"Don't think for a minute that you're getting off the hook that easily. There will definitely be talk about this." Lexi was laughing loud enough I hoped our company couldn't hear.

"I promise you can grill me later, but I have a few things I need to set up tomorrow. You love me too much to risk me messing this up." I gave her my cutest pout and rushed down the hall towards my room.

"Not over. Not even close!" Lexi's voice trailed off as my bedroom door swung closed.

I hadn't taken the boat out in so long I had just about forgotten what I'd need in order to set things up for the promised outing. I arranged for the necessary fishing supplies and called in a favor to dock the boat at Ellis Island. After a few hours of fishing with Bert we would pick the women up and have lunch on the boat. I bet Erica would be up for extending the day a little longer if I offered to take her for a short nautical tour. I checked my schedule and made sure I could move all my work to the late afternoon. Once I had discovered Beth was going to be in town for the week, I'd instructed my secretary to postpone every possible meeting until the following week and cut back my work to the bare minimum.

With my calls made and a few emails sent, I returned to the kitchen. Thankfully, Lexi had listened to me and was now sleeping on the couch, her book open and lying against her chest. I carefully removed the book and covered my sister with a throw blanket. I worked as quietly as possible in the kitchen to put away the remaining dessert, load the dishwasher, and hand wash the pots and pans from dinner.

I let my mind think back through the events of the evening. All had gone well. Beth wasn't her usual self. She hadn't insulted me once. The thought of that made me laugh. I had clearly set the bar incredibly low. However, I also noted that she didn't seem angry with me. A few times her eyes almost seemed sad. She was more withdrawn during dessert, but I'd noticed her talking to Lexi throughout most of dinner. Lexi was so shy I was elated to see her so engaged with a stranger. I hoped she'd be able to keep this friendship with Beth. Of course, I really was hoping for more than that.

37: Beth

I wasn't sure if it was the rocking of the boat or my nerves that was causing the queasy feeling. The day was hot, but the shade from the boat with the breeze was perfectly sublime. The water was dark and brackish. Not quite ocean, but not quite river. The scent of fish, or possibly crab, lingered in the air, not enough to ruin the last of lunch, but not a smell you'd ever hope to find in a candle or lotion. Seagulls swooped down and my aunt tossed a few small pieces of crust toward them in the water.

I thought back to the way Darcy had gently held my hand as I stepped onto the boat, and then how his fingers lingered on my hand as he slowly released his grip. He'd taken the time to arrange for our outing and lunch. He spoke kindly to everyone onboard, including me. He had every reason in the world to treat me with contempt, yet he was a gentleman. I was riddled with guilt, but once again, the company prevented me from making my apology. The more time we spent together, the harder it would be to blurt out what I was feeling. Part of me was thrilled by the delay. I wasn't good with apologies, but I suspected the other part was what made my stomach so uneasy.

"Do you have plans for the Fourth?" Darcy was speaking to me.

Sitting up straight, I looked at him. "I'm not sure. I assume there'll be fireworks somewhere around here. I don't often go when I'm at home, but being in the city, it seems like I'd regret it if we missed them. And with my cousins away there won't be the need to put little ones to bed before dark."

"I'm having a small party at my house. I'd love for you all to join me." With that Darcy turned to my aunt and uncle to make sure they knew they were included. "The view from my roof is one of the reasons I bought the place. I'm not a big fan of the crowds, but Jersey City puts on one of the best celebrations around. If you want to listen to the music, you can join us at any time, but I recommend arriving well before the fireworks start."

Was it possible that my entire week in New York City was actually going to take place in Jersey? I was getting more and more familiar with this side of the Hudson River than I was comfortable with. I started to object, but Aunt Erica caught my eye and rushed to speak first. "Oh, we wouldn't want to interrupt the plans you already have. You've already been far too generous."

"Nonsense. I haven't enjoyed myself so much in quite some time. I'm only having a few friends over." Looking straight into my eyes, "Beth, you've met most of them. Chad and his family, a few friends from church and work. I assure you, your company would be just as welcome to Lexi as to myself." Then to my aunt and uncle he said, "And if this is Beth's first time seeing the fireworks, the view can't be beat. Come for that reason alone."

I knew my aunt. She was making the customary rejection before wholeheartedly accepting. "Well, if it isn't an imposition, we'd love to. Thank you!"

I closed my eyes for just a moment. *Lord, what are you doing? You must be trying to teach me something because this is ludicrous. What am I going to do now?*

**

In the two days between our jaunt on the river and the 4th of July, I spent the majority of my time with Aunt Erica. For almost an entire day we explored the beautiful paths and bridges of Central Park. Not exactly hiking Acadia National Park, but not a terrible compromise. We had stopped to listen to street musicians playing near Bethesda Fountain, when Aunt Erica's phone rang.

"Hi Miles. How was camp today...That's amazing. How far did your rocket fly?...Did you recover it?....I can't wait to see it."

While my aunt continued her daily check in with her kids, my mind wandered. Would I have that someday? I loved my students, but each year I had an entirely new group of kids to love on and care about. But then they were gone. I wanted something deeper. I wanted a partner like Aunt Erica had in Uncle Bert. I wanted to miss my kids as much as Aunt Erica did this past week all the while knowing they were having a wonderful time. I wanted Darcy. Of that, I was sure. Was it possible I could fix this?

"Listen to Jane and be a good girl, Sadie. And save me some of those cookies you're making today. I love you. Bye."

Aunt Erica sighed as she slipped her phone back into her purse. "I miss them."

I pulled her into a side hug. "You're a good mom."

We walked and talked. In all that time, Aunt Erica never once questioned my relationship with Darcy and barely even mentioned his name. I knew my aunt too well to think it was because it was not of interest to her. She was playing it cool, and for that I would be eternally grateful.

**

Independence Day festivities began early in both cities. There were enough street vendors selling food and souvenirs to double the population of the area. Add the tourists, and I was feeling claustrophobic before I even set foot outside my aunt and uncle's apartment. I felt like I was in a livestock car as we worked our way to the PATH station. Uncle Bert laughed at my unease on the crowded train, mocking my need to constantly be holding onto the poles. We exited into Exchange Place like cattle, and I was feeling the dread. I hated the crowds and chaos of events like this.

Aunt Erica sensed my anxiety and suggested that we head to Torico for ice cream. It would get us away from the waterfront. The further away we traveled the more the crowd thinned, but to me it still felt oppressive. I had also never been good with heat, one of the reasons I hated the beach. Excessive heat mixed with crowds and knowing I was going to spend more time with Darcy, I was feeling out of sorts. I felt dizzy and my breathing was shallow. My heart was racing, and I could feel the sweat dripping down my spine. I saw in my uncle's eyes that I looked as terrible as I felt. He made the decision to head over to Darcy's home earlier than planned. Darcy had assured us that we could come any time, but we had told him to expect us closer to dark. It was only seven, but I didn't have it in me to fight this decision. We still had quite a few blocks before we reached the marina and Darcy's building. I questioned if I was going to make it. Once inside, I began to shiver. This was not good.

The look on Lexi's face as she opened the door was more disheartening. She went from shocked happiness to brows furrowed in concern.

"Beth. Are you okay?"

Uncle Bert had offered me his arm, so he pushed me gently forward to our hostess. "Beth was feeling a little under the weather with the heat. She's prone to heat exhaustion. We hope you don't mind that we showed up a little early."

Lexi didn't miss a beat. "Of course not. Come on in. I'll take care of her. This is the perfect place to relax." Lexi took me by the arm and guided me through the great room toward the kitchen. Speaking over her shoulder, she said, "Make yourselves at home." I wasn't sure, but it looked like she was looking at Darcy, but she never stopped. She snagged a bottle of water off the kitchen island and headed straight down the hallway. We entered a room that I was sure must be hers.

Lexi led me to a chair by a desk, opened the bottled water and handed it to me. "Here, drink this. You'll cool down in a few minutes. And you're given me the perfect excuse to step away from the crowd we have in the other room. But don't worry, it's nothing like you just had to pass through to get here."

I offered a faint smile as I drank down the cool water. "I hate crowds, and parties. More than eight people is too many to talk."

"I couldn't agree more, but sadly there's more than eight people out there." Lexi lay back on her bed, but started at a knock at the door. She opened it just a crack, and peered out. Darcy's questioning look was answered with Lexi's exasperated sigh. "Darcy, give us a few minutes of girl time. There are so many people out there. I just wanted a break. We'll be out soon." He nodded and Lexi closed the door. "Darcy's used to me doing this. He's over protective, but it's just because he loves me. And honestly, I think he hates parties too, so he uses checking on me as an excuse to get away. We have each other's backs."

"Thank you for doing that. I don't want to be tonight's spectacle." I was already feeling better and downed the last of the water. "I'm ready to go out if you want."

Lexi's grinned mischievously. "Let's make them wait a little longer. I wasn't kidding. I really hate these things. I get stuck talking to Missy Woods." Lexi made a face. "Chad is nice. He's been like a big brother to me, but his sister. Ugh!"

Like a brother? I wonder if that's true.

**

Darcy hadn't exaggerated. The view of the fireworks was spectacular. Apparently, he owned the entire roof. Thankfully, the outdoor area caught a nice breeze. The rooftop deck was surrounded by strings of lights, which were turned off during the fireworks display, but provided the perfect amount of lighting for the party atmosphere. A bar was attended by staff the entire evening. Tables and chairs were set up in various seating arrangement throughout the area to allow for more intimate conversation. Lexi barely left my side the entire time. I had assured her that whatever her feelings for Missy Woods were, they didn't compare to the degree with which Missy despised me. Lexi was thrilled by this news and considered me her lucky charm to ward away Missy for the night. It worked. Chad came over and sat on the empty stool next to Lexi.

"Hey kiddo, how are you enjoying adulting?"

"I'd explain it to you, but you probably wouldn't understand. You kind of have to experience it to really get it. Maybe one day you'll mature enough to try it." Lexi smirked at him.

"Hey now, I cooked my own dinner once last month, and it didn't come from a box. Seriously though. You doing okay with the transition to CEO? We have been praying for you at Bible study. Darcy's super proud of you, but I know it's a lot to take on." Chad looked at her with kindness.

"Thanks. I appreciate the prayers. Darcy's been great, but the board and Darcy's assistant have been guiding me through every step of the process. The Foundation work will take me longer to get a hold of, but there's no rush."

Chad turned to me. "How have you been? How's Jane? It's been a while." His voice was hesitant.

"It has been. We've missed you in Princeton. It's not the same without you." I hope he understood my meaning behind the "we."

Chad and Lexi chatted for a bit longer. I observed Lexi's statement to seem true. They acted like siblings more than a couple. I wasn't necessarily surprised, but I was relieved, at least a little.

Once the fireworks ended, the majority of guests headed right out, but the Woods family and my family stayed back. Lexi assured them that the PATH would be ridiculously crowded and there was no use being packed in like brown sugar when we could wait a little while and enjoy a much more comfortable trip home. We agreed, but only waited twenty minutes before heading out. Darcy had moved from group to group throughout the evening. Work colleagues and church friends made up the majority of the guests, and Darcy attended to everyone. He checked in regularly with Lexi, each time asking me if I needed anything. When the fireworks began, he moved to stand just behind Lexi and me, but we didn't talk. I couldn't help myself from turning back to check on him from time to time, and each time he turned his head to catch my eye. It was embarrassing and so very middle school. I still hadn't found the time or courage to apologize, and now we were leaving. My one consolation in all of this was the friendship I was developing with Lexi. Unlike her brother, we had exchanged phone numbers and had already texted several times throughout the night to silently communicate about the other guests.

38: Darcy

I closed the door behind Beth and her family, and turned back towards Lexi. The smile on her face told me exactly what I wanted to know. "I like her Darcy. This was the most fun I've had at one of your boring events."

I wrapped my arm around her and kissed her forehead. "I'm glad. The real question is how she feels about me." I gave her a wry smile.

"Well, I spent most of the night cataloging all your faults, but unfortunately we didn't have enough time for me to finish the list."

"Shut up!" I gave her a playful shove. "Let's get back up and finish this night out."

Missy's voice could be heard even over the breeze. Subtle wasn't her strength. "Honestly, she looked sick. So pale. And obviously fragile. I don't think she moved from that one spot over there the entire night."

I was about to speak, but Lexi beat me to it. "I asked her to stay with me. We've become such good friends this week with her coming over to dinner and all. She knows how much I hate all these gossipy parties. It's nice to have someone you can trust."

Missy's face was almost as pale as Beth's when she had arrived tonight. "Um, well, I guess that was thoughtful of her."

I was impressed. Lexi never spoke up. She was shy and hated confrontation. She really must like Beth to stick up for her. "Well, I think considering Lexi's dislike for these events, we should wrap this up so Lexi can recuperate."

Chad immediately stood and shook my hand. "Thank you for tonight. And not just for the party. For the talk. I'm grateful."

I pulled him into a hug and patted him on the back. "I'm sorry for earlier. I'd never have said anything if I hadn't thought it was truly in your best interest. I hope you know how much you mean to me."

"I do, man. I do. Looks like both of us have some work to do. You seem to have a head start on me." I appreciated Chad's cautious wording as we spoke, his sister looking on. No need to light her ire.

"I have a bigger hole to dig myself out of."

Chad laughed. "Yes, you do." He slapped me on the back. "See you at Bible study. Sounds like both of us need it."

Missy looked on our interaction with a furrowed brow. I kissed her on her cheek like always but made sure to make it quick and step out of her reach quickly.

With the party guests all gone, I leaned my back against the closed door and sighed. *Lord, I know you said to be patient, and I know you said to show genuine love, but it's hard. Please give me the wisdom I need for this. And more patience. Seems I'm going to need a ton.*

39: Beth

The next morning, I got a text from Darcy.

Darcy: *Are you free this afternoon?*

My fingers sent a quick reply.

Me: *Yes. Why?*

Darcy: *Interested in going to the library?*

Me: *The library? For books?*

Darcy: *The NYC Public library. You'll see.*

My heart sped up as we settled our plans.

I knew Aunt Erica would be giving me a knowing look the moment I informed her of these new plans. I wasn't worried my aunt would be upset about the loss of my company. We had already planned on a lazy day after so much excitement the previous day, but I was sure her curiosity would be piqued regarding the level of interest the Williams family was showing our family. I was confident she would assume it had nothing to do with her or her husband's charm and everything to do with me.

I received a text from Darcy that he was running a few minutes behind, so rather than wait, I headed out to the front of the building. This would be my chance to clear the air with him. Up until now every time we had been together there was no opportunity to tell him how sorry I was for my behavior and the conclusions I had wrongly jumped to. I'd tell him today, but maybe not right away.

When Darcy's car arrived, he got out and helped me in. I started off with questions about work, and he asked about my day and made sure I was feeling better after such an exhausting evening. I appreciated his not commenting on how bad I appeared. The driver let us off on 5th Avenue outside the main branch of the NYC public library. Darcy led me in and picked up a brochure from the front desk.

"Is this like a museum?" I cocked my head a little to look at the pamphlet.

"Sort of. There's something I think you'll enjoy seeing. Well, a few things really." Darcy led the way up a grand marble staircase and escorted me to a reading room on the top floor. He stopped at a large glass case and pointed.

I could make out that the open volume was a very old Bible. It was an illuminated manuscript with lovely designs. I wasn't exactly sure what was special about this beautiful book, and surely Darcy wouldn't have brought me here just to see a Bible. I turned my eyes to read the description plate. "A Gutenberg Bible? As in an actual Bible from the Gutenberg press?"

I turned toward Darcy. His face was all lit up. "Incredible isn't it? I knew you'd appreciate it. There are a lot of other things to see here as well, or we could sneak a book off the shelf and read for a while."

I thought for a few moments before responding. "I think I'd like to see some of the other things. I suppose I can read any time I'd like."

"My thoughts exactly."

We walked in companionable silence, stopping occasionally to look at old photographs of the construction of this grand building that Carnegie had funded. Sheet music, first editions of rare books, letters. And the building itself was magnificent. They just don't build buildings like this anymore.

"I have one more thing I think you're really going to want to see, but it's down in the children's section on the bottom floor."

"Okay. To be honest, I almost always stop in the children's section of any library or bookstore. I suppose it's the teacher in me. I read an embarrassingly high number of children's books for someone my age."

"I think you'll agree with me that this will be even better than a children's book."

We entered the children's section. I enjoyed the warm atmosphere of the room and the presence of several tiny library patrons sitting with books in their hands, others running down the aisles, and a handful of mothers reading to children. As we turned into the center section, Darcy pointed to another glass case filled with old stuffed animals from the Winnie the Pooh stories. "These are the originals from A.A. Milne." His hushed voice was reverent in tone. We stopped in front of the case, both silent. Darcy had been right. This was better than the books. This was literary history.

How was it that this man could understand me so well? I had misjudged him so much. I wanted to tell him how sorry I was, but I couldn't get the words out. I was ashamed and my heart hurt knowing that I had ruined what might have been a truly great relationship before it had even gotten started. But why had he brought me here? I had been cruel, and he had responded with kindness, detached and cool at times, but kindness nonetheless. Was this his way of repairing the bridge that I had burnt, or was it more an act of heaping hot coals on your enemy's head? I hoped for the former. I needed to speak, but I just couldn't.

40: Darcy

We stood by the glass which encased the collective memories of generations of children. Beth was beautiful as she stared into the case mesmerized. I'd wagered that an elementary school teacher with a love of literature and history would enjoy both the Bible and the Milne stuffed animals, but her silence unnerved me a little. She seemed to be thinking about something farther off than the 1920 storybooks. I didn't want to interrupt her thoughts, so I just watched her as she gazed.

Finally, I spoke. "Would you like to get outside for a bit? We aren't too far from Bryant Park?"

She didn't respond immediately. It was difficult to pull her from her reverie. "I'd like that."

The afternoon carried on into the early evening. We had picked up lemonade, sat in shaded benches overlooking people laying out and playing on the center lawn. We watched kids on the carousel, but the conversation was stilted. She appeared to be searching for words, and I was anxious as to whether those words would be ones I'd want to hear. We sat in the tension, neither of us catching the other's gaze. Beth kept wringing her hands together. Her eyes never seemed to meet mine. Reaching for her cell phone, Beth pulled it out. She pressed the button, but the screen remained dark. She sighed. "My battery died. Do you know what time it is?"

I looked at my phone. "It's almost five-thirty. Do you need to get home?"

"Yes, I don't know if my aunt has been trying to get ahold of me or not. I think we are supposed to be going out to dinner after my uncle gets home."

I called for my car to come around for us. When we got in, I offered her my phone charger. "I think it ought to fit your phone." I assumed correctly and within a few minutes Beth's phone had turned back on and was followed by a series of dings notifying her of numerous text messages.

I laughed. "Popular. I'm glad you had time to spare for me."

Beth's face went white. The look of pain that shown in her eyes made my own heart ache. What could possibly be wrong? I didn't know if my touch would be welcome, but I had to offer her comfort. "Beth, what's the matter?"

As she turned her face to look at me, I could see the tears building up in her eyes, and then the dam broke. She began to sob. I pulled her into an embrace. "What happened?" Rather than speak, she just handed me the phone.

The texts were from Jane. I scrolled up to the first text in the series. It had come in at two-thirty.

Jane: *Have you talked to Lydia?*

Jane: *Please call.*

Jane: *Lydia's missing*

Jane: *She snuck out of the house last night and ran off, Took a bus to Atlantic City*

Jane: *Amy's parents didn't know she was even gone until the girls didn't come for lunch.*

Jane: *With Jon Wade*

I clutched the phone as if to crush it. No, this couldn't be true.

Jane: *Please call. Cat knew*

Jane: *They've been secretly dating since March*

Jane: *She said Lydia's pregnant.*

Jane: *Amy Foster said they're eloping.*

Jane: *What has she done? What about college? Please call.*

I handed the phone back to Beth. I wanted to comfort her, but what could I possibly say to help ease the pain of her sister's choice? Eighteen. Lydia was only eighteen.

"What can I do Beth? What can I do to help?"

She shook her head. Then she pulled back almost as if the shock had just hit her. For a brief moment her eyes locked on to mine, and then her shoulders dropped, her tears returned and her face tilted to the floor. "Nothing. I just need to get home to my aunt and uncle. I have to get home to Jane. I can't call her. Not just yet."

"I'll get you back to your aunt and uncle. It won't be long."

I pulled her back to me. Beth buried her head in my shoulder.

"Father God, we need you now. Please protect Lydia. Bring her safely home. Comfort Beth and Jane and their family. Help them to help Lydia. Lord, she's so young." *And Father, help me to help them. Give me the wisdom to know the best ways to help them right now.*

When we arrived at the building, I gave instructions to my driver to stay close by. I assured him I'd be back shortly. Quickly, I escorted Beth up to the apartment offering her my support to make it through the door. When she entered and her aunt saw her face, Beth's sobs returned. Erica caught her up in her arms. "Dear, what on earth is the matter?"

Beth continued to sob. A few minutes later she was able to pull herself out of the embrace and offer her aunt the much needed but excruciating explanation. "I have to get home."

There was little I could do here to be of use. "I'll leave my driver instructions to take you home. He'll take you straight to Princeton. I am afraid there isn't anything else I can do here, so I'll leave you and your aunt to tend to this family matter. If you need anything, please call."

Wordlessly, Beth nodded, but never looked up at me. I addressed her aunt next. "If you need anything, please, you can call me." Her aunt took my hand in hers and thanked me for my generosity and hospitality.

Leaving the women, I contacted my driver and gave him instructions to take Beth home. I told him that it might be a little while knowing that Beth needed to pack her things, but he should wait out front. Then I called an Uber for myself and headed home. I might not be able to make things right, but I could at least try to mitigate the impact of this disaster.

41: Beth

I don't remember much of the ride home. I'd called Jane shortly after I was in the car on my way. Hesitant to have such a personal conversation with the driver listening, I kept the call short and vague. I sent Darcy a text.

Me: *I can't thank you enough. I'm sorry I keep ruining things.*

Immediately he responded. *I'm praying for you and your family.*

No denial. I hadn't been fishing for reassurance, but that didn't mean I hadn't yearned for some. I cried this time for so much more than for Lydia who was too ignorant to understand the consequences of her own wretched choices. I cried for the baby who did nothing wrong to come into the world like this. I cried for Jane and having to deal with Mom at a time like this without my support. I cried for my own shattered dreams. This scandal would taint the entire family. More than just the gossip, because sometimes the Christian community can be more unforgiving than the world, and I feared Darcy would avoid anyone so intimately connected to Jon Wade. If rumors were true, I'd be Jon's sister-in-law. Darcy Williams was going to cut ties and run.

Lydia was not likely to have matured in such a short time. I clenched my fists and gritted my teeth when I thought of Jon Wade. *Lydia. Oh Lydia. My baby sister. Not such a baby anymore. I should have done better by you. I should have warned you about Jon. This is my fault.* My face was flushed; my energy depleted. I fell asleep and woke to a crick in my neck and the driver's voice alerting me that we had arrived. His face spoke of compassion and concern. I didn't know how much he knew, but he was wise enough to know that whatever tragedy had thrown off his plans for the day must be something grave.

"Thank you for bringing me home. I hope I didn't make you work too late tonight. You must have a long drive home."

"No, ma'am. I just hope everything works out for you. I'll be lifting you up in my prayers."

"Thank you." Once again, I began to tear up. The driver removed my luggage and carried it to the house for me. As I began fumbling for a tip, he waved me off.

"Absolutely not. This is my job, and I'm happy to do it." I nodded. The driver nodded back in return and stepped away.

**

Since moving out with Jane almost two years ago, coming home had felt like a chore, but never more than it had today. Crossing the threshold, I was hit with how sad it made me feel to be back in this house. Home should be a place of comfort, where you go to have your worries melt away, but that hadn't been the case for this place for some time. Never more so than today.

I heard the sound of footsteps clicking across the upstairs hallway, quickening as they hit the steps to descend into the foyer. Jane would certainly be the one to welcome me. It was Jane who has suffered the most during this ordeal. She had not only borne the burden of Lydia's indiscretion, but she'd been caring for our cousins, monitoring our sisters, and undoubtedly bending to the whims of our mother whose mental state could not possibly be anything short of despair.

"Beth!" Jane's voice cut through the air.

"I'm so sorry I wasn't here for you." I pulled her into a hug so fierce it would have been painful had our nerves both not become numb by the events of the day. Jane held on to me, but her tears didn't fall the way mine did. Always the stoic one, able to compartmentalize her emotions and stow them away when needed, Jane's face was somber but sure.

The next hour passed with the retelling of every detail that had been gathered to date. Jane explained to me what the Fosters had related regarding Lydia's stay down the shore. Jon had been staying at a house down the way and was a frequent visitor at their home. Like typical teens, Lydia and Amy slept the morning away and then spent much of the afternoon and evenings at the beach and on the boardwalk. The Fosters had no idea that anything was amiss, but Amy finally confessed to assisting in the plan. Cat had also known what was going on, though no one seemed to know all the details of the plot.

It seemed that Lydia had found out she was pregnant shortly after arriving in Seaside Heights and confided the news to Jon. Her initial panic had given way to the scheme. Unwilling to end the pregnancy, but too embarrassed to confess her condition to our parents, Lydia figured an elopement would solve her problem. There would be no shame in being married and with child. With a husband, she'd have help going to school and taking care of the baby. Jon had confessed to his friends that he wasn't interested in being a parent right now, but the idea of running off with a girl had seemed exciting. He hoped to have a little fun and then push for her to have an abortion. To Lydia, he'd agreed to her plan to run off and get married, which is what Lydia had told Amy. It wasn't until Mr. Foster threatened Jon's friends that the additional information came out. The search was then set for Atlantic City where the couple was supposed to be enjoying their honeymoon. Dad had headed there shortly after the news had reached him this morning. With New Jersey's three-day waiting period for a marriage license, it wasn't possible for them to be married right away. This didn't actually give anyone additional comfort.

I sent a text to Darcy, expecting that his turned back as he exited my aunt's apartment would be the last time I'd see him. But my humiliation as to the situation and my shame of still having not apologized couldn't keep me from expressing my gratitude for all he'd done.

Me: *I arrived home safely a little while ago. Jane has filled me in on the details. My dad is searching for them in Atlantic City. I am incredibly grateful for the use of your car. You can't know how much that helped.*

Darcy: *I'm glad. I'm sorry I couldn't do more.*

I was hopeful that there might be more, but I was sure wanting to do more and being willing to connect yourself with a family like the Becketts were two completely different things.

Neither Mary nor Cat had shown their face the entire evening.

I cleared away the remnants of the sandwiches Jane and I had eaten while Jane had detailed the situation. The crumbs fell off the plate into the trash reminding me of the way my life had begun to feel. Only crumbs remained. I rinsed the plates and placed them in the dishwasher. I gathered the cutlery and glasses that my sisters should have put in the dishwasher and loaded them myself. There wasn't enough room for much else, so I pulled the detergent from under the sink, filled the reservoir, and closed the door. Turning the dishwasher on, I felt as if I was clearing away something old and beginning to put the pieces of my life back in order. A good night's sleep would help wash away this sorrow, and I intended to wake up tomorrow ready to carry Jane's burden and fix what could be fixed of this mess.

42: Beth

I called Dad before I even climbed out of bed. Not being a morning person, mixed with the tossing and turning I had done last night, it was after nine when my eyes could fully register that day had arrived. Dad would surely be up and hopefully made his way to city hall to inquire what he needed to do in order to recover his daughter. Dad answered, but I could tell by his voice that things weren't going well.

My anxiety gave my voice the alertness that my freshly risen self wouldn't normally have. "Dad! What have you found out?"

"Nothing much so far. Because Lydia is eighteen, she's an adult. Even if she walked in the courthouse right this minute, I can't do anything more than talk to her. She isn't considered a missing person, because, again, she's an adult and she told people where she was going and what she was doing. Nothing illegal has happened, so the police won't look into anything for at least 72 hours, and that's assuming her cell phone and social media accounts continue to remain silent. I can try to hire a private detective, and I'm welcome to hang posters or look around town myself. I was assured that no hotel is going to give out information on a guest, so I'd be better off searching public areas like the beach or the casinos. Lydia's too young to gamble, so I'm not sure it's worth much to look there. I'm going to start combing the beach until I get something new to go on."

I had determined to have a better perspective this morning. "Dad, Lydia will show up. She's foolish, but she loves our family. I'm sure she'll be back in a few days. You know she can't live without her cell phone for long." I knew he'd hear the smile in my voice, but I worried that he could also hear how fake it had been. I worried that this time she'd dug her hole so deep she'd be afraid to come home, much like I had been too afraid to speak with Darcy.

My call with my father hadn't lasted long. Neither of us was in the mood to talk about anything outside of Lydia, and there hadn't been much to say on that topic either. I had a lot of thoughts as to how her future was going to play out. The most obvious revolved around marriage and motherhood. Finances were the biggest issues. Who knew what Jon actually did for money, but if Darcy's letter was any indication, there was a very good chance that Jon wasn't gainfully employed. He didn't need to marry Lydia to be required to financially support his child, but that didn't mean he would pay up when the time came, if she was even pregnant, which was still in question. *Dear Lord, don't let her be pregnant.*

My heart told me she was. Where would she live? What about college? What kind of job would she be able to get? She'd been planning on going to a Christian college. Would she lose her spot once the evidence of her sins couldn't be hidden any longer? I forced myself to push these thoughts away. There was no need to borrow trouble from tomorrow, today certainly had enough of its own.

I grabbed up my phone as I left Lydia's room, the room I had crashed in last night. Turning back, I looked at the posters and decorations that had made this room so uniquely Lydia. My heart sank. Maybe if I had been more of a friend, an older wiser friend, rather than some sort of self-appointed advisor to her, she'd have come to me before making such a foolish choice. Maybe being a teacher at the school had made me feel as if it was my job to instruct her rather than love her fully. I would do better when she came home. I'd help her no matter what state she came back in. I was so quick to find fault in others, accuse the church of being judgmental and I was the worst of all. My church had always been filled with gracious and loving people who loved people through tough times. I just found the few exceptions of people to point my finger at and cry foul. *Lord, I am so sorry.* My tears flowed once again.

43: Beth

A call from Uncle Bert late in the morning the following day came as a complete surprise. I wiped the tears from my eyes before I swiped to answer the call.

"Beth, I have Lydia. I'm bringing her home tonight."

"Praise Jesus. Does Dad know? Are you in Atlantic City? Where was she?"

"Slow down. Yes, your father knows. Please pass this on to the rest of the family. I don't want to say more now, but she's safe, and I've got her."

I was pacing my room. "Is she pregnant?" I just had to know.

"Yes, she is." Uncle Bert's tone was solemn.

Tears streamed down my cheeks. "The important thing is that she's safe. We can handle the rest together. As a family."

"That's exactly what I told her."

"Tell her I love her. Please."

I stood still trying to slow my heart rate. "I will. And Beth, be gentle with her when we get there."

And with that Uncle Bert disconnected.

When I hung up the phone, I related the most important pieces of news to Jane and our mother. Aunt Erica and Uncle Bert would be driving down today with Lydia. They'd stay the night and would take their kids home now that the summer camp had ended and our immediate crisis was over.

It was late when Lydia made her appearance. I had tried to prepare myself for my reaction to her entrance. It'd be difficult to mask my true feelings, if even I had been able to sort out exactly what they were. They were a mix of disappointment, frustration, anger, relief, compassion, and love. The negative ones often showed on my face, but in truth they were no greater than the positive ones: they were only a poor presentation for the love I felt for her. Lydia's eyes showed dark circles and redness. Not as if she were recently crying, but as if the weight of her troubles had been keeping her up, and while slightly eased, they were still too heavy for her to bear. She was tan, her ash-blond hair recently highlighted, but her frame was thinner than it had been when she had left only a few weeks ago.

Mother rushed to her first. Her embrace was energetic and tight, her crying absent of any true tears. I could see that she loved her daughter and was glad to have her home, but I wasn't sure the experience had changed her much at all. For some mothers, not changing when their prodigal daughter comes home would have been a beautiful reflection of the grace of God, the Father. For our mother, it was less steadfast love than hope that a pregnant Lydia would mean a married Lydia.

When my turn to greet Lydia finally came, I squeezed her hand and stepped close, waiting for her to lift her eyes to look directly at me. I held her gaze for a moment and whispered words I should have said to her every day. "I love you!" No admonitions. No tears. No promises that everything would be okay. I wasn't sure they would be, but I would do everything to make sure that we would be okay. She and I. Sisters.

The family settled into the living room. All five sisters, our parents, and our aunt and uncle had gathered around. Mary came without a book, which might have spoken of the seriousness of the situation more than anything else. Jane had put a movie on for our two young cousins to keep them occupied as the details of Lydia's escapades were laid out in more graphic detail than would be appropriate for young children to hear.

Lydia barely spoke, having passed the responsibility off to our uncle.

"I received some information from a colleague in the city, that led me to where Lydia was staying. Aunt Erica went over and talked to Lydia. Once we found out she was pregnant, we set up an appointment for her to visit a crisis pregnancy center and talk with a counselor."

"Who on earth did you know who knew to contact you about Lydia?" My voice was too loud, but I was shocked.

"I attribute this to God answering our prayers. God knew where she was, and He used his people to help us." Uncle Bert's tone was soft, calm.

I looked to Lydia, pale faced and curled in a ball at the end of the couch. "Yes. He did. Nothing is as important as having Lydia home." I placed my hand on her barefoot that lay closest to me. Lydia turned her glassy eyes to me for a moment.

Uncle Bert continued, "The pregnancy center gave her an ultrasound. The baby appears healthy. She's due in March. They connected us with a local crisis pregnancy center. She has an appointment next week. Nothing needs to be decided today. She has a lot of very grownup decisions to make, but she has options."

"And she isn't alone." I said my words with conviction. I saw Jane rub Lydia's shoulder from her place on the opposite side of Lydia.

"And what about marriage?" It was the first Mom had spoken during the conversation.

"Well, Jon came to the pregnancy center appointment." I saw the tension in Uncle Bert's face as he spoke through a semi-clenched jaw. "Seems that he's not really interested in marriage. And quite frankly, I don't know how I feel about Lydia married to a man of such low character."

"She can't stay unmarried!" Mom's outrage was surely heard by our cousins.

Lydia's expression remained almost blank. I'm sure emotional fatigue played a part, but it was more than that. Lydia was a different person. I couldn't say for sure yet if that person was wiser, but she was certainly less naïve. I couldn't read a single thing into her expressions.

"The man wants her to abort. He lied about marriage, so she'd join him on a weekend escapade. He has no job. The man is despicable. It's bad enough he'll be a dead-beat dad, he doesn't need to also mooch off of your daughter the rest of his life as well. Honestly, dear, I can't even believe that's what you're worried about." Dad stood up, but before he strode from the room he turned and spoke directly to Lydia. "I'll help you however I can, but know this, your mistakes don't need to define who you are."

And that was that. The conversation was over. Dad might have well have just dropped the mic.

I was glad for Lydia's sake. She needed to rest. I, on the other hand, had a million questions still running through my mind. Would she parent or opt for adoption? Would she still go to college? Would she live here or somewhere else? I was grateful for my aunt and my uncle who made sure throughout all of this, that Lydia knew she had choices, and she wasn't alone. Things would be hard. No one was going to sugarcoat that for her, but she wouldn't be abandoned by her family, even if Jon had done so.

**

I slipped into my father's library knowing he'd still be up. Most men of his generation had man caves with large screen TVs and video game consoles, perhaps a pool table or foosball. Not my father. He had a library with floor to ceiling bookshelves. The collection of books was possibly the most valuable property our family still owned. Each generation has added to the family collection even as tracts of land were being sold off piecemeal. My father saved the best of the best each time the family downsized to a smaller residence. Some of his books dated back to the 1700s, most were collector's editions expertly bound, all of them he had read at least once. It was in this room where my father went to hide away from the frivolous conversations of the women in his life. It was here where deep thought and fervent prayer came together. It was here where I knew I'd find him on a night like this, a night when his youngest child had walked across his threshold unwed and with child.

He spoke first. "I'll never be able to repay your uncle for all he's done. He must have spent a fortune tracking her down and seeing to her care."

I took his hand as I lowered myself in the chair next to his, the chair he reserved especially for me. "He wouldn't want that. He's a good man."

"He's a better man than I am." His voice was filled with remorse and self-condemnation.

"No, Dad. Don't say that. You're a great father. This isn't your fault."

"No, Beth. Don't try and make me feel better. I need to own my responsibility in this. I have made an idol out of a peaceful home. I failed to raise my daughters in a Godly manner. I should have been teaching you all how to be Godly women in this world. I didn't train you up. I simply lived my life and hoped you would follow. That was never the path the Bible laid out for fathers. I was lazy, and I'm reaping the consequences of my sin. Worse, my child is reaping the consequences of my choices. I'm not saying she's blameless, she's not, but the sins of the father most certainly do fall upon their children."

For a moment we both sat there in silence. There was some truth in what he said.

"Things will be different here. I know you girls are all grown now, but I'm going to do better. I'm going to lead better and perhaps Lydia's child will give me another chance to lead a child in the way she should go."

I had nothing to add to my father's words. He was a good man, and I knew he was growing greater still. I stood and placed a kiss on the top of his bowed head. He released my hand, and I slipped away quietly. I recalled the story of Joseph and how after he revealed himself to his brothers he told them that what they had planned for evil, God had planned for good. Even this difficult time, brought on by the sins of several people, God could turn around for the good of all those involved and that would be my prayer.

44: Darcy

I hated to leave Beth like that, but there were things I could do that might help the situation. I headed immediately to my office at Williams Security Services. We were a relatively small company, but I had resources and contacts that most people didn't. I was willing to pull every string available to me. My first thought was to question whether Lydia had actually gone to Atlantic City.

On the way, I called my second in command at WSS. "Jared, I'm going to need your help. It's going to be a long night."

"What do you need?" he asked.

"I need you to contact your army buddy who heads up security at New Jersey Transit. Get him to send you the security footage from the train station at Bay Head and the Bus Terminal in Toms River. Tell him I'll owe him one. I'll get you pictures of the two people I'm looking for. Bring in any help you need. As many as you need. I'll compensate everyone generously."

"Sure. I haven't left yet. I'll start setting up in the conference room."

"Perfect. I'll be there in fifteen. I'm going to pull in help from our social media department and few of the forensics team in the video surveillance department. I'll send them to you."

The social media specialist would be focused on seeing if anything came up on either Lydia or Jon, but I'd provide a few names of people connected to Jon they could check into as well. I knew of a few places Jon still had connections, and maybe one of them would mention something. I also knew that his primary MO was mooching. He'd want to stay with friends who'd foot the bill, not rent a hotel room. Most of those connections were old high school buddies in New York City, not down in AC. If the plan was truly to get married, it didn't make any sense to go to Atlantic City. It wasn't like Vegas. New Jersey had a three-day waiting period for a marriage license, but New York didn't. I hoped that wasn't the plan, because the idea of Lydia married to Jonathan Wade, made my blood burn.

With that portion of the plan in action, I focused on establishing a security net for Lydia. If in fact she was pregnant, I had no reason to believe that a guy like Jon Wade would want to settle down and become a dad. That meant either she wasn't pregnant or he'd be pushing her to have an abortion. I'd start with contacting the crisis pregnancy centers that The Williams Foundation supported. I'd find out what resources they might have for her in relation to counseling, college, and financial help. I hoped Beth's family would be supportive, but there was no guarantee that would be the case. After forty-five minutes on the phone with the director of the center closest to Lydia's home, I was armed with a lot of knowledge and several contacts in both Atlantic City and Jersey City.

I'd already canceled all my other work for the evening. I stopped by the conference room often and made sure the coffee was flowing and food was on hand.

"Thank you all for being here tonight. I consider this a personal favor to me, and I plan to generously compensate you for help. I'm going to step into the other conference room for a few minutes to pray. Anyone who wants to join me is welcome."

I wasn't surprised that nearly everyone joined in. We didn't spend too long bringing our requests to God, but the time settled me and gave me hope.

The first break came with surveillance cameras finding Lydia and Jon on the New Jersey Transit line heading north. Starting there, they followed the surveillance cameras station by station until they saw the couple depart at Penn Station in New York. Lydia seemed elated, laughing and smiling as she stepped onto the platform; Jon more sedate. Tracking them through New York was practically impossible, but it brought the search to a completely different city.

I picked up the phone to contact Beth's uncle. I had no doubt that he was a good and godly man whose discretion I could count on. He didn't seem surprised to hear from me, but that changed once I explained what was going on. I explained what we'd discovered so far, and decided it was best to not include Beth's father in the update just yet. The search area was too large to get his hopes up, but we knew we couldn't keep him in the dark more than a few hours. There were too many courthouses and abortion clinics in the city to even begin at those places, so I explained my plan to hire a private investigator to begin the search with the few connections I knew Jon had in the city, beginning with the closest to Penn Station.

I wasn't completely honest with Bert Vaughn. I had no intention of hiring a single investigator. I called in another favor with a large and well-respected private investigation firm I'd worked with in the past. With several possible locations, I hired people to watch each location as well as a couple extra hands to track down other leads. Time was of the essence and money wasn't. Lydia was older, but not wiser than some of the girls who'd left home with romantic dreams only to find themselves in dire straits. If Jon dropped her cold, would she be too embarrassed to come home? I'd been involved enough with the work of The Williams Foundation that I wasn't ignorant of the danger she could be in. Human trafficking wasn't likely, but it was far too real to ignore.

I'd sent my team home early in the morning, but I stayed in the office. It wasn't any closer to the City than I'd be in my apartment, but I had more computer resources here than at home in the event that something came up. That's where I was when my phone rang in the morning.

"We've got them at the Norris house. We only got eyes on the girl, but there are several people in the house. We think the guy is one of them."

I called Bert first, and we set up a plan to intervene. The investigator would continue to watch this location, but I called off all the other teams. Assuming Lydia stayed put, I'd head over with her Aunt Erica, but stay out of sight. We thought Lydia was more likely to speak with her aunt alone than with anyone else present. They couldn't force her to do anything so persuasion was our best bet.

Bert agreed to contact Mr. Beckett, and I called the pregnancy center to set up an appointment. They weren't open at this hour, but I left a message and headed home to shower. I'd be busy with this for the next few hours at least, but I knew I couldn't show my face right away. Eventually, I'd need to settle things with Jonathan. Hopefully that would include some legal documents to protect Lydia and her child. The lawyer would need to draw up the papers, and at this point I didn't know what papers I'd need her to draft. I hoped this was the right thing to do.

45: Beth

The next night, I heard Lydia's quiet sobs through the wall that separated our two rooms. Jane had needed a breather, so she had gone back to the apartment, and I had stayed to lend a hand.

I crept from the room and tapped on her door. "Lydia, can I come in?" The sobs halted and were followed by the sound of her breath sucking in. Silence.

"Lydia, please."

The whispered agreement came, so I opened the door and crossed to her bed. I sat on the edge and rubbed her back. She was facing the wall, so I couldn't see her eyes, but I felt the pain that seemed to radiate off of her.

"I'm such an idiot. I never should have believed him. He said he loved me. He promised me." The tears returned and her body shook as she let them fall.

"Scoot over." Once Lydia moved, I lay down and snuggled close to her, wrapping my one arm around her and propping my head up with my other arm. "You're not an idiot. You made a mistake. This isn't going to be the end for you. I'm not saying it won't be hard, but it's not the end."

"Darcy said the same thing after the ultrasound. He looked at the picture and said 'This isn't the end, Lydia, this is the beginning. The beginning of something hard, but something beautiful.' I think it was the nicest thing anyone has ever said to me."

Darcy? Darcy Williams? What was he doing there? That didn't make sense. "Darcy who?"

"Darcy Williams." Then she sucked in another breath. "Oh, Beth. Please don't say anything. I promised him I wouldn't mention anything. Ugh! I am an idiot."

I swatted her arm gently. "You're not an idiot. But why was Darcy there?"

Lydia rolled over onto her back and looked up at the ceiling. She took a deep breath and began. "Beth, you can't tell anyone. Please." She looked at me, and I nodded my agreement. "Darcy found us and sent Aunt Erica to the house we were staying in. I don't know exactly how, but I heard something about his company and a private investigator. Jon didn't want to go to the appointment at the pregnancy center, but he finally agreed. When we got there, Darcy was there. Jon was furious, but Darcy took him outside and when they came back in, Jon was quieter, but still angry.

"He came in the session with Aunt Erica and I. Darcy and Uncle Bert stayed out in the waiting room with another woman. After Jon started talking and spewing out his stupid lies about never wanting to get married and wanted me to have an abortion, well things got a little ugly. But the counselor was great. She explained some of the options we had, the legalities of different decisions. When Jon said he didn't want a baby and he'd give up his rights for adoption and parenting, the counselor told him that if I chose to parent he could be required to pay child support whether he wanted to or not. He said that wasn't fair that I got to decide and he had no say. I might not have been so nice at that point. The counselor told him that he might find it better to step into the next office and talk over some of his thoughts with a male counselor that was there for him. He left.

"When I finished up with my counselor, Jon was still next door, but Darcy and Uncle Bert and that other lady weren't in the waiting room. So, we waited, and they all came out together. I'm not sure what exactly happened, but it seems the other woman was a lawyer, and Darcy and his lawyer were meeting with Jon to draw up some legal papers.

"Nothing can be signed until I have the baby and decide what to do, but Darcy made sure that I got the best legal counsel and child support arrangement possible. Jon's going to sign off his rights either way. He wants out, but a child support trust is being set up for me if I want to parent to ensure I'll have the funds to raise this baby."

At that Lydia stopped talking for a moment. Then she turned her head to me. "Darcy isn't as bad as you've made him out to be. He's a good guy. I don't know what the real deal is with him and Jon. Something's not right with Jon's story. I know Jon hates him, and I'm sure he's going to hate him more after all this, but I don't care. I don't know what I would have done without Darcy there."

"Darcy really is a good guy. I'm sorry I ever doubted it." I said the words as flat as possible, but the emotions I was feeling at Lydia's story were anything but neutral. Darcy was one of the most amazing men I'd ever met, and I had been more foolish than Lydia.

"I think I'm going to keep my baby. I know it'll be hard, and despite all my talk, I know I'm not really grown up. I'm just a kid. But I feel like I already love this baby. I want to do right by this little person who didn't do anything wrong to get here. Do you think I can do it, Beth?"

I pulled her closer to me, into almost a hug. "I know you can do it. And you won't have to do it alone. We'll all be there for you. That's what family is for."

"You know what else? Darcy set up a meeting with the pregnancy center here. They work with this Christian college. There's a special program that helps pregnant teens get their college degrees. They have childcare and scholarship money to help them afford the classes. I might still be able to go to college."

"That's amazing."

I was going to be the best sister and aunt I could possibly be. *Lord, help me become more like you. More patient, more loving, more gentle.*

46: Beth

By the middle of August, life in our family had settled down significantly. Lydia had met numerous times with her counselor and had made the decision to parent. The Christian college that worked with the pregnancy center had granted Lydia admission. I had to admit, despite being a Christian, I often was harder on Christians than non-Christians. I was truly surprised that there was a Christian college doing this. My view of Christians was changing, as was my own heart.

I'd taken her in to meet with the admissions counselor to help set up her schedule for the fall. Lydia would take the spring semester off, but would be able to return the following fall with the full support of the college and her family. Everything seemed to be falling into place, except for my issue with Darcy. I couldn't text him, not with the way things had been when I had last seen him. Maybe if I had told him how I felt after I read his letter and apologized while I was there this summer.

No, having not done that and then having the issue with Lydia interrupt our final moments together, I couldn't even hope that he'd want anything to do with me. Yet, knowing what Lydia had told me, I knew I needed to offer him an even greater apology. I needed to make amends. Not knowing how to do that, I hadn't done anything. And each day of silence between us made the chasm grow larger.

******

The first leaves had already begun to turn the yellows and reds of autumn despite the long summer days. It signaled that the time had come for teachers to report back to school. My classroom needed to be set up with binders, books, and nameplates marking student desks. The other teachers and I had spent our first days back mostly in our own rooms, but this afternoon there would be a staff meeting and guest speakers to prepare us for the coming year.

I shouldn't have been surprised when Chad Woods stepped into the multi-purpose room with Heather and Nick Hurst, by his side. I spotted Chad first and reached out to clasp Jane's hand under the table. She'd need the comfort, once she saw. Her face turned to mine and then followed my gaze to Chad. He was talking to Dr. Cooper, but it wasn't long before he turned away and scanned the room with obvious intentionality. When his face caught Jane's, he smiled. Not the genuine smile of joy that crinkled one's eyes, but the kind of smile that asks the question, "Am I allowed to smile at you?" I looked at Jane to see if her face would answer his question and it seems it had. She smiled sweetly and looked down. For myself, I knew my smile was real, but I am sure if Chad could read my face, he could see the apprehension in my eyes. Was Chad back only for business or had he hoped to see Jane?

At the end of Chad's presentation on advanced placement testing, clearly geared more towards the middle and high school teachers, he left the meeting. As teachers, we needed to stay. I had quietly whispered to Jane, "Make an excuse and leave. The restroom or a drink? Bump into him nonchalantly."

Jane was too honest for a ruse, and so she stayed, even though I could tell that she wasn't going to absorb a single thing in this meeting that would help her this year. Her thoughts were with Chad, and once again he was gone. My ears perked up as Dr. Cooper mentioned avoiding the light construction going on in the field north of the main building where concrete was being poured for a sundial that was donated to the school to be used by our science classes. I knew it should be of interest to me, but my focus was on Jane. I'd have to ask about it later.

When the meetings ended, I accompanied Jane back to her classroom and helped her finish up what she had been working on earlier in the day. Bright colored carpet dots and school supplies labeled with both pictures and words had appeared in her room since I was there yesterday. I helped her move the reading table into the corner and then the two of us left side-by-side. Tonight, I'd make her dinner while we talked over what was obviously on her mind. Those plans were completely shot the moment we stepped out the front door of the school to see Chad and Darcy sitting on a bench under the shade trees that lined the play area. Chad jumped to his feet, and there was no mistaking the fact that he'd been waiting for us to emerge. Darcy was slower to rise. My heart began to pound. I was excited for Jane and terrified for myself.

Chad came toward us, so we moved in his direction, meeting in the grass just beyond the circular drive where Darcy and I had first met. At first, the conversation was awkward. There were a lot of "How have you been?" and "What have you been doing?" but after a long silence, Darcy suggested we head down toward the canal. Jane and I had bags in our hands, but as our apartment was on the way, we suggested that we stop there first. The guys opted to remain outside while we ran in. That was perfect as it gave us both a few minutes to compose ourselves before stepping back out into the unknown.

As soon as I closed the apartment door behind me, I leaned back on it and let out a sigh. Then, steadying myself, I turned to Jane who was putting her things down. "Jane, how are you holding up?"

Jane's face was pale, but her answer was more honest than I was used to. "I don't know. I'm so afraid that he's going to break my heart again. I tried so hard to pretend that it didn't matter that he left me like that. I hoped that if I just pretended it didn't matter I could make it true. But it did matter." Her eyes began to fill with tears.

I pulled her into a hug. "Of course, it mattered. I can't promise you that he won't break your heart again, but I can promise you that I'm here. Let's pray before we go back out."

I stepped back and took Jane's hands in mine. "*Lord, you know how this is going to play out. Protect Jane's heart. More than that, give her the desires of her heart. You're the giver of all good gifts. We ask that if Chad is the right man for Jane, you'll give him the courage to pursue her. And if he's not, please take him away from her so she won't hurt any longer. Give us the wisdom to say the right things. Amen.*"

Jane squeezed my hand and headed to the bathroom. When she came out, her eyes were dry and her face looked calm, not happy, but prepared for this.

The four of us meandered down to the canal. Most of the flowers had disappeared, so the path was green with ferns, hostas, and may apples. The mosquitos were a bit bothersome, which threatened to shorten our time out. God used hornets to win a battle, so I suspected he was using mosquitos to cut short this first interaction between Darcy and myself. Jane and Chad had fallen into step, and they seemed to be slowly easing back into their former familiar way with one another. They walked close to one another. Chad's hand brushing against Jane's repeatedly. Not holding hands, but contact.

Darcy and I were not. He kept his distance. I didn't know what to say, and it seemed to me that he was only there on behalf of his friend. Knowing what he had told me in his letter, I wasn't sure if Darcy was there to support Chad in pursuing Jane or if his reservations had him here more to chaperone than to encourage. Had my admission of Jane's affection altered things? I hoped so. Had Darcy told Chad so much? Darcy certainly had nothing to say to me. We ambled along in silence, only pausing while I swatted at a mosquito on my ankles or neck. I must have been a sight. Randomly an arm would flail, attempting to ward off a miniature assault. We followed the path around and back towards our apartment in record time.

"Are you here for a while?" There, I said something.

"Possibly. It depends on things."

Well, that was vague. "How's Lexi?"

Darcy relaxed. A hint of a smile appeared on his otherwise tense face. "She's good. Busy with work. She misses you."

I missed her too. I missed Darcy. I couldn't say that. "Oh."

Jane's soft giggle drew both of our attention to the couple in front of us. Silence again. Our apartment building was directly in front of us.

Nothing earth shattering had come of our meeting, but still it was good. When the men said goodnight and we entered our apartment, I could see that Jane was feeling lighter. "I'm so glad that is over. Now, we've gotten that first awkward meeting out of the way, and we can go back to being friends."

I laughed. "I don't think so Jane. Don't forget that I was right behind you, so I watched you both the entire time. I don't want to get your hopes up, but I'm pretty sure Chad has something other than friendship in mind."

47: Beth

We returned to work that evening for Convocation chapel, which had just ended. Parents were mingling around the old church catching up with one another, chatting about summer vacations and their kids' excitement for the upcoming school year. The week back had been long and arduous. It always was for teachers, so an evening event for faculty and parents had left me exhausted.

I had hoped to make my way to the front door and sneak off to my apartment for a cup of tea and a mindless sitcom. I knew I'd get stopped on my way out by at least a few people: it was the same every year. I hated small talk. I wasn't unsocial, just shy. Parents of my new students introduced themselves to me, offered me any support I needed, and told me they'd be praying for me this year. Really, my job was amazing. How many people can say that? As I neared the chapel doors, I saw Jane in a conversation with another set of parents. Jane would never extract herself without help, so I diverted my path and interjected myself into their conversation. I made our apologies and brought Jane along with me.

The cool August air was refreshing after the stuffiness of the old chapel packed with bodies. The streetlamps were on though the sun hadn't fully set. The woods blocked the light, but the sky still held the color of salmon. It would have been a perfect evening for a stroll had I not been so wiped out. As we approached the apartment, I noticed a car parked out front by the no parking sign that stood beside the building's driveway. At our approach, an older woman stepped from the car, her identity hidden by the shadows. Jane and I both hitched our steps, and then cautiously approached. Recognition dawned on me. What I didn't know was why Dee Burgh was here.

"Mrs. Burgh, what are you doing here? Is Joy alright?" Forgetting my manners, I mentally took a step back and started again. "Jane, you remember Mrs. Burgh? Mrs. Burgh, Jane, my sister."

"Yes, I remember." Mrs. Burgh spit the words out of her mouth.

Jane's pleasant demeanor couldn't be shaken by her curt tone. She always wrote off bad manners as the result of some personal struggle, traffic, that sort of thing. "It's so lovely to see you again. Won't you please come in?"

She shook her head. Her words were terse. "I don't have time. I simply came to speak with your sister." She turned to face me. "Take a walk."

It wasn't a question, but I tamped down my initial irritation at her commanding tone. "Sure." I handed Jane my purse, but slipped my phone into my pocket. Jane questioned me with her eyes. I nodded slightly and then watched as Jane approached our door. I saw her glance back before letting herself in. I watched her, using that time to control my reaction to appear warm and polite.

"Let's head this way." I pointed away from the chapel entrance. Parents and teachers were still swarming around, and I didn't want to be stopped, nor did I want to answer questions about my visitor. We headed toward the sports fields where there were a few lights. "What brings you here, Mrs. Burgh?"

"What brings me here?" The poison in her voice was unmistakable. "As if you don't know."

I pinched my lips together and let the air in my lungs escape slowly. "I have absolutely no idea why you are here. Is there something the matter with Joy or Colin?"

"This has nothing to do with either of them. This has everything to do with you!"

My fists began to automatically clench so I willed them to relax. I didn't know how long I'd be able to keep my frustration in check. "Me? What on earth could have to do with me that would have brought you all the way here?"

She stopped suddenly and swung around to face me. "I wish I didn't need to come all the way here, but you left me no choice.

When I heard the vicious rumors you started about my family, I couldn't let them go. I welcomed you into my home and you repay me with slander, gossip, lies. How dare you?"

My voice rose to reflect my irritation. "Slander? Gossip about your family? I have done nothing of the sort. I have no idea what you are talking about. If you are going to so rudely accuse me, at least have the dignity of explaining the charges. What lies?"

For an older woman, she certainly had a lot of fight left in her. "I cannot believe you would stoop so low as to deny this, but let me lay it out for you. I have heard that you intend to steal away the man my daughter is going to marry. My Anne is marrying Darcy Williams, so the rumors of your engagement most certainly count as slander against my family."

I laughed louder than I should have. The absurdity of this entire conversation was not lost on me. "Engaged to Darcy? Ma'am, first off, if your daughter were actually going to marry Darcy Williams they would have to date first. And considering their ages and the fact that that hasn't happened, I think you're deluding yourself to think otherwise. Really, we aren't living in the 19th century any more. Arranged marriages don't really happen in New Jersey no matter how much mothers want them to."

"You are the most obstinate child I have ever met. How dare you insult me and my daughter? "

"How dare I?"

"You're a pillow toting gold digger and you think you can seduce Darcy away from my daughter. Unconscionable. Did you or did you not start these horrid rumors?"

I paused to decide if I even owed her an answer to her outrageous claims, but it seemed better to answer her and end this humiliation. "I most certainly did not. The first I have heard of this were from your lips just now."

I would have thought that would satisfy her, but the look on her face was anything but satisfied. "Are you engaged to Darcy Williams?"

I wanted to step forward and get right into her face, but even I have enough self-control to know it unforgivable to threaten a little old lady, no matter how badly they were behaving. I held my ground, but my shoulders tensed as I closed my fingers into my palms. "I am not. And really, I can't even believe I am dignifying you with any answers after the way you have treated me. We're done here."

I started to turn around and storm away from her, but she reached out and grabbed my arm. She was clearly pushing her luck. "One more thing. Promise you will never marry Darcy?"

That was it. I spun around fast enough to knock her hand off of my arm. I stepped close enough to make my point, but not enough to make her feel threatened. "I will never make a promise like that to you. Whom I marry is none of your business. My life is my own and your opinion has no bearing on it."

I marched away as quickly as I could before she could respond or dare touch me again. My reserve of patience was depleted, and I wasn't sure even the Holy Spirit could have tolerated that woman. Images of Jesus flipping tables in the temple made me laugh and my shoulders relaxed as I rushed through my front door and slammed it behind me. Okay, maybe being a Godly woman didn't always have to mean sweet and reserved. God made me with fire in my soul, and he was using fire to refine me so I could choose the right path. And tonight, that meant the peaceful one that didn't include cracking any whips. *Unfortunately.*

To Jane's credit she didn't ask me any questions right away. She simply rose from the couch and crossed to our kitchen. I watched her start the teakettle. I knew she was giving me space but offering me a listening ear at the same time. I rested against the door for a few minutes watching her take the tea bags from the canister and place them in our mugs. She pulled the spoons from the drawer and moved the sugar bowl to the table. In a moment, she would place our mugs there, and I would join her. First, I was going to take off my shoes, change into pajamas and let down my hair. Brushing it out after having been in a ponytail all day would hopefully ease some of my tension.

Jane was sitting at the table when I returned. She was the best sister and friend I could have ever asked for. She could have brought the tea to the coffee table, and we could have been slouched on the couch, but Jane must have known that the table would offer the sense of attentiveness that this conversation needed. This was weighty and a sturdy table was needed to carry the burden I was going to lay down.

Jane waited for me to begin.

"She isn't too happy right now. It seems she believes that I am standing in the way of her greatest life goal, which in this case is the wedding of her daughter to Darcy Williams." I looked at Jane to gauge her reaction. She nodded for me to continue. "It seems that somehow a rumor was started that Darcy and I are engaged, which of course is problematic for her plans, and she assumes that I'm the one who started the rumor."

Jane stared off over my shoulder. She was thinking of something deep. "Do you think that someone heard his proposal? He did make it while you were in Philadelphia, right?"

I shook my head. "No. Who could have heard? We were all alone. And that was months ago. Certainly, if that was the case, she would have heard about it before now. This must be new news. No one impulsively drives an hour away at night over something they heard months before."

"And you've told nobody?"

I shook my head again. "I haven't said a single word to anyone except you. And I can't believe Darcy would have said anything. He was angry and insulted. Why he would lead anyone to believe that I had said yes? No, it couldn't have been him."

Tears had threatened to spill from my eyes, but before they fell new pain stabbed me. "Oh, Jane. It just keeps getting worse. I wanted to apologize to him for everything after he sent me that letter. And the longer it goes, the harder that apology is to get out. Then everything happened with Lydia, and I was sure I would never see him again. But then he was here this week, and he was so silent. He barely spoke to me, and I can't blame him. He must have been waiting for me to say I was sorry, and I was so humiliated I didn't. If he hears about these rumors, I'll just die. Especially if he thinks the same way Mrs. Burgh does. How horrible of a person will he think I am? I'll sound cruel and manipulative. Ugh! I know I ruined everything months ago, but there must be some end to how deep I can fall because of it, right?"

Tears ran down my cheeks, but I didn't bother to wipe them away. I had cried so often these past months that I had become comfortable with their presence.

Jane sat with me in silence broken only by the occasional sob that escaped my lips. Jane is a rare soul who can be comfortable with another's pain. She carries it with them to lighten their load. Tonight, she lifted me up with her silence and her prayers.

48: Darcy

Chad had decided it was time to be forthcoming with his intentions towards Jane. We'd talked at length about his feelings and what Beth had revealed to me. I had apologized to him on the Fourth of July for my interference, but Chad was a good friend and understood my rationale behind everything. The thing that most upset him was when I told him that Jane had been in New York at Christmas time and had visited with Missy. I told him that we had kept that information from him for all the reasons we'd interfered with before.

However, when Chad had confronted Missy about things it turned out her actions had gone far beyond anything I had imagined. Under protest, he had forced her to produce the email he had sent to Jane, which alluded to a relationship with Lexi. The fact that Jane hadn't texted him after that suddenly had taken on a totally different meaning than our mutual belief that Jane simply wasn't that interested in pursuing a dating relationship. Chad had forgiven Missy, but had been unwilling to restore the closeness that they had previously enjoyed. Missy had moved into a place of her own, and when Chad came down to stay with Heather and Nick, he didn't bring Missy. He did, however, bring me. He'd have come down earlier, but I urged him to wait a few weeks until the issues with Lydia had a chance to settle. I worried Jane would be too overwhelmed to hear Chad out.

Despite the fact that Chad was supposed to confess his feelings to Jane yesterday and chickened out, the meeting had still bolstered his courage. Today, Chad was going to lay everything on the table with Jane. He'd express his feelings, explain his absence, and ask her out. He wanted me to join him both for moral support and because he figured I could occupy Beth while he spoke with Jane. I knew he wanted me to confess my own affection for Beth, but I wasn't fool enough to open myself up to that same kind of abuse until I got more of a response from her that things had changed. Our time in Jersey City over the summer had given me hope, but then Lydia's crisis had interrupted my plans to soften Beth toward me. I hated to see the pain in her expression, and I hated to walk away that day, but helping her was crucial. Keeping that a secret was even more important. I couldn't have Beth's affection out of obligation. I didn't want her to feel like she owed me. I needed her to love me for who I was. So, when I showed up last week and Beth didn't completely blow me off, I figured I could start back up slowly with my current plans. I had hoped things would move faster, but Beth was worth my patient pursuit.

We arrived on the grounds early in the morning. Chad allowed me an unoccupied office to work in while he worked with Academic Success staff doing training and handling the business end of things. I had finally handed over full control of the family real estate holdings to Lexi, but I was still supporting her in her role. I was pleasantly surprised with where my professional life was headed.

The foundation had always been a family affair, so Lexi and I would both continue on the board of trustees there, making sure to personally oversee as much of the grant work as possible. Letting go of the real estate venture had filled me with relief. It had been a long few years raising Lexi and effectively running three businesses. I was ready to have some more free time, and I knew exactly where I wanted to devote that time.

Chad had gotten the Asbury Christian Academy's faculty schedule for today when he'd arranged a meeting time with their guidance office. He knew when Jane's meeting would let out, so he scheduled his meeting accordingly and planned to be outside the room when Jane emerged. He'd have to do that on his own, because quite frankly I was busy, and he needed to man up. He was going to invite Jane and Beth to go out to dinner tonight. If they agreed, we would head outside of the Princeton area to eat. Chad had determined that Lambertville offered nice restaurants and a great path along the canal. If we knew one thing about the girls, they loved wandering by the canal.

49: Beth

I wasn't surprised that Chad had invited Jane to dinner, but the fact that the invite included me was strange. There was never any question as to whether I would go, but the thought of being the third wheel had me almost as uneasy as if I was going on a first date. Chad knocked on the door and Jane opened it. At the sight of Darcy, I realized I hadn't adequately prepared myself for the level of anxiety that I was going to endure this evening.

I'm not sure if Chad was brilliant, conniving, or lucky, but here we all were eating at a restaurant with the tiniest of tables I had ever seen in an establishment of this caliber. Seriously, this was not the way I had envisioned my evening. My knees occasionally bumped Darcy's. The food was excellent, and the place far more expensive than I would ever have picked. This was every bit a date, which was fine for Jane and Chad, but where did that leave Darcy and me? I watched Jane and Chad throughout the night as they fell into quiet conversation, their chairs so close they barely needed to talk above a whisper to hear one another. Darcy and I ate in near silence. I couldn't think of a single thing I could possibly say before I apologized, and I couldn't apologize in the middle of a crowded restaurant two feet away from my sister and Chad.

My hand froze when he grazed it reaching for the butter. It trembled as I was bringing my water glass to my lips. I tried to watch his reactions from the corner of my eye because I wasn't going to face him. I couldn't make eye contact. A few times he seemed to be smirking, but mostly his face was neutral. I am certain he was bored out of his mind. For my part, I was too uncomfortable to be bored. Time had never moved more slowly.

"How's your food?" Darcy asked.

"Fine." Silence. "Yours?" I knew I was being rude, but my brain wasn't letting me relax.

"Delicious. Tender. Seasoned perfectly. How's the school year looking?" Darcy paused and looked at me. I could see this from the corner of my eye, but I didn't look at him.

"Fine. Yours?"

"Well, I finished setting up all the desks and decorating my bulletin board, but I still have lesson plans to write."

I whipped my head around and stared at him.

Darcy chuckled. "Oh, there you are. I wasn't sure you were even listening to me."

He disarmed me with his charm, but still my stomach fluttered, and my palms sweat.

"Sorry." I looked down again. I heard Darcy let out a sigh and pick his utensils back up again.

After dinner, Chad led Jane north along the canal path, taking them away from the town center. Darcy and I trailed way behind.

Darcy was too much of a gentleman to treat me the way I had treated him; he simply offered me his arm. "Shall we?"

There in the parking lot of the restaurant, with the Delaware River in the background, I finally looked him in the eyes. I didn't take his arm, and I didn't speak. I felt the tears welling up in my eyes, and I knew I needed to say something before the tidal wave released. "I'm so sorry," I blurted out, and that was all I managed before my fortitude crumbled

Darcy reached out with both hands and placed them on my shoulders. He dipped his head down in an attempt to look me in the eyes. My gaze had dropped to the ground. Darcy was so much taller that his efforts were fruitless. He released one of my arms and placed his index finger under my chin, gently lifting it until I could catch his eye. His smile was deep.

"Beth, you know, you're a lot of work."

I started to laugh through my tears at his statement, one he'd said so often to me for obvious reasons. I was a lot of work, and I was sure I wasn't worth it. With that revelation, my smile faded and my tears increased as he directed me down toward a bench that sat by the river. We sat with his arm around my shoulder. He didn't speak. I assume he knew I had a lot on my mind, a lot to say, and either he wasn't going to let me off easy, or he was as clueless as to what I needed to say as I had been with Mrs. Burgh.

It seemed like forever before I regained my composure enough to speak. I wiped my eyes with my hand and fumbled through my purse for a tissue. Darcy released me as I cleaned my face up and paused to speak. I turned to him, but I didn't do more than occasionally glance at his eyes.

"I'm so incredibly sorry. I've been horrible to you and you've been nothing but kind and generous. I have no excuse for my behavior, but please know how sorry I am. I wanted to tell you that in July, but I was embarrassed and then everything happened with Lydia." My words were catching in my throat, and I needed to slow down. "I figured after Philly that I was probably the last person you wanted in your house, yet you were so welcoming. When you left after Lydia disappeared, I missed my chance. I begged God for a new heart. Not just to fix the broken one I have; I need a brand new one. Could you ever forgive me? Please." With those words he frowned. I was bringing up those memories, and I was right to think that he'd no longer want to have a friendship with any family connected to Jonathan Wade.

Darcy faced me more directly and clasped my hands with his. "Beth, of course, I forgive you. I hate that you've been so worried over this. We serve a God whose pleasure is found in creating clean hearts. I like the beautiful heart he gave you. I love that you're letting him refine you. When I heard Aunt Dee had come to your home and treated you so terribly, I was furious. I confronted her and from the sounds of things, I wasn't as kind to her as you. I'm so sorry she did that to you. But a little part of me is glad she did it." He smirked.

"Why's that?"

"Well, I wasn't sure how you felt about me, but when she told me how you refused to promise you'd never marry me, I thought we might still have a chance. I figured if you still hated me you'd have just told her that, but you didn't."

I nodded. "I still don't know where those rumors got started. I promise you I never said a word to anyone but Jane."

Darcy laughed again. "Actually, I think I started them. Well, not exactly. Missy might have heard me talking with Chad, and thought if she shared my feelings with Aunt Dee, she might get another chance with me. Missy has never been one to take no for an answer when it's come to dating me."

I forced myself to go on. "But then you rescued Lydia. There's no other way to describe it." His eyes widened, and I saw the shock on his face. "She told me one night when I found her crying. Please don't be mad at her. She was sorry she broke your trust." The tears that rolled down my cheek at this point were silent and slow, simply the reminder of the passing of painful memories. "But I just can't figure out why you'd have done all that for her. It must have been so awful for you to deal with Jon again, and I can never repay you for all you've done for my family. For me."

"I didn't want you to know. I never wanted you to feel like you owed me. Beth, if you feel the same way about me as you did when we parted in Philly, tell me now and I'll stop. But if your feelings have changed, I have more to say."

I was speechless, but my feelings had changed so very much. "Go on." I smiled through my tears.

"I did it because I love you, but I want you to love me for who I am, not because of some debt." There was hope in his eyes. A smile lit across his face. "And you, Beth Beckett, are the most amazing woman I have ever met." And with that, he slipped off the bench and onto one knee. He pulled a small box out of his inside jacket pocket and opened it to reveal a solitary diamond in a gold setting. Simple and perfect. "Beth Beckett, you are a lot of work." And he laughed. "But you are worth every minute of it. I want to spend the rest of my life loving you and cherishing you and caring for you and giving you everything your heart desires. Please give me the one thing that my heart desires. Please marry me, Beth."

Nothing could have prepared me for the question Darcy had just asked me. A few minutes ago, I thought he hated me and now he was professing his love and asking me for my hand in marriage. This seemed so unlikely, so impossible, only God could orchestrate something so amazing.

"Yes, Darcy, Yes. Nothing would make me happier."

Darcy slipped the ring onto my finger and closed the distance between us. Kneeling, his head was still higher than mine. He cupped my cheeks in his hands and dipped his head down and covered my lips with his. I had never felt such complete bliss in all my life. As Darcy moved his one hand around to the back of my neck and pushed his fingers into my hair, he moved his other hand down my neck, across my shoulder and down my back. He drew me closer and kissed me deeper. I surrendered everything inside me into that kiss. I trusted him completely; just the same way I loved him. When Darcy pulled away from the kiss, I moved my hand to his chest. I could feel his heart pounding beneath his shirt. My breath was jagged, and I felt the warmth covering my cheeks.

He rested his forehead again mine and whispered, "I love you, Beth."

"I love you, Darcy Williams. More than you could ever know."

50: Darcy

By the time Chad and Jane returned, Beth and I had spent time talking through some of the practicalities of being engaged from a distance, but to be honest we spent more time kissing than talking. I explained that Chad wanted to drive out of town to reduce the chance of them bumping into any of their students' parents. I confessed that Chad had been hoping for some kissing, but I was less hopeful. Either way, the privacy seemed prudent. I also admitted to buying the ring back in July, but not having enough hope to put it in my jacket pocket until the visit from Aunt Dee. Lexi had helped me pick it out and had demanded a call once Beth agreed. Being that she didn't know when I was going to ask, she wouldn't be sitting at home waiting for her phone to ring. She hadn't talked to Beth since shortly after she'd left in July, so Lexi was anxiously anticipating getting her friend back.

When Beth saw Jane approach, she jumped from the bench and ran to her sister, tears already falling. The ladies embraced while Chad eyed me suspiciously.

"I went for broke, man, but it paid off. She said yes," I told him.

Chad slapped me on the back and pulled me in for a hug. "Congratulations! Wow, you sure work fast." We both chuckled.

"I guess I do."

Chad's relationship with Jane had been non-existent for long enough that he'd simply proposed that they agree to date. I was sure his other question wouldn't be long in coming, but for the time being we both seemed content with the current state of our happiness. We escorted the ladies back to the car. Everyone was smiling. On the way to dinner, Jane had suggested she and Beth sit in the back. Because of my height, she felt the front would be more comfortable. I refused her suggestion for the way home and allowed Chad to settle her into the passenger seat while I helped Beth into the back. I wasn't the least bit worried about the close quarters.

After bidding goodnight to the ladies, Chad and I retired for the night. I needed to call Lexi, and then spend some time in prayer. There was so much to be thankful for, but this wouldn't be a simple path. We'd still have to pick a wedding date and determine where we'd live with our jobs being so far apart. There was no obstacle we couldn't face together, but the guidance and strength of the Holy Spirit would be greatly appreciated.

51: Beth

"I have an announcement." The tinkling of silver wear stilled, and I drew in a deep breath. "I'm engaged to Darcy Williams." The fact that I needed to include a name on to my announcement wasn't lost on me. What must they all be thinking?

I'm not sure what I expected, but it didn't go quite like I imagined.

Jane took a play from my playbook by reacting just the same way I had at Joy's engagement announcement. I barely stifled my giggle as Jane burst forth, "Congratulations!" .

"Ridiculous." That would be my mother. "There is no way you could be engaged to that man. It's not even funny, Beth. I don't know why you feel the need to joke like this."

"I'm not kidding. He asked me last night." My eyes scanned the table and landed on Lydia. Her mouth hung open. Her eyes wide. Slowly, an understanding smile crept up her cheeks.

"Darcy is a good man. He'll take good care of you," Lydia said.

I nodded my agreement. "He is good."

Lydia surprised me by standing up and coming over to give me a hug.

Cat practically dropped her fork on the plate, her voice shrill. "I want to get married. Nothing interesting ever happens to me."

"Have you set a date?" Jane's question turned the attention from Cat's outburst.

"No, not yet. It's too soon."

I looked to Mary. The only indication that she heard the conversation was that her book lay closed beside her plate.

"I am at a loss here, Beth. This seems so sudden, and so unlike you." Dad almost seemed hurt. "Do you even know this man? His character?"

"I do. I know it probably seems so out of the blue." I giggled a little myself. It certainly was. "But that's only because I never mentioned how much time I've spent with Darcy." Realizing how that sounded I tried again. "I wasn't sneaking around or anything, I just didn't realize until recently how important our time together had been. And honestly, I didn't like him at first, that much is no secret."

My family's nodding embarrassed me. I was part of the reason they had such a low opinion of the man I now loved.

I briefly shared about our time in Jersey City, Philadelphia, and New York over the past year or so. Eventually. Dad seemed convinced that this was not a joke, that I really did know Darcy well. His apprehension seemed to ease.

I decided I would keep Darcy and Lydia's secret from him, but I needed my father to understand the bombshell I had dropped. I found him later that evening. I stepped into the library. "Dad, I know Darcy asked me to marry him before he asked your permission, but I'm sure he's going to want to talk to you, and I'd really like to know you'll give him your blessing."

"Beth, I must say I'm really at a loss here. Last year, you hated this man. And then I hear almost nothing about him, and now you want to marry him. I know Joy married Colin for the change in situation, but I never thought you would do the same. You can't be marrying for money?"

I shook my head. "Daddy, you know me better than that. I love him. I know what I said, and I'm embarrassed by it now. Darcy is a really good man. He's kind and thoughtful and generous. You have no idea how generous he is, and I don't mean his foundation, although he does such amazing work through that as well. He's raised his sister, and she's wonderful. I adore her. You should've seen him with Aunt Erica and Uncle Bert. I think he's more of an introvert than a snob like I thought. And he loves me. He really loves me. I couldn't pick a more Godly man, I'm certain."

The smile that had been growing across my father's face had finally made me stop babbling. I looked at him, wondering if he believed me or was he making fun of me.

"Beth, my love. I never thought there would be a man worthy enough to give him your hand. But, I knew one day a man would come and ask and you'd look at me just the way you are right now, with hope in your eyes. I'll give my blessing to him, because I trust what you say about him. I hope I'll get to see if for myself, but I have never questioned your judgment, and I won't start now. If you love him, and if he is all you claim him to be, then I will consent to his request for your hand."

My heart soared in my chest, and I wrapped my arms around my father's neck. "Oh, thank you, Dad. Thank you!"

52: Darcy

Fall gave way to winter, which was just fine by me. I had waited long enough to marry Beth.

"Beth, relax. Everything is going to be fine." I reached out and grabbed her arm as she paced past me for what seemed like the tenth time. I pulled her onto my lap and held her still. I had been sitting on the couch in the apartment I'd rented in Princeton. I wanted to call it small, but I'd seen Beth's place, and comparatively, this was a palace.

"What if something happens and Lydia or the baby needs me, but I'm so far away? And I'm going to need to help the church plan Lydia's baby shower and Jane's bridal shower, and I still have work. Oh, and I have so much packing left to do."

"First off, I've seen your place. We can have it packed up in a couple of hours. Second, we aren't moving to Jersey City until the summer. By then, both showers will be over and done. You need to relax. You're starting to make me feel like you're not sure you want to marry me." I pouted.

Eyes wide she gasped. "Never. I will never change my mind."

"Good." I tickled her side. I tightened my grip on her as she squirmed in my grasp. Letting up, I continued. "Sit with me for fifteen minutes. I'll even set a timer. And then I'll help you with whatever you want that'll help you feel more relaxed."

A flirtatious smile crossed her face. "Whatever."

"Don't tempt me, woman." I pulled her down for a kiss. "Be nice."

Beth returned my kiss and relaxed into my embrace. "Okay, fifteen minutes."

I took Beth's hands into my own once she settled beside me. "Jesus, you're the Prince of Peace. Give Beth some of that peace right now. Help her to find her rest in you." I could feel Beth relaxing as we prayed.

When the timer went off, Beth was slow to stand up, but then she pulled me to my feet. "I asked Cat and Mary to come over for dinner tonight. Lydia has class. We've gotten so close since the baby, I was feeling awful neglectful of the other girls. Mary declined. Not a surprise, but Cat agreed. I need to run to the grocery store. Then I was hoping to pack a few more boxes to bring over here. Since Chad proposed at Thanksgiving, Jane and I have been sorting through our things we won't need anymore and can save for Lydia and Cat. Honestly, if Lydia just moved into our apartment after Jane's wedding in June, it'd save a lot of energy. We could just leave the furniture and kitchen set up as is. Neither of us will need it. That gets Lydia through the first few months of an infant at home with support, and then she'd have her own space, but still close enough if she needs help."

"Hmm, it's a shame you can't just call up the owner of the apartment building and ask her if she could work that out. I hear she's really busy being a bridesmaid in her brother's wedding in a few days."

"You think Lexi would do that? It's not like Lydia works on the grounds. That's been a requirement. And I haven't talked to Lydia about it. I don't want her to feel like we're babying her or anything, but that could be awesome."

I pulled her into my arms. "Slow down. Your brain is running a mile a minute. Take a breath. I'm sure Lexi would be willing to do that. She loves you more than she loves me. She's so happy she's finally getting a sister you could ask her for anything and she'd say yes. You can call her while we drive to the grocery store."

Beth nodded against my chest. I felt her take several calming breaths and then she released her hold on my waist. "Thanks."

"After dinner with Cat, we need to finalize some plans for next week. Do you want me to stop over with the seating chart? Will it be too late?"

"If you could stop by that would be great. Cat has an early class, so she won't be staying late. I ordered all the poinsettias for the church and my Bible study group is going to string the lights so the sanctuary will be ready for the rehearsal on the 23rd. The only thing Pastor Tim asked is that we are cleared out of the sanctuary on the 24th by 2:00 so they can practice for the Christmas Eve service."

"That won't be a problem. And I confirmed our dinner reservations for the rehearsal dinner with the restaurant. We just need to get the seating chart for the reception to the caterer tomorrow morning. Everything is going to be fine. You have three more days of school as Miss Beckett, and when you return in the New Year, you're going to be Mrs. Williams."

Beth brightened. "I can't believe we're getting married in less than a week."

*****

I couldn't tear my eyes off of my wife. She was radiant. Her black hair a contrast to the white dress. Her veil, now flipped back, revealed her beautiful eyes and lips. She'd been up early today with the hairdresser and getting ready, and while still early I could see she was tired. She'd danced the afternoon away with family and friends, but I was ready to drag her out of here to spend time alone with me.

I whispered into her ear. "Say goodbye to Jane, we need to leave. Our plane is going to be ready soon."

"I thought you chartered a plane. Won't it wait for us?" Always with the sass.

"It doesn't work like that. There are still flight plans to file. Say goodbye." I playfully pinched her side.

Beth looked up at me. The lights of the ballroom reflected off her hazel eyes. "Fine. If we must."

I growled a little. "We must."

Beth crossed the edge of the dance floor, and I watched her hug each of her sisters. She held Jane's embrace the longest. Behind me, a hand came down and landed on my shoulder. Chad.

"This will be you and Jane in a few months. You ready?"

"I'd have married her already if she didn't want to wait a few months to give Beth the limelight." Chad kept his eyes fixed on Jane.

"Beth wouldn't have minded."

"I know. I think Jane just needed to make sure her younger sisters were okay. She didn't want her and Beth both gone so quickly. I understand. That's the kindness I love about her."

"I'm sure everything will be fine, but you know how to reach me if anything happens while we're gone."

"Of course." Chad hugged me and stepped away as Lexi approached.

"Take care of my sister. Bring her back in one piece. I have plans this summer to take her and my annoying brother to some amazing sites around the world that my Foundation supports."

"Excuse me. Our foundation. And I'm taking my wife on a similar trip. Perhaps I'll see you." I pulled Lexi into a giant bear hug.

"Ouch. Let go, you baboon. And you better see me. I've been looking forward to this for a long time. I practically had a party when Beth's passport arrived."

"Well, if she doesn't finish saying goodbye, she's going to miss getting the first stamp."

"I'll go get her." Lexi crossed the room and moments later we were off.

The look on Beth's face when we entered our suite in St. Lucia was exactly how I imagined. An eight-foot evergreen lit up with white lights was framed by a wall of windows though it was too dark to see the view. I watched Beth take in the place. I had sent gifts ahead that were scattered under the tree. It cost extra to have traditional decorations brought in and set up. I knew Beth would consider it wasteful, but I wanted our first Christmas together to be memorable. We were here for the next ten days. I intended to do everything in my power to give Beth the perfect honeymoon.

"Darcy, I can't believe you did all this." Her eyes glistened as she turned to look at me.

I tipped the bell hop and closed the door behind him.

"I wanted it to be perfect. I've been taking notes since the day we met of all the things you love and hate, so I could make this everything you've dreamed."

"Really? I don't know about that. If you were paying attention, you would know that I hate the beach, and here we are on a tropical island."

"Wrong. You don't hate the beach. You hate being overheated and you hate being covered in sand. You love the picturesque view of the water, the sound of the crashing waves, and the smell of the salt air. With the ocean breeze, and it being December, you might even need a sweater. We can open the doors to our patio and enjoy the beach without you touching even a toe into the sand. And while there are tons of things to explore like hiking and historic landmarks, I assure you, I will not be the least bit disappointed if we never leave our room."

Beth gasped at my meaning. I grabbed her around the waist and leaned down to kiss her slowly walking her backwards towards our room.

53: Beth

The sun streamed through the glass walls of our suite. Outside were views of the ocean and the lush green mountains. I had no idea the Caribbean Islands had mountains on them. The view was spectacular, but my attention was drawn to the man lying beside me.

"Tell me, Darcy, when did you first start to like me?"

He turned to face me. "I liked you from the first time I met you."

I scoffed. "You lie. The first time we met, you were horrible to me. You were rude and arrogant." I laughed at the memory.

He grinned. "You asked about my feelings not yours. I loved your feistiness. I was late for a meeting; I'd had a horrible day. I pull up behind a bunch of other parked cars and you start yelling at me. Not anyone else. Just me. I'd never been in a carpool line. I had no idea what it was. Most people treat me with kid gloves. I hate that. I never know where I really stand with someone. But not you. You came storming in, all five feet of you, demanding I move my car. I thought you were adorable. I couldn't help but to rile you up a little more. I knew right then that I wanted to get to know you."

"You've got to be kidding me!"

Darcy drew his finger across his chest in a cross shape. "Cross my heart. I knew you'd be a lot of work, Mrs. Williams, but I figured you'd be worth it."

I put on a fake pout. "Well, were you right about the work? Are you sure it was worth it?"

He rolled over and pulled me close. "I'm always right, and you, my dear, are definitely worth it." I melted into his embrace and thanked God for this man whose life I was so blessed to share.

The End

Click below to join Barbara's mailing list and receive a free copy of Once Upon This Time.

https://www.barbaraseidle.com/free-stuff/[1]

---

1. https://www.barbaraseidle.com/free-stuff/

About the Author

Barbara Seidle is a writer, elementary school teacher, and connoisseur of the absurdities of living in this fallen world. She writes about the humor and joy we can find in life even in the midst of grief and pain, covering a myriad of topics including marriage, mental illness, and the loss of an adult child. When she is not teaching or writing, she enjoys time with her husband of 25 years, Jay, and her three adult children, Caleb, Abigail, and Joel. She enjoys cooking, eating, reading, traveling, and watching chick flicks. She says she enjoys hiking, but she really only means the downhill part.

Read more at https://www.barbaraseidle.com/.